THE CURATE IN CHARGE

MARGARET OLIPHANT

THE CURATE
IN CHARGE

ALAN SUTTON
1987

Alan Sutton Publishing Limited
30 Brunswick Road
Gloucester GL1 1JJ

First published 1985

Copyright © in this edition 1987
Alan Sutton Publishing Limited

British Library Cataloguing in Publication Data

Oliphant, *Mrs.*
  The curate in charge.
  I. Title
  823′.8[F]   PR5113.C9

  ISBN 0-86299-327-X

Cover picture: detail from The Reverend Robert Walker Skating
by Sir Henry Raeburn.
The National Gallery of Scotland, Edinburgh.
Photograph: Bridgeman Art Library

Typesetting and origination by
Alan Sutton Publishing Limited.
Photoset Bembo 9/10.
Printed in Great Britain
by The Guernsey Press Company Limited,
Guernsey, Channel Islands.

CONTENTS

INTRODUCTION

Margaret Oliphant, the author of *The Curate in Charge* and of several other fine novels, was born in Wallyford, near Edinburgh, on 4 April 1828. Little is known of her father, Francis Wilson, an excise official who had a fairly distant relationship with his children. Her mother, whose maiden name had been Margaret Oliphant, was a much more interesting person. 'She had a very high idea . . . . of the importance of the Oliphant family, so that I was brought up with the sense of belonging (by her side) to an old, chivalrous, impoverished race.' The lords Oliphant, who may or may not have been related to her, had lived at Kellie Castle in Fife and had the motto '*À tout pourvoir*' – to provide for all. Their namesake was to grow up both chivalrous and impoverished, and was to take this motto seriously. There were also two boys, Frank and Willie, who were several years older than their sister.

Margaret and a 'recluse childhood', constantly moving about with her family, spending four years in Glasgow and then, at the age of ten, going to Liverpool where her father had a job in the Customs House. She probably never went to school but was educated at home on a diet of Shakespeare, the Bible, and the traditional classics and history of Scotland. When she began to write her first novels in her teens she was highly intelligent and highly inexperienced:

> 'We lived in the most singularly secluded way. I never was at a dance till after my marriage, never went out, never saw anybody at home. Our pleasures were books of all and every kind, newspapers and magazines.'

She did her work at a corner of the family table 'as if I had been making a shirt instead of writing a book'. It never occurred to her parents and brothers that she might need privacy.

Her first novel, *Margaret Maitland* 1849, was published when she was only twenty-one, and from then on she never looked back, bringing out at least two books a year for the rest of her life. As her career blossomed, her brother Willie's declined. He was lovable and intelligent, but had a drinking problem and was quite unable to hold down a job. He qualified as a minister in the Free Presbyterian Church, which had seceded from the Church of Scotland in 1843. But after only a few months he broke down and came back in disgrace to his family. He would have, Margaret wrote, 'to be guarded and provided for as if disease had disabled him'. Not surprisingly, many of her novels are concerned with weak men and the women who look after them. She is fascinated, too (as we can see from *The Curate in Charge* and other books) by the figure of the failed priest.

When this happened she was about to marry her cousin, Frank Oliphant, a painter and designer of stained-glass windows. She was twenty-four, and already the author of several novels, when the wedding took place on 4 May 1852. The future seemed bright. But they had only been married a few months when her parents came to live near them in London, bringing Willie, who spent his time drinking, smoking and reading old novels. There were bitter quarrels, and Margaret's feelings for her husband were ambiguous from that time on.

Her daughter, Maggie, was born in 1853, followed by a son, Cyril, in 1856, but three more babies died at or near birth. As well as being constantly pregnant Margaret had to work harder than ever before, for her husband, generous and devoted to his art, was not the kind of man to make money. She produced several more novels and became a regular writer for *Blackwood's*, the famous Scottish-based magazine with which she was to be connected all her life. In 1858 Frank became gravely ill with tuberculosis and the family travelled to Italy in the hope that it would do him some good. Her Autobiography gives a poignant account of how she nursed him through a long cold winter in Florence and then a summer on the Campagna before he finally died in Rome at the end of 1859. A few weeks later her last child, Francis Romano (always known as Cecco) was born.

She came back to England a young widow of thirty-one, in

debt, and with only 'my head and my hands to provide for my children'. By this time her own and Frank's parents were all dead. During that agonising year abroad she had learned to cope with any crisis that came along. She decided not to marry again, although at least one man was attracted to her, and to devote the rest of her life to her children. A description of her at this time reads:

> A slight figure, draped in black; a very calm and gentle manner; a low and pleasant voice, marked with that homely Scottish accent which she never lost or wished to lose; a pair of the most delicate and beautiful hands I had ever seen; and such eyes as I had never looked into, large, intensely dark, and lambent, with a pure and steady flame.

After a year's hard struggle, when she feared that no one would accept her work, *Blackwood's* began to publish her well-known series of novels, the *Chronicles of Carlingford*. For a time they were so popular that George Eliot was forced to deny that she was the author. Set in an imaginary English country town, they resemble Trollope in having clergymen among their central characters (the Victorians were fascinated by religious subjects), and also show her serious interest in the problems of women. They include the famous *Salem Chapel* 1864, and two impressive short novels, *The Rector* and *The Doctor's Family* (published together in 1863).

At the end of 1863, a popular and successful novelist, she took the three children back to Rome to visit Willie, who was living there, still shiftless and alcoholic, with friends of her husband's. And there she suffered another appalling tragedy when her daughter Maggie, a bright and promising child of ten, caught gastric fever and died on 27 January 1864. For the next eighteen months she wandered wretchedly about Europe with the two little boys, writing one of her best novels, *Miss Marjoribanks* (she was never allowed the luxury of a break from work). This seems to have hit her much harder than Frank's death, and around this time her Christian beliefs, which she never quite lost, were strained to the limit.

She came back to England at the end of 1865 and settled in Windsor so that her sons, Cyril and Cecco, could attend Eton as day-boys. The pleasant house in Clarence Crescent, a short walk from the Castle, where she lived for the next thirty-odd years is still standing. Stoically, she told almost no one about her sorrow and gave the impression of a woman who had nothing to do but enjoy life. In fact, she was working very hard – often sitting up far into the night – to pay for the boys' education. Money was always a problem, for she spent it lavishly and was never again as highly paid as she had been for the *Chronicles of Carlingford*. Her popularity declined after yet another crisis hit the family.

Margaret had always believed that her elder brother, Frank Wilson, was a much more stable character than Willie. A clerk in the Bank of England, he lived in Birkenhead with his wife Jeanie and their four children, whom she hardly knew. Suddenly, in 1868, she learned that he had 'got into great trouble about money, and was, in fact, a ruined man'. She offered to help in any way she could, and took his teenage son Frank home with her to be educated with her own boys. But almost as soon as he had found another job his wife died, and he and his two daughters – little girls of five and six, much younger than his other children – moved in with her, for life.

'Of course I had to face a prospect considerably changed by this great addition to my family', Margaret wrote afterwards. 'I had been obliged to work pretty hard before to meet all the too great expenses of the house. Now four people were added to it, very small two of them, but the others not inexpensive members of the house. I remember making a kind of pretence to myself that I had to think it over, to make a great decision, to give up what hopes I might have had of doing now my very best, and to set myself steadily to make as much money as I could, and do the best I could for the three boys . . . . I don't think, however, that there was any reality in it. I never did nor could, of course, hesitate for a moment as to what had to be done.'

It was bad enough that she, who had been compared to George Eliot, should be forced to write pot-boilers (throughout the 1870's she worked ferociously, grinding out novels and articles at an inhuman pace). It was even worse that she could feel no real affection for the three people who had taken over her home. Her brother was prematurely old and quite unfit to work:

> 'He settled down to a kind of quiet life, read his newspaper, took his walk, sat in his easy-chair . . . . He and I, who had been so much to each other once, were nothing to each other now. I sometimes thought he looked at me as a kind of stepmother to his children, and we no longer thought alike on almost any subject: he had drifted one way and I another.'

The little girls, Madge and Denny, were 'very chilly, scared, distrustful little things'. They must have seemed a poor substitute for her much-loved daughter.

This is the background to *The Curate in Charge*, which was written in the early months of 1875 as a relief from hack-work. The figures of her brother and his two children can easily be recognised, and the woman who gets 'all the trouble of them' is, of course, Margaret herself. 'The artist and the housekeeper', Mab and Cicely, are two aspects of her own personality. The rare china which the hero collects symbolises a life incompatible with that of most women, who have to look after children and struggle to pay the bills. By this time Margaret had become very sympathetic to the movement for women's suffrage, although like most Victorians she had thought it a mad idea at first. As she grew older she identified strongly with ordinary women, and felt that society undervalued their work.

Over the next few years, there were changes. Her brother died; the girls went away to school and gradually built up a close and loving relationship with their aunt. Willie, who had never been able to support himself since his failure to become a clergyman, also died in Rome in 1885. Margaret continued to write at full stretch – no one knows quite how many millions of words – telling herself that 'to bring up the boys for the service of God was better than to write a fine novel'.

There is a well-known photograph, taken in 1874, of her and the three boys on the steps of their house in Windsor. They were all bright, attractive and highly-educated; no one could have guessed how dark their future would be. Her nephew Frank, the most reliable of them, tragically died of fever in India at the age of twenty-five. Her sons, who had done brilliantly at school, wasted their time at Oxford and by the beginning of the 1880's she had begun to fear that they would never be off her hands.

Around this time she began to do superb work again, although she never got as much praise as she had done for the *Chronicles of Carlingford*. Her many bereavements had caused her to think seriously for years about questions of life and death. With *A Beleaguered City* 1880, she began a series of short 'supernatural' pieces – ghost stories of an entirely new kind. The best of them are '*The Open Door*' (often anthologised), '*Old Lady Mary*', '*The Library Window*' and '*The Land of Darkness*', a surprisingly modern vision of hell. These stories, unlike the rest, were not written for the market; 'I can produce them only when they come to me'.

Other, realistic novels written in the 1880's reflect her disillusionment, the pain of her family relationships and her concern about the treatment of women. The most outstanding of these are *The Ladies Lindores* 1883, *A Country Gentleman and his Family* 1886, and her masterpiece, *Kirsteen* 1890. Also notable are *Hester* 1883, *Sir Tom* 1884, *The Marriage of Elinor* 1892, and *Old Mr Tredgold* 1896.

The boys' characters deteriorated as they stayed at home year after year, overshadowed by their mother's fame, unable and perhaps unwilling to strike out for themselves. Cyril, in particular, wrung her heart by his self-indulgence and idleness. 'My dearest, bright, delightful boy missed somehow his footing,' she wrote (carefully concealing the sordid details), 'how can I tell how? I often think that I had to do with it, as well as what people call inherited tendencies, and, alas! the perversity of youth, which he never outgrew. He had done everything too easily in the beginning of his boyish career . . . . and when he came to that stage in which hard work was necessary against the competition of the hard working, he could not believe how much more effort was necessary.' As time went on it became obvious that they had inherited their father's bad health. After years in which Margaret had pulled every string, exploited every contact with the rich and powerful to find jobs for them, Cyril got an appointment in

Ceylon, but was shipped home after a few months because it turned out that he would not live in the climate. Cecco, a natural academic, very nearly found a place at the British Museum, but he too was rejected on health grounds after he had begun to show the early signs of tuberculosis. Her nieces, grown up now, also needed an expensive training and were used to an easy, even luxurious lifestyle. Fearing that this could not go on for ever, Margaret wrote in a diary in 1887:

> 'All the things I seem to want are material things. I want money. I want work – work that will pay enough to keep the house going which there is no other one to provide for but me . . . . Here are all these helpless people, boys who ought to be earning their own living, girls who can't but will somehow if I am out of the way, servants, dependants, all accustomed to have everything that is wanted and only me to supply all, and I will be sixty in a few months and my work is failing, whether my strength is or not . . . . And it does not seem God's will for me that I should ever have any very unusual success – I suppose I did in the Carlingford days, but never had any such praise as Trollope and many others. . . . And now I suspect the stream is ebbing away from me altogether, and yet I have nothing before me but to work till I die.'

Her great autobiographical short story, '*Mr Sandford*', written at this time, was inspired by the fear that her work would stop selling and that she would then be unable to support herself or the children. She fully realised that she might seem old-fashioned, perhaps even ridiculous, as the novel began to change towards the end of the century. Many new developments repelled her; she praised some of the younger writers like Kipling and Stevenson but denounced the 'grossness' of Hardy's *Jude and Obscure* and said she preferred to read about 'a world which is round and contains everything, not "the relations between the sexes" alone'.

Her greatest wish, that her sons should make something good of their lives, was never fulfilled. Cyril died in 1890, when he was not quite thirty-four, having achieved nothing and leaving only bitter memories for his mother. She fought very hard to save Cecco, who had to spend every winter abroad and needed constant nursing, but he too died in 1894. Ironically, the two nieces whom she had not wanted to bring up were her great consolation in her last years. Madge, the elder, married and went to live in Dundee; her grandchildren and great-grandchildren are Margaret's only living relatives. Denny remained with her aunt and drew a fine picture of her which is now in the Scottish National Portrait Gallery. In 1896 they left the Windsor house which was full of memories of the boys and moved to a small house on Wimbledon Common.

She went on working mechanically, as there was nothing else to do, and wrote the two-volume *Annals of a Publishing House* 1897, a history of the firm of Blackwood with which she had been connected for forty-five years. She somehow managed to wear a hold in one finger by repeated use of her pen. The publisher J.M. Dent, who met her about this time, recorded:

> 'She was a lady under middle height, with a beautiful low broad forehead, and very dark keen eyes which held you strongly. You felt somehow that no suffering would break her spirit, and that her body must obey to the last ounce of its strength her indomitable will. This I felt although I did not know her story until afterwards.'

Her friends knew, though, that she did not want to live any longer than she could help. She died on 25 June 1897, at the height of Queen Victoria's jubilee celebrations, and was buried next to the boys at Eton cemetery. 'She was to me one of those people who *make* life,' commented Anne Thackeray Ritchie, — so many un-make it.'

Her reputation soon withered, as she had known it would. 'No one even will mention me in the same breath as George Eliot,' she had written. 'And that is just.' Perhaps the book by which she is best remembered is her *Autobiography*, which came out, edited by her cousin Annie Coghill, in 1899. It shows that she was strongly tempted to compare herself with the other great woman novelist who had had none of her troubles and responsibilities:

'How I have been handicapped in life! Should I have done better if I had been kept, like her, in a mental greenhouse and taken care of? . . . . It is a little hard sometimes not to feel. . . . that the men who have no wives, who have given themselves up to their art, have had an almost unfair advantage over us.'

If she is remembered at all, it is as a tragic example of a writer whose talents were destroyed by the incessant claims on her as mother and breadwinner. Yet the amazing thing is that anyone who wrote so much (a hundred and twenty full-length books and no one knows how many articles) could also write so well. As the novelist Howard Sturgis wrote, 'One mistake which many of her critics make is the supposition that her work at its best was injured by her immense productiveness. Her best work was of a very high order of merit. The harm that she did to her literary reputation seems rather the surrounding of her best with so much which she knew to be of inferior quality, that her high peaks of achievement, instead of rising out of the plain, as it were, suffer diminution by the neighbourhood of so many foothills'.

Most of her work, it is true, did not deserve to survive. But over the last few years more and more of the better novels have been rescued from oblivion; the *Chronicles of Carlingford*, *Hester*, *Kirsteen* and many of the supernatural stories are all back in print. And she did, after all, make something good out of her bitter experiences; *The Curate in Charge* and *The Doctor's Family* are both about women who are not allowed to choose their way of life. It is well worth reading these books and getting to know a remarkable novelist who, as J.M. Barrie said, 'was of an intellect so alert that one wondered she ever fell asleep'.

MERRYN WILLIAMS

CHAPTER ONE

THE PARISH OF BRENTBURN

The parish of Brentburn lies in the very heart of the leafy county of Berks. It is curiously situated on the borders of the forest, which is rich as Arden on one side, and on the edge of a moorland country abounding in pines and heather on the other; so that in the course of a moderate walk the wayfarer can pass from leafy glades and luxuriant breadth of shadow, great wealthy oaks and beeches, and stately chestnuts such as clothe Italian hill-sides, to the columned fir-trees of a Scotch wood, all aromatic with wild fragrant odours of the moor and peat-moss. On one hand, the eye and the imagination lose themselves in soft woods where Orlando might hang his verses, and heavenly Rosalind flout her lover. On the other, knee-deep in rustling heather and prickly billows of the gorse, the spectator looks over dark undulations of pines, standing up in countless regiments, each line and rank marked against the sky, and an Ossianic breeze making wild music through them. At the corner, where these two landscapes, so strangely different, approach each other most closely, stand the church and rectory of Brentburn. The church, I am sorry to say, is new spick-and-span nineteenth century Gothic, much more painfully correct than if it had been built in the fourteenth century, as it would fain, but for its newness, make believe to be. The rectory is still less engaging than the church. It is of red brick, and the last rector, so long as he lived in it, tried hard to make his friends believe that it was of Queen Anne's time – that last distinctive age of domestic architecture; but he knew very well all the while that it was only an ugly Georgian house, built at the end of the last century. It had a carriage entrance with the ordinary round 'sweep'· and clump of laurels, and it was a good-sized house, and comfortable enough in a steady, ugly, respectable way. The other side,

1

however, which looked upon a large garden older far than itself, where mossed apple-trees stood among the vegetable beds in the distant corners, and a delicious green velvet lawn, soft with immemorial turf, spread before the windows, was pleasanter than the front view. There was a large mulberry-tree in the middle of the grass, which is as a patent of nobility to any lawn; and a few other trees were scattered about – a gnarled old thorn for one, which made the whole world sweet in its season, and an apple-tree and a cherry at the further corners, which had of course, no business to be there. The high walls were clothed with fruit trees, a green wavy lining, to their very top – or in spring rather a mystic, wonderful drapery of white and pink which dazzled all beholders. This, I am sorry to say, at the time my story begins, was more lovely than profitable; for, indeed, so large a garden would have required two gardeners to keep it in perfect order, while all it had were the chance attentions of a boy of all work. A door cut in this living wall of blossoms led straight out to the common, which was scarcely less sweet in spring; and a little way above, on a higher elevation, was the church surrounded by its graves. Beyond this, towards the south, towards the forest, the wealthy warm English side, there were perhaps a dozen houses, an untidy shop, and the post-office called Little Brentburn, to distinguish it from the larger village, which was at some distance. The cottages were almost all old, but this hamlet was not pretty. Its central feature was a duck-pond, its ways were muddy, its appearance squalid. There was no squire in the parish to keep it in order, no ben-evolent rich proprietor, no wealthy rich clergyman; and this brings us at once to the inhabitants of the rectory, with whom we have most concern.

The rector had not resided in the parish for a long time – between fifteen and twenty years. It was a college living, of the value of four hundred and fifty pounds a year, and it had been conferred upon the Rev. Reginald Chester, who was a fellow of the college, as long ago as the time I mention. Mr Chester was a very good scholar, and a man of very refined tastes. He had lived in his rooms at Oxford, and in various choice regions of the world, specially in France and Italy, up to the age of forty, indulging all his favourite (and quite virtuous) tastes, and living a very pleasant if not a very useful life. He had a little fortune of his own, and he had his fellowship, and was able to keep up congenial society, and to indulge himself in all the indulgences he liked. Why he should have accepted the living of Brentburn it would be hard to say; I suppose there is always an attraction, even to the most philosophical, in a few additional hundreds a year. He took it, keeping out poor Arlington, who had the next claim, and who wanted to marry, and longed for a country parish. Mr. Chester did not want to marry, and hated everything parochial; but he took the living all the same. He came to live at Brentburn at the beginning of summer, furnishing the house substantially, with Turkey carpets , and huge mountains of mahogany – for the science of furniture had scarcely been developed in those days; and for the first few months, having brought an excellent cook with him, and finding his friends in town quite willing to spend a day or two by times in the country, and being within an hour's journey of London, he got on tolerably well. But the winter was a very different matter. His friends no longer cared to come. There was good hunting to be sure, but Mr Chester's friends in general were not hunting men, and the country was damp and rheumatic, and the society more agricultural than intellectual. Then his cook, still more important, mutinied. She had never been used to it, and her kitchen was damp, and she had no means of improving herself 'in this hole,' as she irreverently called the rectory of Brentburn. Heroically, in spite of this, in spite of the filthy roads, the complaints of the poor, an indifferent cook, and next to no society, Mr Chester held out for two long years. The damp crept on him, into his very bones. He got incipient rheumatism, and he had a sharp attack of bronchitis. This was in spring, the most dangerous season when your lungs are weak; and in Mr Chester's family there had at one time been a girl who died of consumption. He was just at the age when men are most careful of their lives, when, awaking out of the confidence of youth, they begin to realize that they are mortal, and one day or other must die. He took fright; he consulted a kind of physician, who was quite ready to certify that his health required Mentone or Spitzbergen, whichever the patient wished; and then Mr Chester advertised for a curate. The parish was so small that up to this moment he had not had any occasion for such an article. He got a most superior person, the Rev. Cecil St. John, who was very ready and happy to undertake all the duties for less than half of the stipend. Mr Chester was a liberal man in his way. He let Mr St. John have the rectory to live in, and the use of all his furniture, except his best Turkey carpets, which it must be allowed were too good for a curate; and then, with heart relieved, he took his way into the south and the sunshine. What a relief it was! He soon got better at Mentone and went on to more amusing and attractive places; but as it was on account of his health that he had got rid of his parish, consistency required that he should continue to be 'delicate.' Nothing is more easy than to manage this when one has money enough and nothing to do. He bought a small villa near Naples, with the best possible aspect, sheltered from the east wind. He became a great authority on the antiquities of the neighbourhood, and in this way had a constant change and variety of the very best society. He took great care of himself; was never out at sunset, avoided the sirocco, and took great precautions against fever. He even began to plan a book about Pompeii. And thus the years glided by quite peacefully in the most refined of occupations, and he had almost forgotten that he ever was rector of Brentburn. Young fellows of his college recollected it from time to time, and asked querulously if he never meant to die. 'You may be sure he will never die if he can help it,' the Provost of the learned community replied, chuckling, for he knew his man. And meantime Mr St. John, who was the curate in charge, settled down and made himself comfortable, and forgot that he was not there in his own right. It is natural a man should feel so who has been priest of a parish for nearly twenty years.

This Mr St. John was a man of great tranquillity of mind, and with little energy of disposition. Where he was set down there he remained, taking all that Providence sent him very dutifully, without any effort to change what might be objectionable or amend what was faulty; nobody could be more accomplished than he was in the art of 'putting up with' whatsoever befell him. When once he had been established anywhere, only something from without could move him – never any impulse from within. He took what happened to him, as the birds took the crumbs he threw out to them, without question or preference. The only thing in which he ever took an initiative was in kindness. He could not bear to hurt any one's feelings, to make any one unhappy, and by dint of his submissiveness of mind he was scarcely ever unhappy himself. The poor people all loved him; he could never refuse them anything, and his reproofs were balms which broke no man's head. He was indeed, but for his sympathy, more like an object in nature – a serene, soft hillside touched by the lights and shadows of changeable skies, yet never really affected by them except for the moment – than a suffering and rejoicing human creature.

> 'On a fair landscape some have looked
> And felt, as I have heard them say,
> As if the fleeting time had been
> A thing as steadfast as the scene
> On which they gazed themselves away.'

This was the effect Mr St. John produced upon his friends and the parish; change seemed impossible to him – and that he could die, or disappear, or be anything different from what he was, was as hard to conceive as it was to realize that distinct geological moment when the hills were all in fusion, and there was not a tree in the forest. That this should be the case in respect to the curate in charge , whose position was on sufferance, and whom any accident happening to another old man in Italy, or any caprice of that old man's fancy, could sweep away out of the place as if he had never been, gave additional quaintness yet power to the universal impression. Nobody could imagine what Brentburn would be like without Mr St. John, and he himself was of the same mind.

At the period when this story commences the curate was a widower with 'two families.' He had been so imprudent as to marry twice; he had two daughters grown up, who were coming to him, but had not arrived, and he had two little baby boys, whose mother had recently died. But how this mother and these boys came about, to Mr St. John's great surprise – and who the daughters were who were coming to take charge of him – I must tell before I go on any further. The whole episode of his second marriage was quite accidental in the curate's life.

CHAPTER TWO

THE PREVIOUS HISTORY OF MR ST. JOHN

The Reverend Cecil St. John started in life, not so much under a false impression himself, as conveying one right and left wherever he moved. With such a name it seemed certain that he must be a man of good family, well-connected to the highest level of good connections; but he was not. I cannot tell how this happened, or where he got his name. When he was questioned about his family he declared himself to have no relations at all. He was his father's only child, and his father had been someone else's only child; and the result was that he had nobody belonging to him. The people at Weston-on-Weir, which was his first curacy, had a tradition that his grandfather had been disowned and disinherited by his family on account of a romantic marriage; but this, I fear, was pure fable invented by some parish authority with a lively imagination. All the years he spent at Weston nobody, except an old pupil, ever asked for him; he possessed no family possessions, not even an old seal, or bit of china. His father had been a curate before him, and was dead and gone, leaving no ties in the world to his only boy. This had happened so long ago that Mr St. John had long ceased to be sad about it before he came to Weston; and though the ladies there were very sorry for his loneliness, I am not sure that it occurred to himself to be sorry. He was used to it. He had stayed in Oxford for some years after he took his degree, working with pupils; so that he was about five and thirty when he took his first curacy, moved, I suppose, by some sense of the monotony of an unprogressive life. At five and thirty one has ceased to feel certain that everything must go well with one, and probably it occurred to him that the Church would bring repose and quiet, which he loved, and possibly some quiet promotion. Therefore he accepted the curacy of Weston-on-Weir, and got lodgings in

Mrs Joyce's, and settled there. The parish was somewhat excited about his coming, and many people at first entertained the notion that his proper title was Honourable and Reverend. But, alas! that turned out, as I have said, a delusion. Still, without the honourable, such a name as that of Cecil St. John was enough to flatter a parish, and did so. Even the sight of him did not dissipate the charm, for he was handsome, very tall, slight, serious, and interesting. 'Like a young widower,' some of the ladies thought; others, more romantic, felt that he must have a history, must have sustained a blight; but if he had, he never said anything about it, and settled down to his duties in a calm matter-of-fact way, as if his name had been John Smith.

Everybody who knows Weston-on-Weir is aware that Mrs Joyce's cottage is very near the vicarage. The vicar, Mr Maydew, was an old man, and all but incapable of work, which was the reason why he kept a curate. He was a popular vicar, but a selfish man, whose family had always been swayed despotically by his will, though scarcely any of them were aware of it, for his iron hand was hidden in the velvetest of gloves, and all the Maydews were devoted to their father. He had sent one son to India, where he died, and another to Australia, where he had been lost for years. His eldest daughter had married a wealthy person in Manchester, but had died too, at an early age, for none of them were strong; thus his youngest daughter, Hester, was the only one left to him. Her he could not spare; almost from her cradle he had seen that this was the one to be his companion in his old age and inexorably he had guarded her for this fate. No man had ever been allowed to approach Hester, in whose eyes any gleam of admiration or kindness for her had appeared. It had been tacitly understood all along that she was never to leave her father, and as he was very kind in manner, Hester accepted the lot with enthusiasm, and thought it was her own choice, and that nothing could ever tempt her to abandon him. What was to become of her when her father had left her, Hester never asked herself, and neither did the old man, who was less innocent in his thoughtlessness. 'Something will turn up for Hester,' he said in his cheerful moods, 'and the Lord will provide for so good a daughter,' he said in his solemn ones.

But he acted as if it were no concern of his, and so, firm in doing the duty that lay nearest her hand, did she, which was less wonderful. Hester had lived to be thirty when Mr St. John came to Weston. She was already called an old maid by the young and gay, and even by the elder people about. She was almost pretty in a quiet way, though many people thought her *quite* plain. She had a transparent, soft complexion, not brilliant but pure; soft brown eyes, very kind and tender; fine silky brown hair, and a trim figure; but no features to speak of, and no style, and lived contented in the old rotten tumbledown vicarage, doing the same thing every day at the same hour year after year, serving her father and the parish, attending all the church services, visiting the schools and the sick people. I hope good women who live in this dutiful routine get to like it, and find a happiness in the thought of so much humble handmaiden's work performed so steadily; but to the profane and the busy it seems hard thus to wear away a life.

When Mr St. John came to the parish it was avowedly to relieve old Mr Maydew of the duty, not to help him in it. Now and then the old vicar would show on a fine day, and preach one of his old sermons; but, except for this, everything was left to Mr St. John. He was not, however, allowed on that account to rule the parish. He had to go and come constantly to the vicarage to receive directions, or advice which was as imperative; and many a day walked to church or into the village with Miss Hester, whom nobody ever called Miss Maydew, though she had for years a right to the name. The result, which some people thought very natural, and some people quite absurd, soon followed. Quietly, gradually, the two fell in love with each other. There were people in the parish who were quite philanthropically indignant when they heard of it, and very anxious that Mr St. John should be undeceived, if any idea of Hester Maydew having money was in his thoughts. But they might have spared themselves the trouble. Mr St. John was not thinking of money. He was not even thinking of marriage. It never occurred to him to make any violent opposition, when Hester informed him, timidly, fearing I know not what demonstration of lover-like impatience, of her promise never to leave her father. He was willing to wait. To spend every evening in the vicarage, to see her two or three times a day, going and coming; to consult her on everything, and inform her of everything that happened to him, was quite enough for the curate. He used to tell her so; while Hester's heart, wrung with pleasure and pain together, half stood still with wonder, not knowing how a man could bear it, yet glad he should. How much there is in the hearts of such good women which never can come into words! She had in her still soul a whole world of ideal people – the ideal man as well as the ideal woman – and her ideal man would not have been content. Yet *he* was, and she was glad; or rather I should say thankful, which is a different feeling. And thus they went on for ten years. Ten years! an eternity to look forward to – a lifetime to look back upon; yet slipping away so softly , day upon day, that Mr St. John at least never realized the passage of time. He was a very good clergyman, very kind to the poor people and to the children, very ready to be of service to any one who wanted his services, seeking no diversion or ease except to go down to the vicarage in the evening by that path which his patient feet had made, to play backgammon with the vicar and talk to Hester. I cannot see, for my part, why they should not have married, and occupied the vicarage together; but such an arrangement would not have suited Mr Maydew, and Hester was well aware of the impossibility of serving two masters. So year came after year, and hour after hour, as if there were no changes in human existence, but everything was as steady and immovable as the surface of that tranquil rural world.

When Mr Maydew died at last it was quite a shock to the curate; and then it was evident that something must be done. They hoped for a little while that Lord Weston might have given the living to Mr St. John, who was so much beloved in the parish; but it had been promised years before to his old tutor, and there was an end of that expectation. I think Hester had almost come to doubt whether her curate had energy to marry her when she was thus set free; but there she did him injustice. Though he had not a notion how they were to live, he would have married her on the spot had decorum permitted. It was some time, however, before he heard of anything which would justify them in marrying. He had little interest out of the parish, and was shy of asking anything from the few people he did know. When they were told of Brentburn, and the rector's bad health, they both felt it a special providence that Mr Chester's lungs should be weak. There was the rectory to live in, and two hundred pounds a year, which seemed a fortune to them both; and they married upon it with as much confidence as if it had been two thousand. They were almost old people when they set off from the little church at Weston bride and bridegroom; yet very young in the tranquillity of their souls. Mr St. John was thoroughly happy – not much more happy indeed than when he had walked down across the grass to the vicarage – but not less so; and if Hester felt a thrill of disappointment deep down in her heart at his calm, she loved him all the same, and knew his goodness, and was happy too. She was a woman of genius in her way – not poetical or literary genius – but that which is as good, perhaps better. She managed to live upon her two hundred a year as few of us can do upon three or four times the sum. Waste was impossible to her; and want appeared as impossible. She guided her house as well, as only genius can – without any pitiful economies, without any undue sparing, making a kind, warm, beneficent, living house of it, and yet keeping within her income. I don't pretend to know how she did it, any more than I can tell you how Shakespeare wrote *Hamlet*. It was quite easy to him – and to her; but if one knew how, one would be as great a poet as he was, as great an economist as she. Mr St. John was perfectly happy; perhaps even a little more happy than when he used to walk nightly to her father's vicarage. The thought that he was only curate in charge, and that his rector might get better and come back, or get worse and die, never troubled his peace. Why should not life always go as it was doing? why should anything ever happen? Now and then he would speak of the vicissitudes of mortal existence in his placid little sermons; but he knew nothing of them, and believed still less. It seemed to him as if this soft tranquillity, this sober happiness was fixed like the pillars of the earth, and would never come to an end.

Nor is it possible to tell how it was, that to this quiet pair two such restless atoms of humanity as the two girls whose story is to be told here should have been born. Hester's old nurse, indeed, had often been heard to tell fabulous stories of the energy and animation of her young mistress in the days of her youth, but these had always been believed in Weston to be apocryphal. The appearance of her children, however, gave some semblance of truth to the tale. They were the most living creatures in all the parish of Brentburn. These two children, from the time they were born, were ready for anything – nothing daunted them or stilled them – they did not know what fear was. Sometimes there passed through the mind of their mother a regret that they were not boys; but then she would think of her husband and the regret was never expressed. Their very vitality and activity made them easy to train, and she taught them, poor soul, and spent her strength upon them as if she knew what was coming. She taught them her own household ways, and her economy as far as children could learn it, and to read and write, and their notes on the old piano. This was all she had time for. She died when Cicely was twelve and Mab eleven. God help us! what it must be when a woman has to consent to die and leave her little children to fight their own way through this hard world, who can venture to tell? For my part, I cannot so much as think of it. Something comes choking in one's throat, climbing like Lear's *hysterica passio*. Ah, God help us indeed! to think of it is terrible, to do it – Poor Hester had to accept this lot and cover her face and go away, leaving those two to make what they could of their life. Her death stupefied Mr St. John. He could not believe it, could not understand it. It came upon him like a thunderbolt, incredible, impossible; yet, to be sure, he had to put up with it like other men. And so tranquil was his soul, that by-and-by he quite learned to put up with it, and grew calm again, and made himself a path across the common to the churchyard gate which led to her grave, just as he had made himself a path to her father's door. Everything passes away except human character and individuality, which outlive all convulsions. The parish of Brentburn, which like him was stupefied for the moment, could not contain its admiration when it was seen how beautifully he bore it – 'Like a true Christian,' the people said – like himself I think; and he was a good Christian, besides being so placid a man.

The two children got over it too in the course of nature; they had passions of childish anguish, unspeakable dumb longings which no words could utter; and then were hushed and stilled, and after a while were happy again; life must defend itself with this natural insensibility or it could not be life at all. And Mr. St. John's friends and parishioners were very kind to him, especially in the matter of advice, of which he stood in much need. His 'plans' and what he should do were debated in every house in the parish before poor Hester was cold in her grave; and the general conclusion which was almost unanimously arrived at was – a governess. A governess was the right thing for him, a respectable, middle-aged person who would have no scheme for marrying in her head – not a person of great pretensions, but one who would take entire charge of the girls (whom their mother, poor soul, had left too much to themselves), and would not object to give an eye to the housekeeping – of ladylike manners, yet perhaps not *quite* a lady either, lest she might object to the homelier offices cast upon her. Mrs Ascott, of the Heath, happened to know exactly the right person, the very thing for poor Mr St. John and his girls. And Mr St. John accepted the advice of the ladies of the parish with gratitude, confessing piteously that he did not at all know what to do. So Miss Brown arrived six months after Mrs St. John's death. She was not too much of a lady. She was neither old nor young, she was subject to neuralgia; her complexion and her eyes were grey, like her dress, and she had no pretensions to good looks. But with these little drawbacks, which in her position everybody argued were no drawbacks at all, but rather advantages, she was a good woman, and though she did not understand them, she was kind to the girls. Miss Brown, however, was not in any respect a woman of genius, and even had she been so, her gifts would have been neutralized by the fact that she was not the mistress of the house, but only the governess. The maid who had worked so well under Hester set up pretensions to be housekeeper too, and called herself the cook, and assumed airs which Miss Brown got the better of with great difficulty; and the aspect of the house changed. Now and then indeed a crisis arrived which troubled Mr St. John's peace of mind very much, when he was appealed to one side or the other. But yet the life of the household had been so well organized that it went on *tant bien que mal* for several years. And the two girls grew healthy, and handsome, and strong. Miss Brown did her very best for them. She kept them down as much as she could, which she thought was her duty, and as what she could do in this way was but small, the control she attained to was an unmixed advantage to them. Poor Hester had called her eldest child Cecil, after her father, with a touch of tender sentiment; but use and fondness, and perhaps a sense that the more romantic appellation sounded somewhat weak-minded, had long ago improved it into Cicely. Mabel got her name from a similar motive, because it was pretty. It was the period when names of this class came into fashion, throwing the old-fashioned Janes and Elizabeths into temporary eclipse; but as the girls grew up and it came to be impossible to connect her with any two-syllabled or dignified word, the name lent itself to abbreviation and she became Mab. They were both pretty girls. Cicely had her mother's softness, Mab her father's more regular beauty. They spent their lives in the pure air, in the woods, which were so close at hand, in the old-fashioned garden which they partly cultivated, or, when they could get so far, on those bleaker commons and pine forests, where the breezes went to their young heads like wine. Miss Brown's friends in the parish 'felt for her' with two such wild creatures to manage; and she occasionally 'felt for herself', and sighed with a gentle complacency to think of the 'good work' she was doing. But I don't think she found her task as hard as she said. The girls did not look up to her, but they looked very kindly down upon her, which came to much the same thing, taking care with youthful generosity not to let her see how much insight they had, or how they laughed between themselves at her mild little affectations. Children are terribly sharp-sighted, and see through these innocent pretences better than we ourselves do. They took care of her often when she thought she was taking care of them; and yet they learned the simple lessons she gave them with something like pleasure; for their natures were so vigorous and wholesome that even the little tedium was agreeable as a change. And for their father they entertained a kind of half-contemptuous – nay, the word is too hard – a kind of condescending worship. He was a god to them, but a god who was very helpless, who could do little for himself, who was inferior to them in all practical things, though more good, more kind, more handsome, more elevated than any other mortal. This was, on the whole, rather safe ground for two such active-minded young persons. They were prepared to see him do foolish things now and then. It was 'papa's way,' which they accepted without criticism, smiling to one another, but in their minds he was enveloped in a sort of feeble divinity, a being in whom certain weaknesses were understood, but whose pedestal of superiority no other human creature could approach. Thus things went on till Cicely was fifteen, when important changes took place in their lives, and still more especially in their father's life.

CHAPTER THREE

AUNT JANE

The St. Johns had one relative, and only one, so far as they
knew. This was Miss Jane Maydew, who lived in London, the
aunt of their mother, a lady who possessed in her own right –
but, alas, only in the form of an annuity – the magnificent sum
of two hundred and fifty pounds a year. To think that this old
lady, with only herself to think of, should have fifty pounds
more yearly than a clergyman with a family, and all the parish
looking to him! More than once this idea had crossed even
Hester's mind, though she was very reasonable and could
make her pounds go further than most people. Miss Maydew
was not very much older than her niece, but yet she was an
old lady, sixty-five, or thereabouts. She liked her little comforts as well as most people, yet she had laid by fifty pounds of
her income for the last twenty years, with the utmost
regularity. A thousand pounds is a pretty little sum of money,
but it does not seem much to count for twenty years of
savings. A stockbroker might make it easily in a morning by a
mere transfer from one hand to another; and to think how
much wear and tear of humanity can it be on the other hand! It
is discouraging to poor economists to feel how little they can
do, labour as they may; but I don't think Miss Maydew had
anything of this feeling. She was on the contrary very proud
of her thousand pounds. It was her own creation, she had
made it out of nothing; and the name of it, a thousand pounds!
was as a strain of music in her ears, like the name of a favourite
child. Perhaps it was the completion of this beautiful sum,
rounded and finished like a poem, which gave her something
of that satisfaction and wish for repose which follows the
completion of every great work; and this brought about her
visit to Brentburn, and all that directly and indirectly followed
it. She had not seen the St. Johns since Hester's death, though

they were her nearest relatives, the natural heirs of the fortune she had accumulated. And the summer was warming into June, and everything spoke of the country. Miss Maydew lived in Great Coram Street, Russell Square. She had two charming large rooms, her bedroom at the back, her sitting-room at the front, the two drawing rooms in better days of the comfortable Bloomsbury mansion. But even when your rooms are airy and cool, it is hard to fight against that sense of summer which drops into a London Street in the warm long days, waking recollections of all kinds, making eyelids drowsy, and the imagination work. Even the cries in the street, the 'flowers a blowing and a growing' of the coster-mongers, the first vegetables, the 'groundsel for your birds,' and the very sight of the greengrocer opposite with his groves of young cabbages and baskets of young potatoes awoke this sensation of summer in the heart of the solitary woman at her window. Her youth, which was so full of summer, stirred in her once more, and old scenes all framed in waving foliage of trees and soft enclosures of greensward, came before her closed eyes as she dozed through the long, long sunny afternoon. A frugal old maiden, lodging in two rooms in a noisy Bloomsbury street, and saving fifty pounds a year, is as little safe as any poet from such visitations. As she sat there musing in that strange confusion of mind which makes one wonder sometimes whether the things one recollects ever were, or were merely a dream, Hester and Hester's children came into Miss Maydew's mind. She had not seen them since her niece's death, and what might have become of the poor children left with that incapable father? This thought simmered in her fancy for a whole week, then suddenly one morning when it was finer than ever, and the very canaries sang wildly in their cages, and the costermongers' cries lost all their hoarseness in the golden air, she took the decided step of going off to the railway and taking a ticket for Brentburn. It was not very far, an hour's journey only, and there was no need to take any luggage with her, as she could return the same night; so the excursion was both cheap and easy, as mild an extravagance as a heart could desire.

The air was full of the wild sweet freshness of the pines as she landed on the edge of the common; the seed pods on the gorse bushes were crackling in the heat, the ragged hedges on the roadside hung out long pennons of straggling branches, blossomed to the very tips with wild roses delicately sweet. Miss Maydew was not long in encountering the objects of her interest. As she went along to the rectory, carrying her large brown sunshade open in one hand, and her large white pocket-handkerchief to fan herself in the other, her ears and her eyes were alike attracted by a little group, under the shadow of a great tree just where the gorse and the pines ended. There were two tall girls in print frocks of the simplest character, and large hats of coarse straw; and seated on the root of the tree slightly raised above them, a plain little woman in a brown gown. Some well worn volumes were lying on the grass, but the book which one of the girls held in her hand, standing up in an attitude of indignant remonstrance, was a square slim book of a different aspect. The other held a huge pencil, one of those weapons red at one end and blue at the other which schoolboys love, which she twirled in her fingers with some excitement. Miss Maydew divined at once who they were, and walking slowly, listened. Their voices were by no means low, and they were quite unconscious of auditors and indifferent who might hear.

'What does "nice" mean?' cried the elder, flourishing the book. 'Why, is it not ladylike? If one is clever, and has a gift, is one not to use it? Not *nice*? I want to know what *nice* means?'

'My dear,' said the governess, 'I wish you would not always be asking what everything means. A great many things are understood without explanation in good society — '

'But we don't know anything about good society, nor society at all. Why is it not nice for Mab to draw? Why is it unladylike?' cried the girl, her eyes sparkling. As for the other one, she shrugged her shoulders, and twirled her pencil, while Miss Brown looked at them with a feeble protestation, clasping her hands in despair.

'Oh, Cicely! never anything but why? – why?' she said, with lofty, yet pitying disapproval. 'You may be sure it is so when I say it.' Then, leaving this high position for the more dangerous exercise of reason. 'Besides, the more one thinks of it, the more improper it seems. There are drawings of *gentlemen* in that book. Is that nice, do you suppose? Gentlemen! Put it away; and, Mabel, I desire you never to do anything so very unladylike again.'

'But, Miss Brown!' said the younger; 'there are a great many gentlemen in the world. I can't help seeing them, can I?'

'A young lady who respects herself, and who has been brought up as she ought, never looks at gentlemen. No, you can't help seeing them; but to draw them you must *look* at them; you must study them. Oh!' said Miss Brown with horror, putting up her hands before her eyes, 'never let me hear of such a thing again. Give me the book. Cicely. It is too dreadful. I ought to burn it; but at least I must lock it away.'

'Don't be afraid, Mab; she shan't have the book,' said Cicely, with flashing eyes, stepping back, and holding the volume behind her in her clasped hands.

Just then Miss Maydew touched her on the sleeve. 'I can't be mistaken,' said the old lady; 'you are so like your poor mother. Are you not Mr St. John's daughter? I suppose you don't remember me?'

'It is Aunt Jane,' whispered Mab in Cicely's ear, getting up with a blush, more conscious of the interruption than her sister was. The artist had the quickest eye.

'Yes, it is Aunt Jane; I am glad you recollect.' said Miss Maydew. 'I have come all the way from town to pay you a visit, and that is not a small matter on such a hot day.'

'Papa will be very glad to see you,' said Cicely, looking up shy but pleased, with a flood of colour rushing over her face under the shade of her big hat. She was doubtful whether she should put up her cheek to kiss the stranger, or wait for that salutation. She put out her hand, which seemed an intermediate measure. 'I am Cicely,' she said, 'and this is Mab; we are very glad to see you, Aunt Jane.'

Miss Brown got up hastily from under the tree, and made the stranger a curtsy. She gave a troubled glance at the girls' frocks, which were not so fresh as they might have been. 'You will excuse their schoolroom dresses,' she said, 'we were not expecting any one; and it was so fine this morning that I indulged the young ladies, and let them do their work here. Ask your aunt, my dears, to come in.'

'Work!' said Miss Maydew, somewhat crossly, 'I heard nothing but talk. Yes, I should like to go in, if you please. It is a long walk from the station – and so hot. Why, it is hotter here than in London, for all you talk about the country. There you can always get shade on one side of the street. This is like a furnace. I don't know how you can live in such a blazing place;' and the old lady fanned herself with her large white handkerchief, a sight which brought gleams of mischief into Mab's brown eyes. The red and blue pencil twirled more rapidly round than ever in her fingers, and she cast a longing glance at the sketch-book in Cicely's hand. The girls were quite cool, and at their ease under the great beech-tree, which threw broken shadows far over the grass, – shadows which waved about as the boughs did, and refreshed the mind with soft visionary fanning. Their big hats shadowed two faces, fresh and cool like flowers, with that downy bloom upon them which is the privilege of extreme youth. Miss Brown, who was concerned about their frocks, saw nothing but the creases in their pink and white garments; but what Miss Maydew saw was (she herself said) 'a picture;' two fair slim things in white, with touches of pink, in soft shade, with bright patches of sunshine flitting about them, and the green background of the common rolled back in soft undulations behind. Poor lady! she was a great contrast to this picture; her cheeks flushed with the heat, her bonnet-strings loosed, fanning herself with her handkerchief. And this was what woke up those gleams of fun in Mab's saucy eyes.

'But it is not hot,' said Mab. 'How can you speak of a street when you are on the common? Don't you smell the pines, Aunt Jane, and the honey in the gorse? Come under the trees near to us; it is not the least hot here.'

'You are a conceited little person,' said Aunt Jane.

'Oh no! she is not conceited – she is only decided in her opinions,' said Cicely. 'You see *we* are not hot in the shade. But come in this way, the back way, through the garden, which is always cool. Sit down here in the summer-house, Aunt Jane, and rest. I'll run and get you some strawberries. They are just beginning to get ripe.'

'You are a nice little person,' said Miss Maydew, sitting down with a sigh of relief. 'I don't want any strawberries, but you can come and kiss me. ,You are very like your poor mother. As for that thing, I don't know who she is like – not our family, I am sure.'

'She is like the St. John's.' said Cicely solemnly; 'she is like papa.'

Mab only laughed. She did not mind what people said. 'I'll kiss you too,' she said, 'Aunt Jane, if you like; though you don't like me.'

'I never said I didn't like you. I am not so fond of my family as that. One can see you are a pickle, though I don't so much mind that either; but I like to look at this one, because she is like your poor mother. Dear, dear! Hester's very eyes, and her cheeks like two roses, and her nice brown wavy hair!'

The girls drew near with eager interest, and Mab took up in her artist's fingers a great handful of the hair which lay upon her sister's shoulders. 'Was mamma's like that?' she said in awe and wonder; and Cicely, too, fixed her eyes upon her own bright locks reverentially. It gave them a new strange feeling for their mother to think that she had once been a girl like themselves. Strangest thought for a child's mind to grasp; stranger even than the kindred thought, that one day those crisp half-curling locks, full of threads of gold, would be blanched like the soft braids under Mrs St. John's cap. 'Poor mamma!' they said simultaneously under their breath.

'Brighter than that!' said Miss Maydew, seeing across the mists of years a glorified vision of youth, more lovely than Hester had ever been. 'Ah well!' she added with a sigh, 'time goes very quickly, girls. Before you know, you will be old, too, and tell the young ones how pretty you were long ago. Yes, Miss Audacity! you mayn't believe it, but I was pretty, too.'

'Oh yes, I believe it!' cried Mab, relieved from the momentary gravity which had subdued her. 'You have a handsome nose still, and not nearly so bad a mouth as most people. I should like to draw you, just as you stood under the beech-tree; that was beautiful!' she cried, clapping her hands. Miss Maydew was pleased. She recollected how she had admired the two young creatures under that far-spreading shade; and it did not seem at all unnatural that they should in their turn have admired her.

'Mabel! Mabel!' said Miss Brown, who knew better, lifting

a warning finger. Miss Maydew took up the sketch-book which Cicely had laid on the rough table in the summer-house. 'Is this what you were all talking about?' she said. But at this moment the governess withdrew and followed Cicely into the house. She walked through the garden towards the rectory in a very dignified way. She could not stand by and laugh faintly at caricatures of herself as some high-minded people are capable of doing. 'I hope Miss Maydew will say what she thinks very plainly,' she said to Cicely, who flew past her in a great hurry with a fresh clean white napkin out of the linen-press. But Cicely was much too busy to reply. As for Mab, I think she would have escaped too, had she been able; but as that was impossible, she stood up very demurely while her old aunt turned over the book, which was a note-book ruled with blue lines, and intended for a more virtuous purpose than that to which it had been appropriated; and it was not until Miss Maydew burst into a short but hearty laugh over a caricature of Miss Brown that Mab ventured to breathe.

'You wicked little thing! Are these yours?' said Miss Maydew; 'and how dared you let that poor woman see them? Why, she is there to the life!'

'Oh! Aunt Jane, give me the book! She has never seen them: only a few innocent ones at the beginning. Oh! *please* give me the book! I don't want her to see them!' cried Mab.

'You hate her, I suppose?'

'Oh! no, no! give me the book, Aunt Jane! We don't hate her at all; we like her rather. Oh! please give it me before she comes back!'

'Why do you make caricatures of her, then?' said Miss Maydew, fixing her eyes severely on the girl's face.

'Because she is such fun!' cried Mab; 'because it is such fun. I don't mean any harm, but if people will look funny, how can I help it? Give me the book, Aunt Jane!'

'I suppose I looked funny too,' said Miss Maydew, 'under the beech-tree, fanning myself with my pocket handkerchief. I thought I heard you giggle. Go away, you wicked little thing! Here is your sister coming. I like her a great deal better than you!'

'So she is a great deal better than me,' said Mab, picking up her book. She stole away, giving herself a serious lecture, as

Cicely tripped into the summer-house carrying a tray. 'I must not do it again,' she said to herself. 'It is silly of me. It is always getting me into scrapes; even papa, when I showed that one of himself!' Here Mab paused to laugh, for it had been very funny – and then blushed violently; for certainly it was wrong, very wrong to caricature one's papa. 'At all events,' she said under her breath, 'I'll get a book with a lock and key as soon as ever I have any money, and show them only to Cicely; but oh! I must, I must just this once, do Aunt Jane!'

Cicely meanwhile came into the summer-house carrying the tray. 'It is not the right time for it, I know,' she said, 'but I felt sure you would like a cup of tea. Doesn't it smell nice – like the hay-fields? Tea is always nice, is it not, Aunt Jane?'

'My darling, you are the very image of your poor mother!' said Miss Maydew with tears in her eyes. 'She was always one who took the trouble to think what her friends would like best. And what good tea it is, and how nicely served! Was the kettle boiling? Ah! I recognize your dear mother in that. It used always to be a saying with us at home that the kettle should always be boiling in a well-regulated house.'

Then the old lady began to ask cunning questions about the household: whether Cicely was in the habit of making tea and carrying trays about, as she did this so nicely; and other close and delicate cross-examinations, by which she found out a great deal about the qualities of the servant and the governess. Miss Maydew was too clever to tell Cicely what she thought at the conclusion of her inquiry, but she went in thoughtfully to the house, and was somewhat silent as the girls took her all over it – to the best room to take off her bonnet, to their room to see what a pretty view they had, and into all the empty chambers. The comments she made as she followed them were few but significant. 'It was rather extravagant of your papa to furnish it all; he never could have wanted so large a house,' she said.

'Oh! but the furniture is the Rector's, it is not papa's,' cried her conductors, both in a breath.

'I shouldn't like, if I were him, to have the charge of other people's furniture,' Miss Maydew replied; and it seemed to the girls that she was rather disposed to find fault with all poor papa's arrangements, though she was so kind to them. Mr St.

John was 'in the parish,' and did not come back until it was time for the early dinner; and it was late in the afternoon when Miss Maydew, knocking at his study door, went in alone to 'have a talk' with him, with intention of 'giving him her mind' on several subjects, written fully in her face. The study was a well-sized room looking out upon the garden, and furnished with heavy book-shelves and bureaux in old dark coloured mahogany. The carpet was worn but those mournful pieces of furniture defied the action of time. She looked round upon them with a slightly supercilious critical glance.

'The room is very well furnished,' she said, 'Mr St. John; exceedingly well furnished; to rub it up and keep it in order must give your servant a great deal of work.'

'It is not my furniture, but Mr Chester's, my rector,' said the curate; 'we never had very much of our own.'

'It must give the maid a deal of work all the same, and that's why the girls have so much housemaiding to do, I suppose,' said Miss Maydew sharply. 'To tell the truth, that was what I came to speak of. I am not at all satisfied, Mr St. John, about the girls.'

'The girls? They are quite well, I think, quite well,' said Mr St. John meekly. He was not accustomed to be spoken to in this abrupt tone.

'I was not thinking of their health; of course they are well; how could they help being well with so much fresh air, and a cow, I suppose, and all that? I don't like the way they are managed. They are nice girls, but that Miss Brown knows just about as much how to manage them as you – as that table does, Mr St. John. It is ridiculous. She has no control over them. Now I'll tell you what is my opinion. They ought to be sent to school.'

'To school!' he said, startled. 'I thought girls were not sent to school.'

'Ah, that is when they have a nice mother to look after them – a woman like poor Hester; but what are those two doing? You don't look after them yourself, Mr. St. John?'

'I suppose it can't be said that I do,' he said, with hesitation: 'perhaps it is wrong, but what do I know of girls' education? and then they all said I should have Miss Brown.'

'Who are "they all?" You should have asked me. I should
never have said Miss Brown. Not that I've anything against
her. She is a good, silly creature enough – but pay attention to
me, please, Mr. St. John. I say the girls should go to school.'

'It is very likely you may be right,' said Mr. St. John, who
always yielded to impetuosity, 'but what should I do with
Miss Brown?'

'Send her away – nothing could be more easy – tell her that
you shall not want her services any longer. You must give her
a month's notice, unless she was engaged in some particular
way.'

'I don't know,' said the curate in trepidation. 'Bless me, it
will be very unpleasant. What will she do? What do you think
she would say? Don't you think, on the whole, we get on very
well as we are? I have always been told that it is bad to send
girls to school; and besides it costs a great deal of money,' he
added after a pause. 'I don't know if I could afford it; that is a
thing which must be thought of,' he said, with a sense of
relief.

'I have thought of that,' said Miss Maydew triumphantly:
'the girls interest me, and I will send them to school. Oh,
don't say anything. I don't do it for thanks. To me their
improving will be my recompense. Put all anxiety out of your
mind; I will undertake the whole – '

'But, Miss Maydew!'

'There are no buts in the matter,' said Aunt Jane, rising; 'I
have quite settled it. I have saved a nice little sum, which will
go to them eventually, and I should like to see them in a
position to do me credit. Don't say anything, Mr. St. John.
Hester's girls! – poor Hester! – no one in the world can have so
great a claim upon me; and no one can tell so well as I what
they lost in poor Hester, Mr. St. John – and what you lost as
well.'

The curate bowed his head. Though he was so tranquil and
resigned, the name of his Hester went to his heart, with a dull
pang, perhaps – for he was growing old, and had a calm
impassioned spirit – but still with a pang, and no easy words
of mourning would come to his lip.

'Yes, indeed,' said Aunt Jane, 'I don't know that I ever
knew any one like her; and her girls shall have justice, they

shall have justice, Mr. St. John. I mean to make it my business to find them a school – but till you have heard from me finally,' she added, turning back after she had reached the door, 'it will be as well not to say anything to Miss Brown.'

'Oh no,' said the curate eagerly, 'it will be much best to say nothing to Miss Brown.'

Miss Maydew nodded at him confidentially as she went away, and left him in all the despair of an unexpected crisis. *He* say anything to Miss Brown! What should he say? That he had no further occasion for her services? But how could he say so to a lady? Had he not always gone upon the amiable ground that she had done him the greatest favour in coming there to teach his daughters, and now to dismiss her – to *dismiss* her! Mr. St. John's heart sunk down, down to the very heels of his boots. It was all very easy for Aunt Jane, who had not got it to do; but he, *he!* how was he ever to summon his courage and say anything like this to Miss Brown?

CHAPTER FOUR

MISS BROWN

Mr St. John's mind was very much moved by this conversation. It threw a shadow over his harmless life. He could not say good night or good morning to Miss Brown without feeling in his very soul the horror of the moment when he should have to say to her that he had no further need of her services. To say it to Hannah in the kitchen would have been dreadful enough, but in that case he could at least have employed Miss Brown, or even Cicely, to do it for him, whereas now he could employ no one. Sometimes, from the mere attraction of horror, he would rehearse it under his breath when he sat up late, and knew that no one was up in the rectory, or when he was alone on some quiet road at the other extremity of the parish. 'I shall have no further need for your services.' Terrible formula! the mere thought of which froze the blood in his veins. This horror made him less sociable than he had ever been. He took no more of those evening walks which he had once liked in his quiet way, – when, the two girls speeding on before, with their restless feet, he would saunter along the twilight road after them, at ease and quiet, with his hands under his coat-tails; while little Miss Brown, generally a step or two behind, came trotting after him with her small steps, propounding little theological questions or moral doubts upon which she would like to have his opinion. The evening stillness, the shadowy, soft gloom about, the mild, grey mist of imperfect vision that made everything dreamy and vague, suited him better than the light and colour of the day. As he wandered on, in perfect repose and ease, with the two flitting figures before him, darting from side to side of the road, and from bush to bush of the common, their voices sounding like broken links of music; notwithstanding all that he had had in his life to wear him down, the curate was

26

happy. Very often at the conclusion of these walks he would go through the churchyard and stand for a moment at the white cross over his wife's grave. But this act did not change his mood; he went there as he might have gone had Hester been ill in bed, to say softly, 'Good night, my dear,' through the closed curtains. She made him no reply; but she was well off and happy, dear soul! and why should not he be so too? And when he went into supper after, he was always very cheerful; it was with him the friendliest moment of the day.

But this was all over since Miss Maydew's visit; the thought of the moment, no doubt approaching, when he would have to say, 'I shall have no further need for your services,' overwhelmed him. He had almost said it over like a parrot on several occasions, so poisoned was his mind by the horror that was to come. And Miss Maydew, I need not say, did not let any grass grow under her feet in the matter. She was so convinced of Miss Brown's incapacity, and so eager in following out her own plan, and so much interested in the occupation it gave her, that her tranquil life was quite revolutionized by it. She went to call upon all her friends, and consulted them anxiously about the young ladies' schools they knew. 'It must not be too expensive, but it must be very good,' she told all her acquaintances, who were, like most other people, struck with respect by the name of St. John. Almost an excitement arose in that quiet, respectable neigh- bourhood, penetrating even into those stately houses in Russell Square, at two or three of which Miss Maydew visited. 'Two very sweet girls, the daughters of a clergyman, the sort of girls whom it would be an advantage to any establishment to receive,' Miss Maydew's friend said; and the conclusion was, that the old lady found 'vacancies' for her nieces in the most unexpected way in a school of very high pretensions indeed, which gladly accepted, on lower terms than usual, girls so well recommended, and with so well- sounding a name. She wrote with triumph in her heart to their father as soon as she had arrived at this summit of her wishes, and, I need not say, carried despair to his. But even after he had received two or three warnings, Mr St., John could not screw his courage to the sticking point for the terrible step that was required of him; and it was only a letter from Miss

Maydew, announcing her speedy arrival to escort the girls to
their school, and her desire that their clothes should be got
ready, that forced him into action. A more miserable man was
not in all the country than, when thus compelled by fate, the
curate was. He had not been able to sleep all night for thinking
of this dreadful task before him. He was not able to eat any
breakfast, and the girls were consulting together what could
be the matter with papa when he suddenly came into the
schoolroom, where Miss Brown sat placidly at the large deal
table, setting copies in her neat little hand. All his movements
were so quiet and gentle that the abruptness of his despair
filled the girls with surprise and dismay.

'Papa came flouncing in,' Mab said, who was partly touched
and partly indignant – indignant at being sent off to school,
touched by the sight of his evident emotion. The girls believed
that this emotion was called forth by the idea of parting with
them; they did not know that it was in reality a mixture of
fright and horror as to how he was to make that terrible
announcement to Miss Brown.

'My dears,' he said, faltering, 'I have got a letter from your
Aunt Jane. I am afraid it will take you by surprise as – as it has
done to me. She wants you to – go to school.'

'To school!' they cried both together, in unfeigned horror
and alarm. Miss Brown, who had been ruling her copybooks
very nicely, acknowledging Mr St. John's entrance only by a
smile, let the pencil drop out of her hand.

'It is – very sudden.' he said, trembling – 'very sudden.
Your poor aunt is that kind of woman. She means to be very
kind to you, my dears; and she has made up her mind that you
must be educated – '

'Educated! Are we not being educated now? Miss Brown
teaches us everything – everything we require to know,' said
Cicely, her colour rising, planting herself in front of the
governess; as she had sprung up to defend her sister, when
Miss Maydew saw her first. At that age Cicely was easily
moved to indignation, and started forward perhaps too
indiscriminately in behalf of any one who might be assailed.
She was ready to put Miss Brown upon the highest pedestal,
whenever a word was said in her disfavour.

'So I think, my dear; so I think.' said the frightened curate.

'I made that very remark to your aunt; but it is very difficult to struggle against the impetuosity of a lady, and – and perhaps being taken by surprise, I – acquiesced more easily than I ought.'

'But we won't go – we can't go cried Mab. 'I shall die, and Cicely will die, if we are sent away from home.'

'My dears!' said poor Mr St. John – this impetuosity was terrible to him – 'you must not say so; indeed you must not say so. What could I say to your aunt? She means to give you all she has, and how could I oppose her? She means it for the best. I am sure she means it for the best.

'And did you really consent,' said Cicely, seriously, looking him straight in the eyes, 'without ever saying a word to us, or to Miss Brown? Oh, papa, I could not have believed it of you! I hate Aunt Jane! Miss Brown, dear!' cried the girl, throwing her arms suddenly round the little governess, 'it is not Mab's fault nor mine!'

Then it was Miss Brown's turn to fall upon the unhappy curate and slay him. 'My dear love,' she said, 'how could I suppose it was your fault or Mab's? Except a little levity now and then, which was to be expected at your age, you have been very good, very good children. There is no fault at all in the matter,' she continued, turning with that magnanimity of the aggrieved which is so terrible to an offender, to Mr St. John. 'Perhaps it is a little sudden; perhaps a person so fond of the girls as I am might have been expected to be consulted as to the best school; for there is a great difference in schools. But Miss Maydew is very impetuous, and I don't blame your dear papa. When do you wish me to leave, sir?' she said, looking at him with a smile, which tortured the curate, upon her lips.

'Miss Brown, I hope you will not think badly of me,' he said. 'You can't think how hard all this is upon me.'

The little woman rose up, and waved her hand with dignity. 'We must not enter into such questions,' she said; 'if you will be so very kind as to tell me when you would like me to go.'

I don't know what incoherent words the curate stammered forth: that she should stay as long as she liked; that she must make her arrangements entirely to suit herself; that he had never thought of wishing her to go. This is what he said in

much disturbance and agitation of mind instead of the other
formula he had rehearsed about having no further need for her
services. All this Miss Brown received with the pale smiling of
the injured and magnanimous; while the girls looked fiercely
on their father, leaving him alone and undefended. When he
got away he was so exhausted that he did not feel able to go
out into the parish, but withdrew to his study, where he
lurked, half paralyzed, all the rest of the day, like the criminal
abandoned by woman and by man, which he felt himself to
be.

And I will not attempt to describe the commotion which
this announcement raised in the rest of the house. Miss Brown
kept up that smile of magnanimous meekness all day. She
would not give in. 'No, my dears,' she said, 'there is nothing
to be said except that it is a little sudden. I think your papa is
quite right, and that you are getting beyond me.'

'It is not papa,' said Cicely; 'it is that horrible Aunt Jane.'

'And she was quite right,' said the magnanimous governess;
'quite right. She saw that I was not strong enough. It is a little
sudden, that is all; and we must not make mountains out of
molehills, my dears.' But she, too, retired to her room early,
where, sitting forlorn at the window, she had a good cry, poor
soul; for she had begun to grow fond of this rude solitude, and
she had no home.

As for the girls, after their first dismay and wrath the tide
turned with them. They were going out into the unknown,
words which sound so differently to different ears – so
miserable to some, so exciting to others. To Cicely and Mab
they were exciting only. A new world, new faces, new people
to know, new places to see, new things to hear; gradually they
forgot their wrath alike and their emotion at this thought. A
thrill of awe, of fear, of delicious curiosity and wonder ran
through them. This checked upon their very lips those
reproaches which they had been pouring forth, addressed to
their father and Aunt Jane. Would they be miserable after all?
should not they, rather, on the whole, *like* it, if it was not
wrong to say so? This first silenced, then insinuated into their
lips little broken words, questions and wonderings which
betrayed to each the other's feelings. 'It might be – fun,
perhaps,' Mab said at last; then looked up frightened at Cicely,

wondering if her sister would metaphorically kill her for
saying so. But then a gleam in Cicely's eyes looked as if she
thought so too.

Miss Brown set about very bravely next morning to get
their things in order. She was very brave and determined to be
magnanimous, but I cannot say that she was cheerful. It is true
that she kept smiling all day long, like Malvolio, though with
the better motive of concealing her disappointment and pain
and unjust feeling; but the effect of this smile was depressing.
She was determined, whatever might happen, to do her duty
to the last: and then, what did it matter what should follow?
With this valiant resolution she faced the crisis and nobly took
up all its duties. She bought I don't know how many dozens of
yards of nice 'long-cloth,' and cut out and made up, chiefly
with the sewing machine, garments which she discreetly
called 'under-clothing' for the girls; for her delicacy shunned
the familiar names of those indispensable articles. She found it
needful that they should have new Sunday frocks, and
engaged the parish dressmaker for a week, and went herself to
town to buy the stuff, after the girls and she had spent an
anxious yet not unpleasant afternoon in looking over patterns.
All this she did, and never a word of murmur escaped her lips.
She was a heroic woman. And the busy days pursued each
other so rapidly that the awful morning came, and the girls
weeping, yet not uncheerful, were swept away by the 'fly'
from the station – where Miss Maydew, red and excited, met
them, and carried them off remorseless on their further way –
before any one had time to breathe, much less to think. Mr St.
John went to the station with his daughters, and coming back
alone and rather sad, for the first time forgot Miss Brown; so
that when he heard a low sound of the piano in the
schoolroom he was half frightened, and, without thinking,
went straight to the forsaken room to see what it was. Poor
curate! – unfortunate Mr St. John! and not less unfortunate
Miss Brown. The music had ceased before he reached the
door, and when he went in nothing was audible but a
melancholy little sound of sobbing and crying. Miss Brown
was sitting before the old piano with her head bowed down in
her hands. Her little sniffs and sobs were pitiful to hear. When
he spoke she gave a great start, and got up trembling, wiping

her tears hastily away with her handkerchief. 'Did you speak, sir?' she said, with her usual attempt at cheerfulness. 'I hope I did not disturb you; I was – amusing myself a little, until it is time for my train. My th-things are all packed and r-ready,' said the poor little woman, making a deplorable effort at a smile. The sobs in her voice struck poor Mr St. John to the very heart.

'I have never had time,' he said in the tone of a self-condemned criminal, 'to ask where you are going, Miss Brown.'

'Oh yes, I have a pl-place to go to,' she said. 'I have written to the Governesses' Institution, Mr St. John, and very fo-fortunately they have a vacant room.'

'The Governesses' Institution! Is that the only place you have to go to?' he said.

'Indeed it is a very nice place,' said Miss Brown; 'very quiet and lady-like, and not d-dear. I have, excuse me. I have got so fo-fond of them. I never meant to cry. It is in Harley Street, Mr St. John, very nice and respectable, and a great b-blessing to have such a place, when one has no h-home.'

Mr St. John walked to the other end of the room, and then back again, twice over. How conscience-stricken he was! While poor Miss Brown bit her lips and winked her eyelids to keep the tears away. Oh, why couldn't he go away, and let her have her cry out? But he did not do that. He stopped short at the table where she had set so many sums and cut out so much underclothing, and half-turning his back upon her said, faltering, 'Would it not be better to stay here, Miss Brown?'

The little governess blushed from head to foot, I am sure, if any one could have seen; she felt thrills of confusion run all over her at such a suggestion. 'Oh, no, no,' she cried, 'you are very kind, Mr St. John, but I have nobody but myself to take care of now, and I could not stay here, a day, not now the girls are gone.'

The poor curate did not move. He took off the lid of the big inkstand and examined it as if that were what he was thinking of. The Governesses' Institution sounded miserable to him, and what could he do? 'Miss Brown,' he said in a troubled voice, 'if you think you would like to marry me, I have no objection; and then you know you could stay.'

'Mr St. John!'

'Yes; that is the only thing I can think of,' he said with a sigh. 'After being here for years, how can you go to a Governesses' Institution? Therefore, if you think you would like it, Miss Brown — '

How can I relate what followed? 'Oh, Mr St. John, you are speaking out of pity, only pity!' said the little woman, with a sudden romantic gleam of certainty that he must have been a victim of despairing love for her all this time, and that the school-going of the girls was but a device for bringing out his passion. but Mr St. John did not deny this charge, as she expected he would. 'I don't know about pity,' he said, confused, 'but I am very sorry, and – and I don't see any other way.'

This was how it happened that three weeks after the girls went to school Mr St. John married Miss Brown. She went to the Governesses' Institution after all, resolute in her propriety, until the needful interval had passed, and then she came back as Mrs St. John, to her own great surprise, and to the still greater surprise and consternation of the curate himself, and of the parish, who could not believe their ears. I need not say that Miss Maydew was absolutely furious, or that it was a great shock to Cicely and Mab when they were told what had happened. They did not trust themselves to say much to each other on the subject. It was the only subject, indeed, which they did not discuss between themselves; but by-and-by even they got used to it, as people do to everything, and they were quite friendly, though distant, to Mrs St. John.

Only one other important event occurred to that poor little woman in her life. A year after her marriage she had twin boys, to the still greater consternation of the curate; and three years after this she died. Thus the unfortunate man was left once more with two helpless children on his hands, as helpless himself as either of them, and again subject as before to the advice of all the parish. They counselled him this time 'a good nurse,' not a governess; but fortunately other actors appeared on the scene before he had time to see the excellent creature whom Mrs Brockmill, of Fir Tree House, knew of. While he listened hopelessly, a poor man of sixty-five, casting piteous looks at the two babies whom he had no right, he knew, to have helped into the world, Cicely and Mab, with bright faces and flying feet, were already on the way to his rescue; and here, dear reader, through you may think you already know something of it, this true story really begins.

CHAPTER FIVE

THE GIRLS AT SCHOOL

The school to which Miss Maydew sent the girls was in the outskirts of a seaside town, and it was neither the best nor the worst of such establishments. There were some things which all the girls had to submit to, and some which bore especially on the Miss St. Johns, who had been received at a lower price than most of the others; but on the whole the Miss Blandys were good women, and not unkind to the pupils. Cicely and Mab, as sisters, had a room allotted to them in the upper part of the house by themselves, which was a great privilege – a bare attic room, with, on one side, a sloping roof, no carpet, except a small piece before each bed, and the most meagre furniture possible. But what did they care for that? They had two chairs on which to sit and chatter facing each other, and a little table for their books and their work. They had a peep at the sea from their window, and they had their youth – what could any one desire more? In the winter nights, when it was cold sitting up in their fireless room, they used to lie down in those two little beds side by side and talk, often in the dark, for the lights had to be extinguished at ten o'clock. The had not spoken even to each other of their father's marriage. This unexpected event had shocked and bewildered them in the fantastic delicacy of their age. The could not bear to think of their father as so far descended from his ideal elevation, and shed secret tears of rage more than sorrow when they thought of their mother thus superseded. But the event was too terrible for words, and nothing whatever was said of it between them. When the next great occurrence, the birth of the two babies, was intimated to them, their feelings were different. They were first indignant, almost annoyed; then amused; in which stage Mab made such a sketch of Miss Brown with a baby in each arm, and Mr St. John pathetically looking on, that they

both burst forth into laughter, and the bond of reserve on this
event was broken; and then all at once an interest of which
they were half ashamed arose in their minds. The fell silent
both together in a wondering reverie, and then Mab said to
Cicely, turning to her big eyes of surprise —

'They belong to us too, I suppose. What are they to us?'

'Of course our half-brothers,' said Cicely; and then there
was another pause, partly of awe at the thought of a
relationship so mysterious, and partly because it was within
five minutes of ten. Then the candle was put out, and they
jumped into their beds. On the whole, perhaps, it was more
agreeable to talk of their father's other children in the dark,
when the half-shame, half-wonder of it would not appear in
each face.

'Is one expected to be fond of one's half-brother?' said Mab
doubtfully.

'There is one illusion gone,' said Cicely, in all the seri-
ousness of sixteen. 'I have always been cherishing the idea that
when we were quite grown up, instead of going out for
governesses or anything of that sort, we might keep together,
Mab, and take care of papa.'

'But then,' said Mab, 'what would you have done with Mrs
St. John? I don't see that the babies make much difference. *She*
is there to take care of papa.'

On this Cicely gave an indignant sigh, but having no
answer ready held her peace.

'For my part, I never thought of that,' said Mab. 'I have
always thought it such a pity I am not a boy, for then I should
have been the brother and you the sister, and I could have
painted and you could have kept my house. I'll tell you what I
should like,' she continued, raising herself on her elbow with
the excitement of the thought; 'I should like if we two could
go out into the world like Rosalind and Celia.

> "Were it not better
> Because that I am more than common tall,
> That I did suit me all the points like a man?"'

'But you are not more than common tall,' said Cicely, with
unsympathetic laughter; 'you are a little, tiny, insignificant
thing.'

Mab dropped upon her pillow half-crying. 'You have no feeling,' she said. 'Aunt Jane says I shall go on growing for two years yet. Mamma did — '

'If you please,' said Cicely, 'you are not the one who is like mamma.'

This little passage of arms stopped the chatter. Cicely, penitent, would have renewed it after an interval, but Mab was affronted. Their father's marriage, however, made a great difference to the girls, even before the appearance of the 'second family;' the fact that he had now another housekeeper and companion, and was independent of them affected the imagination of his daughters, though they were scarcely conscious of it. They no longer thought of going home, even for the longer holidays; and settling down at home after their schooling was over had become all at once impossible. Not that this change led them immediately to make new plans for themselves; for the youthful imagination seldom goes so far unguided except when character is very much developed; and the two were only unsettled, uneasy, not quite knowing what was to become of them; or rather, it was Cicely who felt the unsettledness and uneasiness as to her future. Mab had never any doubt about hers since she was ten years old. She had never seen any pictures to speak of, so that I cannot say she was a heaven-born painter, for she scarcely understood what that was. But she meant to draw; her pencil was to be her profession, though she scarcely knew how it was to be wielded, and thus she was delivered from all her sister's vague feelings of uncertainty. Mab's powers, however, had not been appreciated at first at school, where Miss Maydew's large assertions as to her niece's cleverness had raised corresponding expectations. But when the drawing-master came with his little stock of landscapes to be copied, Mab, quite untutored in this kind, was utterly at a loss. She neither knew how to manage her colours, nor how to follow the vague outlines of the 'copy,' and I cannot describe the humiliation of the sisters, nor the half disappointment, half triumph, of Miss Blandy.

'My dear, you must not be discouraged; I am sure you did as well as you could; and the fact is, we have a very high standard here,' the school-mistress said.

It happened, however, after two or three of these failures that Cicely, sent by Miss Blandy on a special message into that retired and solemn chamber, where Miss Blandy the elder sister sat in the mornings supervising and correcting everything, from the exercises to the characters of her pupils, found the head of the establishment with the drawing-master looking over the productions of the week. He had Mab's drawing in his hand, and he was shaking his head over it.

'I don't know what to say about the youngest Miss St. John. This figure is well put in, but her sky and her distance are terrible,' he was saying. 'I don't think I shall make anything of her.'

When Cicely heard this she forgot that she was a girl at school. She threw down a pile of books she was carrying, and flew out of the room without a word, making a great noise with the door. What she ought to have done was to have made a curtsy, put down the books softly by Miss Blandy's elbow, curtsied again, and left the room noiselessly, in all respects save that of walking backward as she would have done at Court. Need I describe the look of dismay that came into Miss Blandy's face?

'These girls will be my death,' she said. 'Were there ever such colts? – worse than boys.' This was the most dreadful condemnation Miss Blandy ever uttered. 'If their aunt does not insist upon drawing, as she has so little real talent, she had better give it up.

At this moment Cicely burst in again breathless, her hair streaming behind her, her dress catching in the door, which she slammed after her. 'Look here!' she cried; 'look here, before you say Mab has no talent!' and she tossed down on the table the square blue-lined book, which her sister by this time had almost filled. She stood before them glowing and defiant, with flashing eyes and flowing hair; then she recollected some guilty recent pages, and quailed, putting out her hand for the book again. 'Please it is only the beginning, not the end, you are to look at,' she said, peremptory yet appealing. Had Miss Blandy alone been in the seat of judgement, she would, I fear, have paid but little attention to this appeal; but the old drawing-master was gentle and kind, as old professors of the arts so often are (for Art is Humanity, I think, almost oftener than letters), and besides, the young petitioner was very pretty in her generous enthusiasm, which affected him both as a man and an artist. The first page at once gave him a guess as to the inexpediency of examining the last; and the old man perceived in a moment at once the mistake he had made, and the cause of it. He turned over the first few pages, chuckling amused approbation. 'So these are your sister's,' he said, and laughed and nodded his kind old head. When he came to a sketch of Hannah, the maid-of-all-work at the rectory, the humour of which might seem more permissible in Miss Blandy's eyes than the caricatures of ladies and gentlemen, he showed it to her; and even Miss Blandy, though meditating downright slaughter upon Cicely, could not restrain a smile. 'Is this really Mabel's?' she condescended to ask. 'As you say, Mr Lake, not at all bad; much better than I could have thought.'

'Better? it is capital!' said the drawing-master; and then he shut up the book close, and put it back in Cicely's hands. 'I see there are private scribblings in it,' he said, with a significant look; 'take it back, my dear. I will speak to Miss Mabel to-morrow. And now, Miss Blandy, we will finish our business, if you please,' he said benevolently, to leave time for Cicely and her dangerous volume to escape. Miss Blandy was vanquished by this stratagem, and Cicely, beginning to tremble at the thought of the danger she had escaped, withdrew very demurely, having first piled up on the table the books she had thrown down in her impetuosity. I may add at once that she did not escape without an address, in which withering irony alternated with solemn appeal to her best feelings, and which drew many hot tears from poor Cicely's eyes, but otherwise so far as I am aware did her no harm.

Thus Mab's gifts found acknowledgement at Miss Blandy's. The old drawing-master shook his fine flexible old artist hand at her. 'You take us all off, young lady,' he said; 'you spare no one; but it is so clever that I forgive you; and by way of punishment you must work hard, now I know what you can do. And don't show that book of yours to any one but me. Miss Blandy would not take it so well as I do.'

'Oh, dear Mr Lake, forgive me,' said Mab, smitten with compunction; 'I will never do it again!'

'Never, till the next time,' he said, shaking his head; 'but, anyhow, keep it to yourself, for it is a dangerous gift.'

And from that day he put her on 'the figure' and 'the round'
– studies, in which Mab at first showed little more proficiency
than she had done in the humbler sphere of landscape; for
having leapt all at once into the exercise of something that felt
like original art, this young lady did not care to go back to the
elements. However, what with the force of school discipline,
and some glimmerings of good sense in her own juvenile
bosom, she was kept to it, and soon found the ground steady
under her feet once more, and made rapid progress. By the
time they had been three years at school, she was so proficient,
that Mr Lake, on retiring, after a hard-worked life, to
well-earned leisure, recommended her as his successor. So that
by seventeen, a year before Mrs St. John's death, Mab had
released Miss Maydew and her father from all responsibility
on her account. Cicely was not so clever; but she, too, had
begun to help Miss Blandy in preference to returning to the
rectory and being separated from her sister. Vague teaching of
'English' and music is not so profitable as an unmistakable and
distinct art like drawing; but it was better than setting out
upon a strange world alone, or going back to being a useless
inmate of the rectory. As teachers the girls were both worse
off and better off than as pupils. They were worse off because
it is a descent in the social scale to come down from the level of
those who pay to be taught, to the level of those who are paid
for teaching – curious though the paradox seems to be; and
they were better off, in so far as they were free from some of
the restrictions of school, and had a kind of independent
standing. They were allowed to keep their large attic, the bare
walls of which were now half covered by Mab's drawings,
and which Cicely's instinctive art of household management
made to look more cheery and homelike than any other room
in the house. They were snubbed sometimes by 'parents,' who
thought the manners of these Miss St. John's too easy and
familiar, as if they were on an equality with their pupils; and
by Miss Blandy, who considered them much too independent
in their ways; and now and then had mortifications to bear
which are not pleasant to girls. But there were two of them,
which was a great matter; and in the continual conversation
which they carried on about everything, they consoled each

other. No doubt it was hard sometimes to hear music
sounding from the open windows of the great house in the
square, where their old schoolfellow, Miss Robinson, had
come to live, and to see the carriages arriving, and all the glory
of the ball-dresses, of which the two young governesses got a
glimpse as they went out for a stroll on the beach in the
summer twilight, an indulgence which Miss Blandy disap-
proved of.

'Now, why should people be so different?' Cicely said,
moralizing; 'why should we have so little, and Alice Robinson
so much? It don't seem fair.'

'And we are not even prettier than she is, or gooder – which
we ought to be, if there is any truth in compensation,' said
Mab, with a laugh.

'Or happier,' said Cicely, with a sigh. 'She has the upper
hand of us in everything, and no balance on the other side to
make up for it. Stay, though; she has very droll people for
father and mother, and we have a very fine gentleman for our
papa.'

'Poor papa!' said Mab. They interchanged moods with each
other every ten minutes, and were never monotonous, or for a
long time the same.

'You may say why should people be so different,' said
Cicely, forgetting that it was herself who said it. 'There is
papa, now; he is delightful, but he is trying. When one thinks
how altered everything is – and those two little babies. But
yet, you know, we ought to ask ourselves, "Were we happier
at home, or are we happier here?"'

'We have more variety here,' said Mab decisively; 'there is
the sea, for one thing; there we had only the garden.'

'You forget the common; it was as nice as any sea, and
never drowned people, or did anything dangerous; and the
forest, and the sunset.'

'There are sunsets here,' said Mab, – very fine ones. We are
not forgotten by the people who manage these things up
above. And there is plenty of work; and the girls are amusing,
and so are the parents.'

'We should have had plenty of work at home,' said Cicely;
and then the point being carried as far as was necessary the
discussion suddenly stopped. They were walking along the

sands, almost entirely alone. Only here and there another group would pass them, or a solitary figure, chiefly trades-people, taking their evening stroll. The fresh sea-breeze blew in their young faces, the soft dusk closed down over the blue water, which beat upon the shore at their feet in the softest whispering cadence. The air was all musical, thrilled softly by this hush of subdued sound. It put away the sound of the band at Miss Robinson's ball out of the girls' hearts. And yet balls are pleasant things at eighteen, and when two young creatures, quite deprived of such pleasures, turn their backs thus upon the enchanted place where the others are dancing, it would be strange if a touch of forlorn sentiment did not make itself felt in their hearts, though the soft falling of the dusk, and the hush of the great sea, and the salt air in their faces, gave them a pleasure, had they but known it, more exquisite than any mere ball, as a ball ever confers. One only knows this, however, by reflection, never by immediate sensation; and so there was, as I have said, just a touch of pathos in their voices, and a sense of superiority, comfortable only in that it was superior, but slightly sad otherwise, in their hearts.

'I don't know what makes me go to thinking of home.' said Cicely, after a pause. 'If we had been at home we should have had more pleasure, Mab. The people about would have asked us – a clergyman's daughters always get asked; and there are very nice people about Brentburn, very different from the Robinsons and their class.'

'We should have had no dresses to go in,' said Mab. 'How could we ever have had ball-dresses off papa's two hundred a year?'

'Ball-dresses sound something very grand, but a plain white tarlatan is not dear when one can make it up one's self. However, that is a poor way of looking at it,' said Cicely, giving a little toss to her head, as if to throw off such unelevated thoughts. 'There are a great many more important things to think of. How will he ever manage to bring up the two boys?'

Mab made a pause of reflection. 'To be sure Aunt Jane is not their relation,' she said, 'and boys are more troublesome than girls. The want to have tutors and things, and to go to the university; and then what is the good of it all if they are not clever? Certainly boys are far more troublesome than girls.'

'And then, if you consider papa,' said Cicely, 'that he is not very strong, and that he is old. One does not like to say anything disagreeable about one's papa, but what *did* he want with those children? Surely we were quite enough when he is so poor.'

'There is always one thing he can do,' said Mab. Everybody says he is a very good scholar. He will have to teach them himself.'

'We shall have to teach them,' said Cicely with energy; 'I know so well that this is what it will come to. I don't mean to teach them ourselves, for it is not much Latin I know, and you none, and I have not a word of Greek – but they will come upon us, I am quite sure.'

'You forget Mrs St. John, said Mab.

Cicely gave a slight shrug of her shoulders, but beyond that she did not pursue the subject. Mrs St. John's name stopped everything; they could not discuss her, nor express their disapprobation, and therefore they forbore religiously, though it was sometimes hard work.

'Blandina will think we are late,' at last she said, turning round. This was their name for their former instructress, their present employer. Mab turned dutifully, obeying her sister's touch, but with a faint sigh.

'I hope they will be quiet at the Robinsons as we are passing,' the girl said. 'What if they are in full swing, with the "Blue Danube" perhaps! I hate to go in from a sweet night like this with noisy fiddles echoing through my head.'

Cicely gave a slight squeeze of sympathy to her sister's arm. Do not you understand the girls, young reader? It was not the "Blue Danube" that was being played, but the old Lancers, the which to hear is enough to make wooden legs dance. Cicely and Mab pressed each other's arms, and glanced up at the window, where dancing shadows and figures were visible. They sighed, and they went into their garret, avoiding the tacit disapproval of Miss Blandy's good-night. She did not approve of twilight walks. Why should they want to go out just then like tradespeople, a thing which ladies never did? But if Miss Blandy had known that the girls were quite saddened by the sound of the music from the Robinsons', and yet could not sleep for listening to it, I fear she would have thought them very improper young persons indeed. She had forgotten how it felt to be eighteen – it was so long ago.

On the very next morning the news came of their step-mother's death. It was entirely unexpected by them, for they had no idea of the gradual weakness which had been stealing over that poor little woman, and they were moved by deep compunction as well as natural regret. It is impossible not to feel that we might have been kinder, might have made life happier to those that are gone – a feeling experienced the moment that we know them to be certainly gone, and inaccessible to all kindness. 'Oh, poor Mrs St. John!' said Mab, dropping a few natural tears. Cicely was more deeply affected. She was the eldest and had thought the most; as for the young artist, her feeling ran into the tips of her fingers, and got expansion there; but Cicely had no such medium. She went about mournfully all day long, and in the evening Mab found her seated at the window of their attic, looking out with her eyes big with tears upon the darkening sea. When her sister touched her on the shoulder Cicely's tears fell. 'Oh, poor Miss Brown!' she said, her heart having gone back to the time when they had no grievance against their kindly little gov-erness. 'Oh, Mab, if only one could tell her how one was sorry! if she could only see into my heart now!'

'Perhaps she can,' said Mab, awe-stricken and almost under her breath, lifting her eyes to the clear wistful horizon in which the evening star had just risen.

&'And one could have said it only yesterday' said Cicely, realizing for the first time that mystery of absolute severance; and what light thoughts had been in their minds yesterday! Sighs for Alice Robinson's ball, depression of soul and spirit caused by the distant strains of the Lancers, and the 'Blue Danube' – while this tragedy was going on, and the poor soul who had been good to them, but to whom they had not been good, was departing, altogether and for ever out of reach. Cicely in her sorrow blamed herself unjustly, as was natural, and mourned for the mystery of human shortsightedness as well as for Mrs St. John. But I do not mean to say that this grief was very profound after the first sting, and after that startling impression of the impossibility of further intercourse was over. The girls went out quietly in the afternoon, and bought black stuff to make themselves mourning, and spoke to each other in low voices and grave tones. Their youthful vigour was subdued – they were overawed to feel as it were the wings of the great Death-Angel overshadowing them. The very sunshine looked dim, and the world enveloped in a cloud. But it was within a week or two of Miss Blandy's 'breaking up,' and they could not go away immediately. Miss Blandy half audibly expressed her satisfaction that Mrs St. John was only their stepmother. 'Had she been their own mother, what should we have done?' she said. So that it was not until the end of July, when the establishment broke up, that the girls were at last able to get home.

CHAPTER SIX

THE GIRLS AT HOME

We are so proud in England of having a word which means home, which some of our neighbours we are pleased to think have not, that, perhaps, it is a temptation to us to indulge in a general rapture over the word which has sometimes little foundation in reality. When Cicely and Mab walked to the rectory together from the station a suppressed excitement was in their minds. Since they first left for school, they had only come back for a few days each year, and they had not liked it. Their stepmother had been very kind, painfully kind; and anxious above measure that they should find everything as they had left it, and should not be disappointed or dull; but this very anxiety had made an end of all natural ease and they had been glad when the moment came that released them. Now, poor woman, she had been removed out of their way; they were going back to take care of their father as they might have done had there been no second Mrs St. John; and everything was as it had been, with the addition of the two babies, innocent little intruders, whom the girls, you may be sure, could never find it in their hearts to be hard upon. Cicely and Mab took each other's hands instinctively as they left the station. It was the very first of August, the very prime and glory of summer; the woods were at their fullest, untouched by any symptom of decay. The moorland side of the landscape was more wealthy and glorious still in its flush of heather. The common was not indeed one sheet of purple, like a Scotch moor; but it was all lighted up between the gorse bushes with fantastic streaks and bands of colour blazing in the broad sunshine, and haunted by swarms of bees which made a hum in the air almost as sweet and all-pervading as the murmur of the sea. As they drew near the house their hearts began to beat louder. Would there be any visible change upon it? Would it

look as it did when they were children, or with that indefin-
able difference which showed in *her* time? They did not
venture to go the familiar way by the garden, but walked up
solemnly like visitors to the front door. It was opened to them
by a new maid, whom they had never seen before, and who
demurred slightly to giving them admittance, 'Master ain't
in,' said the girl; 'yes, miss, I know as you're expected,' but
still she hesitated. This was not the kind of welcome which the
daughters of a house generally receive. They went into the
house nevertheless, Betsy following them. The blinds were
drawn low over the windows, which were all shut, and
though the atmosphere was stifling with heat, yet it was cold,
miserably cold to Cicely and Mab. Their father's study was
the only place with any life in it. The rectory seemed full of
nothing but old black heavy furniture, and heavier memories
of some chilled and faded past.

'What a dreadful old place it is,' said Mab; 'it is like coming
home to one's grave,' and she sat down on the black haircloth
easy-chair and shivered and cried; though this was coming
home, to the house in which she had been born.

'Now it will be better,' said Cicely pulling up the blinds and
opening the window. She had more command of herself than
her sister. She let the sunshine come down in a flood across the
dingy carpet, worn with the use of twenty years.

'Please, miss,' said Betsy interposing, 'missis would never
have the blinds up in this room 'cause of spoiling the carpet. If
master says so, I don't mind; but till he do – ' and here Betsy
put up her hand to the blind.

'Do you venture to meddle with what my sister does?' cried
Mab, furious, springing from her chair.

Cicely only laughed. 'You are a good girl to mind what your
mistress said, but we are your mistresses now; you must let
the window alone, for don't you see the carpet is spoiled
already? I will answer to papa. What is it? Do you want
anything more?

'Only this, miss,' said Betsy, 'as it's the first laugh as has
been heard here for weeks and weeks, and I don't like it
neither, seeing missis is in her grave only a fortnight to-day.'

'I think you are a very good girl,' said Cicely: and with that
the tears stood in that changeable young woman's eyes.

No Betsy that ever was heard of could long resist this sort of treatment. 'I tries to be, miss,' she said with a curtsy and a whimper. 'Maybe you'd like a cup of tea?' and after following them suspiciously all over the house, she left them at last on this hospitable intent in the fading drawing-room, where they had both enshrined the memory of their mother. Another memory was there now, A memory as faded as the room, which showed in all kinds of feeble feminine decorations, bits of modern lace, and worked cushions and foolish footstools. The room was all pinafored and transmogrified, the old dark picture-frames covered with yellow gauze, and the needlework in crackling semi-transparent covers.

'This was how she like things, poor soul! Oh, Mab,' cried Cicely, 'how strange that she should die!'

'No stranger than that any else should die,' said Mab, who was more matter of fact.

'A great deal stranger It was not strange at all that little Mary Seymour should die. One saw it in her eyes; she was like an angel; it was natural; but poor Miss Brown, who was quite happy working cushions and covering them up, and keeping the sun off the carpets, and making lace for the brackets! It looks as if there was so little sense in it,' said Cicely. 'She won't have any cushions to work up there.'

'I dare say there won't be anything to draw up there,' said Mab; 'and yet I suppose I shall die too in time.'

'When there are the four walls for Leonardo, and Michel Angelo and Raphael and poor Andrea,' said the other. 'How you forget! Besides, it is quite different. Hark! what was that?' she cried, putting up her hand.

What it was soon became very distinctly evident – a feeble little cry speedily joined by another; and then a small weak chorus, two voices entangled together. 'No, no; no ladies. Harry no like ladies,' mixed with a whimpering appeal to 'papa, papa,'

'Come and see the pretty ladies. Harry never saw such pretty ladies,' said the encouraging voice of Betsy in the passage.

The girls looked at each other, and grew red. They had made up their minds about a great many things, but never how they were to deal with the two children. Then Betsy appeared at the door, pushing it open before her with the tea-tray she carried. To her skirts were hanging two little boys, clinging to her, yet resisting her onward motion, and carried on by it in spite of themselves. They stared at the new-comers with big blue eyes wide open, awed into silence. They were very small and very pale, with light colourless limp locks falling over their little black dresses. The girls on their side stared silently too. There was not a feature in the children's faces which resembled their elder sisters. They were both little miniatures of Miss Brown.

'So these are the children,' said Cicely, making a reluctant step forward; to which Harry and Charley responded by a renewed clutch at Betsy's dress.

'Yes, miss; them's the children! and darlings they be,' said Betsy, looking fondly at them as she set down the tea. Cicely made another step forward slowly, and held out her hands to them; when the little boys set up a scream which rang through the house, and hiding their faces simultaneously in Betsy's gown howled to be taken away. Mab put up her hands to her ears, but Cicely, more anxious to do her duty, made another attempt. She stooped down and kissed, or tried to kiss the little tear-stained faces, to which caress each small brother replied by pushing her away with a repeated roar.

'Don't you take no notice, miss. Let 'em alone, and they'll get used to you in time,' said Betsy.

'Go away, go away! Harry no like 'oo,' screamed the spokesman brother. No one likes to be repulsed even by a child. Cicely stumbled to her feet very red and uncomfortable. She stood ruefully looking after them as they were carried off after a good preliminary 'shake,' one in each of Betsy's red hands.

'There is our business in life,' she said in a solemn tone. 'Oh, Mab, Mab, what did papa want with these children? All the trouble of them will come on you and me.'

Mab looked at her sister with a look of alarm, which changed, however, into laughter at sight of Cicely's solemn looks and the dreary presentiment in her face.

'You are excellent like that,' she said; 'and if you had only seen how funny you all looked when the little demons began to cry. The will do for models at all events, and I'll take to painting children. They say it's very good practice, and nursery pictures always sell.'

These lighter suggestions did not, however, console, Cicely. She walked about the room with clasped hands and a very serious face, neglecting her tea.

'Papa will never trouble himself about them,' she said half to herself; 'it will all fall on Mab and me. And boys! that they should be boys. We shall never be rich enough to send them to the University. Girls we might have taught ourselves; but when you think of Oxford and Cambridge — '

'We can't tell,' said Mab; how do you know I shan't turn out to be a great painter, and be able to send them wherever you like? for I am the brother and you are the sister, Ciss. You are to keep my house and have the spending of all my money. So, don't be gloomy, please, but pour out some tea. I wish, though, they were not quite so plain.'

'So like their mother,' said Cicely with a sigh.

'And so disagreeable; but it is funny to hear one speak for both as if the two were Harry. I am glad they are not girls. To give them a share of all we have I don't mind; but to teach them! with those white little pasty faces — '

'One can do anything when one makes up one's mind to it,' said Cicely with a sigh.

At this moment the hall door opened, and after an interval Mr St. John came in with soft steps. He had grown old in these last years; bowed down with age and troubles. He came up to his daughters and kissed them, laying his hand upon their heads.

'I am very glad you have come home,' he said, in a voice which was pathetic in its feebleness. 'You are all I have now.'

'Not all you have, papa,' said Mab; 'we have just seen the little boys.'

A momentary colour flushed over his pale face. 'Ah, the babies,' he said. 'I am afraid they will be a great deal of trouble to you, my dears.'

Cicely and Mab looked at each other, but they did not say anything – they were afraid to say something which they ought not to say. And what could he add after that? He took the cup of tea they offered him, and drank it standing, his tall frame with a stoop in it, which was partly age and partly weakness, coming against one tall window and shutting out the light. 'But that you are older looking,' he said at last, 'all this time might seem like a dream.'

'A sad dream, papa,' said Cicely, not knowing what to say.

'I cannot say that, my dear. I thank God I have had a great deal of happiness in my life; because we are sad for the moment we must not forget to thank Him for all His mercies,' said Mr St. John; and then with a change in his voice, he added, 'Your aunt sends me word that she is coming to see you. She is a very strong woman for her years; I look older than she does; and it is a trouble to me now to go to town and back in one day.'

'You have not been ill, papa?'

'No, Cicely, not ill; a little out of my usual,' he said, 'that is all. Now you are here, we shall fall into our quiet way again. The changes God sends we must accept; but the little worries are trying, my dear. I am getting old, and am not so able to brave them; but all will be well now you are here.'

'We shall do all we can,' said Cicely; 'but you must remember, papa, we are not used to housekeeping, and if we make mistakes at first — '

'I am not afraid of your mistakes,' said Mr St. John, looking at her with a faint smile. He had scarcely looked full at her before and his eyes dwelt upon her face with a subdued pleasure. 'You are your mother over again,' he said. 'You will be a blessing to me, Cicely, as she was.'

The two girls looked at him strangely, with a flood of conflicting thoughts. How dared he speak of their mother? Was he relieved to be able to think of their mother without Miss Brown coming in to disturb his thoughts? If natural reverence had not restrained them, what a cross-examination they would have put him to! but as it was, their eager thoughts remained unsaid. 'I will do all I can, papa, and so will Mab,' said Cicely, faltering. And he put down his cup, and said, 'God bless you, my dears.' and went to his study as if they had never been absent at all, only out perhaps, as Mab said, for a rather long walk.

'I don't think he can have cared for her,' said Cicely; 'he is glad to get back to the idea of mamma; I am sure that is what he means. He is always kind, and of course he was kind to her; but there is a sort of relief in his tone – a sort of ease.'

'That is all very well for us,' said Mab; but if you will think of it, it seems a little hard on poor Miss Brown.'

This staggered Cicely, who loved justice. 'But I think she should not have married him,' she said. 'It was easy to see that anybody could have married him who wished. I can see that now, though I never thought of it then. And kind as it was of Aunt Jane, perhaps we should not have left him unprotected. You ought to have gone to school, Mab, because of your talent, and I should have stayed at home.'

They decided, however, after a few minutes, that it was needless to discuss this possibility now, so long after it had become an impossibility. And then they went upstairs to take off their travelling-dresses and make themselves feel at home. When they came down again, with their hair smooth, Cicely carrying her work-basket and Mab her sketch-book, and seated themselves in the old faded room, from which the sunshine had now slid away, as the sun got westward, a bewildered feeling took possession of them. Had they ever been absent? had anything happened since that day when Aunt Jane surprised them in their pinafores? The still house, so still in the deep tranquillity of the country, after the hum of their schoolroom life and the noises of a town, seemed to turn round with them, as they looked out upon the garden, upon which no change seemed to have passed. 'I declare,' cried Mab, 'there is exactly the same number of apples – and the same branch of that old-plum-tree hanging loose from the wall!'

Thus the first evening passed like a dream. Mr St. John came from his study to supper, and he talked a little, just as he had been in the habit of talking long ago, without any allusion to the past. He told them a few pieces of news about the parish, and that he would like them to visit the school. 'It has been very well looked after lately,' he said. Perhaps this meant by his wife – perhaps it did not; the girls could not tell. Then Betsy came in for prayers, along with a small younger sister of hers who had charge of the little boys; and by ten o'clock, as at Miss Blandy's, the door was locked. and the peaceful house wrapped in quiet. The girls looked out of their window upon the soft stillness with the strangest feelings. The garden paths were clearly indicated by a feeble veiled moon, and the trees which thickened in clouds upon the horizon. There was not a sound anywhere in the tranquil place except the occasional bark of that dog, who somewhere, far or near, always indicates existence in a still night in the country. The stillness fell upon their souls. 'He never asked what we were going to do,' said Mab, for they were silenced too, and spoke to each other only now and then, chilled out of the superabundance of their own vitality. 'But he thinks with me that the children are to be our business in life,' said Cicely, and then they went to bed, taking refuge in the darkness. For two girls so full of conscious life, tingling to the finger points with active faculties and power, it was a chilly home-coming, yet not so unusual either. When the young creatures come home, with their new lives in their hands to make something of, for good or evil, do not we often expect them to settle down to the level of the calm old lives which are nearly worn out, and find fault with them if it is a struggle? Mr St. John felt that it was quite natural his girls should come home and keep his house for him, and take the trouble of the little boys, and visit the schools – so naturally that when he had said, 'Now you are here again,' it seemed to him that everything was said that needed to be said.

In the morning the children were found less inaccessible, and made friends with by dint of lumps of sugar and bits of toast, of which Mab was prodigal. They were very tiny, delicate, and colourless, with pale hair and pale eyes; but they were not wanting in some of the attractions of children. Charley was the backward one, and had little command of language. Harry spoke for both; and I will not say it was easy for these girls, unaccustomed to small children, to understand even him. Mr St. John patted their heads and gave them a smile each by way of blessing; but he took little further notice of the children. 'I believe Annie, the little maid, is very kind to them,' he said. 'I cannot bear to hear them crying, my dears; but now you are here all will go well.'

'But, papa,' said Cicely, 'will it be right for us to stay at home, when you have them to provide for, and there is so little money?'

'Right for you to stay? Where could you be so well as at home?' said the curate, perturbed. The girls looked at each other, and this time it was Mab who was bold, and ventured to speak.

'Papa, it is not that. Supposing that we are best at home' (Mab said this with the corners of her mouth going down, for it was not her own opinion), 'yet there are other things to consider. We should be earning something — '

Mr St. John got up almost impatiently for him. 'I have never been left to want,' he said. 'I have been young, and now I am old, but I have never seen the righteous forsaken, nor his seed begging their bread. Providence will raise up friends for the children; and we have always had plenty. If there is enough for me, there is enough for you.'

And he went out of the room as nearly angry as it was possible for his mild nature to be. Cicely and Mab once more looked at each other wondering. 'Papa is crazy, I think,' said Mab, who was the most self-assertive; But Cicely only heaved a sigh, and went out to the hall to brush his hat for him, as she remembered her mother used to do. Mr St. John like this kind of tendance. 'You are a good girl, Cicely; you are just such another as your mother,' he said, as he took the hat from her; and Cicely divined that the late Mrs St. John had not shown him this attention, which I think pleased her on the whole.

'But, papa, I am afraid Mab was right,' she said. 'You must think it over, and think what is best for Mab.'

'Why should she be different from you?' said Mr, St. John, feeling in his breast pocket for the familiar prayer-book which lay there. It was more important to him to make sure it was safe, than to decide what to do with his child.

'I don't know why, but we *are* different. Dear papa, you must think, if you please, what is best.'

'It is nonsense. Cicely; she must stay where she is , and make herself happy. A good girl is always happy at home,' said Mr St. John; 'and, of course, there is plenty – plenty for all of us. You must not detain me, my dear, nor talk about business this first morning. Depend upon it,' said Mr St. John, raising his soft, feeble hand to give emphasis to his words, 'it is always best for you to be at home.'

What a pity that children and women are not always convinced when the head of the house thus lays down the law! Cicely went back into the dining-room where they had breakfasted, shaking her head, without being aware of the gesture. 'Why should I depend upon it?' she said. 'Depend upon it! I may be quite willing to do it, for it is my duty; but why should I depend upon it as being the best?'

'What are you saying, Cicely?'

'Nothing, dear; only papa is rather odd. Does he think that two hundred a year is a great fortune? or that two of us, and two of them, and two maids (though they are little ones), and himself, can get on upon two hundred a year?'

'I must paint,' said Mab; 'I must paint. I'll tell you what I shall do. You are a great deal more like a Madonna than most of the women who have sat for her. I will paint a Holy Family from you and *them* — They are funny little pale things, but we could light them up with a little colour; and they are *real* babies, you know,' Mab said, looking at them seriously, with her head on one side, as becomes a painter. She had posed the two children on the floor: the one seated firmly with his little legs stretched out, the other leaning against him; while she walked up and down, with a pencil in her hand, studying them. 'Stay still a moment longer, and I will give you a lump of sugar,' she said.

'Harry like sugar,' said the small spokesman, looking up at her. Charley said nothing. He had his thumb, and half the little hand belonging to it, in his mouth, and sucked it with much philosophy. 'Or perhaps, I might make you a peasant woman,' said Mab, 'with one of them on your back. They are nature, Ciss. You know how Mr Lake used to go on, saying nature was what I wanted. Well, here it is.'

'I think you are as mad as papa,' said Cicely, impatient; 'but I must order the dinner and look after the things. That's nature for me. Oh, dear – oh, dear! We shall not long be able to have any dinner, if we go on with such a lot of servants. Two girls, two boys, two maids, and two hundred a year! You might as well try to fly,' said Cicely, shaking her pretty head.

CHAPTER SEVEN

NEWS

Perhaps it had been premature of the girls to speak to their father of their future, and what they were to do, on the very first morning after their return; but youth is naturally impatient, and the excitement of one crisis seems to stimulate the activity of all kinds of plans and speculations in the youthful brain; and then perhaps the chill of the house, the rural calm of the place, had frightened them. Cicely, indeed, knew it was her duty and her business to stay here, whatever happened; but how could Mab bear it, she said to herself – Mab, who required change and novelty, whose mind was full of such hopes of seeing and of doing? When their father had gone out, however, they threw aside their grave thoughts for the moment, and dawdled the morning away, roaming about the garden, out and in a hundred times, as it is so pleasant to do on a summer day in the country, especially to those who find in the country the charm of novelty. They got the children's hats, and took them out to play on the sunny grass, and run small races along the paths.

'Please, miss, not to let them run too much,' said little Annie, Betsy's sister, who was the nurse, though she was but fifteen. lease, miss, not to let them roll on the grass.'

'Why, the grass is as dry as the carpet; and what are their little legs good for but to run with?' said Cicely.

Whereupon little Annie made up a solemn countenance, and said, 'Please, miss, I promised missis — '

Mab rushed off with the children before the sentence was completed. 'That's why they are so pale,' cried the impetuous girl; 'poor little white faced things! But we never promised missis. Let us take them into our own hands.'

'You are a good girl to remember what your mistress said,' said Cicely with dignity, walking out after her sister in very stately fashion. And she reproved Mab for her rashness, and led the little boys about, promenading the walks. 'We must get rid of these two maids,' she said, 'or we shall never be allowed to have anything our own way.'

'But you said they were good girls for remembering,' said Mab, surprised.

'So they were; but that is not to say I am going to put up with it.' said Cicely, drawing herself to her full height, and looking Miss St. John, as Mab asserted she was very capable of doing when she pleased.

'You are very funny, Cicely,' said the younger sister; 'you praise the maids, and yet you want to get rid of them; and you think what "missis" made them promise is nonsense, yet there you go walking about with these two mites as if you had promised missis yourself.'

'Hush!' said Cicely, and then the tears came into her eyes. 'She is dead!' said this inconsistent young woman, with a low voice full of remorse. 'It would be hard if one did not give in to her at first about her own little boys.'

After this dawdling in the morning, they made up their minds to work in the afternoon. Much as they loved the sunshine, they were obliged to draw down the blinds with their own hands, to the delight of Betty, to whom Cicely was obliged to explain that this was not to save the carpet. It is difficult to know what to do in such circumstances, especially when there is nothing particular to be done. It was too hot to go out; and as for beginning needlework in cold blood the first day you are in a new place, or have come back to an old one, few girls of eighteen and nineteen are so virtuous as that. One thing afforded them a little amusement, and that was to pull things about, and alter their arrangement, and shape the room to their own mind. Cicely took down a worked banner-screen which hung from the mantelpiece, and which offended her fastidious taste; or rather, she began to unscrew it, removing first the crackling semi-transparent veil that covered it. 'Why did she cover them up so?' cried Cicely, impatiently.

'To keep them clean, of course' said Mab.

'But why should they be kept clean? We are obliged to fade and lose our beauty. It is unnatural to be spick and span, always clean and young, and new. Come down, you gaudy thing!' she cried. Then with her hand still grasping it, a compunction seized her. 'After all, why shouldn't she leave something behind her – something to remember her by? She ought to leave some trace of her existence here.'

'She has left her children – trace enough of her existence!' cried Mab.

Cicely was struck by this argument. She hesitated a minute, with her hand on the screen, then hastily detached it, and threw it down. Then two offensive cushions met her eye, which she put in the same heap. 'The little boys might like to have them when they grow up.' she added, half apologetically, to herself.

And with these changes something of the old familiar look began to come into the faded room. Mab had brought out her drawing things, but the blinds were fluttering over the open windows, shutting out even the garden; and there was nothing to draw. And it was afternoon, which is not a time to begin work. She fixed her eyes upon a large chiffonier, with glass doors, which held the place of honour in the room. It was mahogany, like everything in the house.

'I wonder what sort of a man Mr Chester is?' she said; 'or what he meant by buying all that hideous furniture – a man who lives in Italy, and is an antiquary, and knows about pictures. If it was not for the glass doors, how like a hearse that chiffonier would be. I mean a catafalque. What is a catafalque, Cicely? A thing that is put up in churches when people are dead? I hope Mr Chester, when he dies will have just such a tomb.'

'It is not so bad as the big bookcase in the study,' said Cicely; certainly things are better now-a-days. If I had plenty of money, how I should like to furnish this room all over again, with bright young things, not too huge; little sofas that would move anywhere when you touched them, and soft chairs. They should be covered in amber — '

'No – blue!' cried Mab.

'Soft amber – amber with a bloom of white in it —'

'In this sunny room,' cried Mab. 'What are you thinking of? No; it must be a cool colour – a sort of moonlighty blue – pale, pale; or tender fairy green.'

'What is fairy green? Amber is my colour – it would be lovely; of course, I don't mean to say it wouldn't fade. But then if one were rich the pleasure would be to let it fade, and then have all the fun over again, and choose another,' said Cicely, with a sigh over this impossible delight.

'Things sometimes improve by fading,' said the artist. 'I like the faded tints – they harmonize. Hush, Cicely! – oh, stop your tidying – there is someone at the door.'

'It cannot be any one coming to call so soon?' said Cicely, startled.

'But it is – listen! I can hear Betsy saying, "This way, ma'am; this way."' And Mab closed her sketch-book, and sat very upright and expectant on her chair; while Cicely, throwing (I am ashamed to say) her spoils under a sofa, took up her needlework by the wrong end, and, putting on a portentous face of gravity and absorbed occupation, waited for the expected visitor.

A moment after the door was flung open, but not by Betsy; and Miss Maydew, flushed with her walk from the station, as when they had first seen her, with the same shawl on, and I almost think the same bonnet (but that was impossible), stood before them, her large white handkerchief in her hand. She was too hot to say anything, but dropped down on the first chair she came to, leaving the door open, which made a draught, and blew about her ribbons violently. 'I know it is as much as my life is worth,' said Miss Maydew; 'but, oh, how delicious it is to be in a draught!'

'Aunt Jane!' the girls cried, and rushed at her with unfeigned relief. They were more familiar with her now than they had been four years ago. They took off her great shawl for her, and loosed her bonnet strings. 'Papa told us you were coming,' they cried; 'but we did not hope for you so soon. How kind of you to come to-day.'

'Oh, my dears,' said Aunt Jane, 'I did not mean to come to-day; I came to see how you were taking it; and what your papa means to do. As soon as I saw it in the paper I thought, oh my poor, poor children, and that helpless old man! What are they to do?'

'Do you mean about Mrs St. John?' said Cicely, growing grave. 'Papa is very composed and kind, and indeed I can do all he wants. Aunt Jane — '

'About Mrs St. John? Poor woman, I have nothing to say

against her – but she is taken away from the evil to come,' said Miss Maydew. 'No, no, it was not about Mrs St. John I was thinking, it was about something much more serious. Not that anything could be more serious than a death; but in a wordly point of view!'

'What is it?' they both said in a breath. The idea of news was exciting to them, even though, as was evident from their visitor's agitation, it was disagreeable news they were about to hear. Miss Maydew drew with much excitement from her pocket a copy of the *Times*, very tightly folded together to enable it to enter there, and opened it with trembling hands.

'There it is! Oh, my poor, poor, children! imagine my feelings – it was the first thing I saw when I took up my paper this morning,' she said.

The girls did not immediately take in the full meaning of the intimation which they read with two startled faces close together over the old lady's shoulder. "At Castellamare, on the 15th July, the Rev. Edward Chester, Rector of Brentburn, Berks."

'But we don't know him,' said Mab, bewildered.

Cicely, I think, had a remark of the same kind on her lips; but she stopped suddenly and clasped her hands together and gave a low cry.

'Ah, *you* understand, Cicely!' said Miss Maydew, wiping her forehead with her handkerchief; 'now let us consult what is to be done. What is the date? I was so agitated I never thought of the date! The 15th. Oh, my dear, here is a fortnight lost!'

'But what can be done?' said Cicely, turning a pathetic glance upon the old room which had seemed so melancholy to her yesterday, and the tons of mahogany which she had just been criticizing. How kind, and friendly, and familiar they had become all at once; old, dear friends, who belonged to her no more.

'Mr Chester, the rector!' said Mab, with sudden apprehension. 'Do you mean that something will happen to papa?'

'There is this to be done,' said the old lady, 'your poor good father has been here for twenty years; the people ought to be fond of him – I do not know whether they are, for a parish is an incomprehensible thing, as your poor dear grandfather always used to say – but they ought to be; I am sure he has trudged about enough, and never spared himself, though I never thought him a good preacher, so far as that goes. But he ought to have a great many friends after living here for twenty years.'

'But, Aunt Jane, tell us, tell us – what good will that do?'

'It might do a great deal if they would exert themselves. They might get up a petition, for instance – at once – to the Lord Chancellor; they might employ all their influence. It is not a rich parish, or a large parish, but there are always gentry in it. Oh, a great deal might be done if only people would exert themselves! It is dreadful to think that a fortnight has been lost.'

Cicely, who was not much consoled by this hope, sat down with a very pale countenance and a sudden constriction of heart. She was almost too much bewildered to realize all that it meant; enough lay on the surface to fill her soul with dismay. Mab, who had less perception of the urgent character of the calamity, was more animated.

'I thought you meant *we* could do something,' she said. 'Oh, Aunt Jane, could not we go to the Chancellor, if that is the man. The parish? I don't see why they should take the trouble. It will not hurt them. They will have a young, well-off man instead of an old, poor man. Couldn't *we* go to the Lord Chancellor, Aunt Jane?'

Miss Maydew's eyes lighted up for a moment. She seemed to see herself approaching that unknown potentate as lovely ladies went to kings in the days of romance, with a child in each hand. She felt how eloquent she could be, how convincing. She felt herself capable of going down on her knees and asking him whether the father of those two sweet girls was to starve in his old age? All this appeared before her like a dream. But alas! common sense soon resumed its sway; she shook her head. 'I don't know if that would do any good,' she said.

'And *we* could not get up a petition from the parish,' said Cicely; 'whatever the people may do we cannot stir in it. Oh, Aunt Jane, how foolish, how wrong of us never to think of this! I have thought that papa was old and that we should have to maintain ourselves and the two babies if – anything happened; but I never remembered that it all hung upon some one else's life. Oh, it does seem hard!' cried the girl, clasping her hands. 'Papa has done all the work since ever I was born, but yet he has only been here on sufferance, ready to be turned out at a moment's notice. Oh, it is wrong, it is wrong!'

'Not exactly at a moment's notice,' said Miss Maydew; 'there is six weeks or three months, or something, I forget how long.'

And then there was a painful pause. Mab cried a little, having her feelings most upon the surface, but Cicely sat quite silent and pale with her eyes fixed upon the white blinds which flapped against the open windows. All at once she got up and drew one of them up with a rapid impatient hand. 'I want air, I want light,' she said,' she said in a stifled voice, and put herself full in the intrusive sunshine, which made Miss Maydew blink her old eyes.

'You will give yourself a headache, my dear, and that will not mend matters,' she said.

Cicely's heart was very heavy. She drew down the blind again and walked up and down the room in her agitation.

'Five of us to provide for now – and that is not the worst; what is papa to do? How can he live with everything taken from him? Oh, go to the Chancellor, or anyone, if it will do any good! It is terrible for papa.'

It was while they were still in this agitated state that Betsy threw open the door again, and Mrs Ascott, of the Heath, one of the greatest ladies in the parish came in. She was not heated, like poor old Miss Maydew, with walking, but fresh and well dressed from her carriage, and tranquil as prosperity and comfort could make her. The girls made that sudden effort, which women so often have to make, to receive her as if nothing had happened, as if their minds were as easy and their circumstances as agreeable as her own. She inquired about their journey, about their school, about how they found their papa looking, about the 'sad trials' he had gone through, all in a sweet even tone, with smiles or serious looks, as became her words, and hoped that now they had come back she should see them often at the Heath. 'You are the musical one, Cicely,' she said; 'I know Mab draws. It is always nice when sisters have each their distinction, that people can't mistake. My husband always says girls are so like each other. What is your voice?

contralto? oh, a good second is such a want here. We are all more or less musical you know.'

'My voice is not much one way or the other,' said Cicely. 'Mab sings better than I do, though she is the one who draws.'

'But I fear,' said Miss Maydew, clearing her throat and interfering, 'unless something is done they will not be here long to be of use to anyone. We have just had news — '

'Ah, about poor Mr Chester,' said Mrs Ascott, with the slightest of glances at the stranger; 'I saw it in the papers. Will that affect your papa?'

'Unless' – Miss Maydew put herself forward squarely and steadily – 'something is done.'

Mrs Ascott looked at the old lady for the first time. She had thought her an old nurse at first – for the good woman was not of a patrician appearance, like the girls, who were St. Johns. 'Unless — something is done? I am sure we will all do anything that is possible. What can be done?'

'Hush! my dear, hush!. She does not know I belong to you.' whispered Miss Maydew. 'I think a great deal might be done. If Mr St. John's friends were to get up a petition to the Lord Chancellor at once – stating how long he had been here, and how much beloved he was, and the whole state of the case. I don't personally know his lordship,' said the old lady; 'but he can't be a bad man or he never would have risen to that position. I can't believe but what if the case were put fully before him, he would give Mr St. John the living. It seems so much the most natural thing to do.'

'Dear me, so it does!' said Mrs Ascott. 'How clever of you to have thought of it. I will speak to my husband, and see what he says.'

'And if there is any one else whom you can influence – to do good it should be general – from the whole parish,' said Miss Maydew – 'from all classes; and it ought to be done at once.'

'To be sure,' said Mrs Ascott. 'I assure you I will speak to my husband.' She got up to take her leave, a little frightened by the vehemence of the stranger, and rather elated at the same time by the sense of having a mission. Miss Maydew went with her to the very door.

'At once,' she said, 'at once! It is a fortnight already since the rector died. If the parish means to do anything, you should not lose a day.'

'No: I see, I see! I will go at once and speak to my husband,' cried the visitor, escaping hastily. Miss Maydew returned to her seat breathing a sigh of satisfaction. 'There, girls! I have set it agoing at least. I have started it. That was a nice woman – if she exerts herself, I don't doubt that it will be all right. What a blessing she came while I was here.'

'I hope it is all right,' said Cicely doubtfully; 'but she is not very — not very, *very* sensible, you know. But she is always kind. I hope she will not do anything foolish. Is that papa she is talking to?' cried the girl alarmed, for there were sounds of commotion in the hall. A silence fell upon even the chief conspirator, when she felt that Mr St. John was near – the possibility that her tactics might not be quite satisfactory alarmed her. She withdrew into a corner, instinctively getting the girls and a considerable mass of furniture between herself and any one coming in at the door.

'I do not know what Mrs Ascott is talking of,' said the curate. 'Is tea ready, my dear, for I have a great deal to do? What have you been putting into that good woman's head? She is talking of a petition, and of the Lord Chancellor, and of bad news. I hope you are not a politician, Cicely. What is it all about'

'Here is Aunt Jane, papa,' said Cicely, who was not more comfortable than Miss Maydew. And the old lady had to get up and stretch out her hand to Mr St. John over the sofa, which was her bulwark in chief.

'But I wonder what she meant about bad news,' he went on; 'she seemed to think it affected us. My dears, have you heard anything?'

'Oh, papa, very bad news,' said Cicely with tears in her eyes. 'It is in the paper. Mrs Ascott has seen it, and that is what we were talking about. Oh, dear papa, don't be cast down. Perhaps it may not be so bad as we think. Something may be done; or at the very worst we are both able and willing to work – Mab and I.'

'I don't know what you mean,' said Mr St. John, and he read the announcement without much change of countenance.

'Dear me, so he is gone at last!' he said. 'I have long expected this. His health has been getting worse and worse for years. Poor Chester! has he really gone at last? I remember him at college. He was a year younger than I but always sickly. Poor fellow! and he was a great deal better off then I am, but never got the good of it. What a lesson it is, my dears!'

'But, oh, papa,' cried Mab, who was the most impatient, 'it is a great deal more than a lesson. Think what consequences it will bring to you – and us – and everybody.'

He looked at her with a half smile. 'Little Mab,' he said, 'teaching her elders. Harry will begin soon. Yes, to be sure; we have got fond of this place; it seems hard that we should have to go.'

'But, papa, where shall we go? What shall we do? What is to become of us?' said Cicely.

Mr St. John shook his head. 'If you will consider that I have only just seen it this moment,' he said, 'you will see that I cannot be expected all at once – Was this what Mrs Ascott was talking of? And what did she mean by petitions, and the Lord Chancellor? I hope you have not been putting anything into her head?'

There was a pause – the girls looked at each other, and blushed as if they were the culprits; then Miss Maydew came boldly to the front. 'It was not the fault of the girls, Mr St. John; on the contrary, they were against it. But I thought there was no harm in saying that a petition from the parish – to the Lord Chancellor – a well signed petition, as there must be so many people here who are fond of you – and that no doubt he would give you the living if he understood the circumstances.'

'I a beggar for a living!' said Mr St. John. 'I who have never asked for anything in my life!' A deep flush came upon his delicate pale face. He had borne a great many more serious blows without wincing. Death had visited him, and care dwelt in his house – and he had borne these visitations placidly; but there was one flaw in his armour, and this unlooked-for assault found it out. A flame of injured pride blazed up in him, swift as fire and as glowing. 'I thought I should have died without this,' he said with a groan, half fierce, half bitter. 'What was it to you? I never asked you for anything! Oh, this is hard – this is very hard to bear.'

In the memory of man it had never been known that Mr
St. John thus complained before. The girls had never heard
his voice raised or seen the flush of anger on his face; and they
were overawed by it. This kind of sentiment too has always a
certain fictitious grandeur to the inexperienced. Never to ask
for anything; to wait – patient merit scorning all conflict with
the unworthy – till such time as its greatness should be
acknowledged. This sounds very sublime in most cases to the
youthful soul.

'Well, Mr St. John,' said Miss Maydew, 'you may say I have
no right to interfere; but if you had stooped to ask for
something it might have been a great deal better for your
family. Besides, you have not asked for anything now. I am not
responsible for my actions to anyone, and I hope I may do either
for you or anybody else whatever I please in the way of service.
If the Lord Chancellor does give you the living — '

Mr St. John smiled. 'I need not make myself angry,' he
said, 'for it is all sheer ignorance. The living is a college
living. I don't know what your ideas are on the subject, but
the Lord Chancellor has as much to do with it as you have.
Cicely, let us have tea.'

Miss Maydew shrivelled up upon her chair. She sat very
quiet, and did not say a word after this revelation. What she
had done would have troubled her mind little; but that she
had done nothing after risking so much was hard to bear.
After this little ebullition, however, the curate fell back into
his usual calm. He spoke to them in his ordinary way. His
voice resumed its tranquil tone. He took his tea, which was a
substantial meal, doing justice to the bread and butter, and on
the whole showed signs of being more concerned for Mr
Chester than he was for himself.

'I remember him at college – we were of the same college,'
he said; 'but he always the richest, much the best off. How
little that has to say to a man's happiness! Poor Chester was
never happy; he might have been very well here. How much
I have had to be thankful for here! but it was not his
disposition. He was good-looking too when he was young,
and did very well in everything. Any one would have said he
had a far better chance for a happy life than I had.'

The gentle old man grew quite loquacious in this contrast,

though he was in general the most humble-minded of men; and the two girls sat and listened, giving wondering glances at each other, and blushing red with that shame of affection which lively girls perhaps are particularly disposed to feel when their parents maunder. This sort of domestic criticism, even though unexpressed, was hard upon Mr St. John, as upon all such feeble good men. His last wife had adored him at all times, as much when he was foolish as when he was wise. She would have given him the fullest adhesion of her soul now, and echoed every word he said; but the girls did not. They would have preferred to silence him, and were ashamed of his gentle self-complacency. And yet it was quite true that he felt himself a happier man than Mr Chester, and higher in the scale of merit though not of fortune; and the calm with which he took this event, which was neither more nor less than ruin to him, was fine in its way.

'But what are we to do, papa?' Cicely ventured to ask him, looking up into his face with big anxious eyes, as he took his last cup of tea.

'My dear, we must wait and see,' he said. 'There is no very immediate hurry. Let us see first who is appointed, and what the new rector intends to do.'

'But, Mr St. John, you are a very learned man – and if it is a college living' — suggested Miss Maydew.

'It is my own college, too,' he said reflectively; 'and I suppose I am now one of the oldest members of it. It would not be amiss if they let me stay here the rest of my days. But I never was distinguished. I never was a Fellow, or anything. I never could push myself forward. No – we must just wait and see what is going to happen. A few days or a few weeks will make little difference. Compose yourselves, my dears,' said Mr St. John. 'I am not very anxious after all.'

'I wonder if he would be anxious if you were all starving,' cried Miss Maydew, as the girls walked with her to the station in the evening. 'Oh, Cicely, I know I oughtn't to say anything to you about your papa. But if he has not been anxious, others have been anxious for him. Your poor mother! how she slaved to keep everything as it ought to be; and even poor Miss Brown. It did not cost him much to marry her – but it cost her her life.'

'Aunt Jane!' cried both the girls indignant.

'Well, my dears! She might have been living now, a respectable single woman, doing her duty, as she was capable of doing; instead of which what must she do but bring a couple of white-faced babies into the world that nobody wanted, and die of it. Yes, she did die of it. You don't understand these things – you are only children. And all because he was what you call kind-hearted, and could not bear to see her cry, forsooth. As if the best of us were not obliged both to cry ourselves and to see others cry often enough! but they never thought what they were doing; and the ones to suffer will be you.'

'Aunt Jane, you ought not to speak so of papa,'

'I know I shouldn't my dear – and I humbly beg your pardons,' said Aunt Jane, drying her eyes.

'And we ought not to have left him unprotected,' said Cicely, with a sigh.

CHAPTER EIGHT

THE NEW RECTOR

The news which so much disturbed the inhabitants of the rectory of Brentburn was already old news in Oxford, where indeed it was known and decided who Mr Chester's successor was to be. The august body in whose hands the appointment lay was absolutely unconscious of the existence of Mr St. John. Several members of it, it is true, were his own contemporaries, and had been his acquaintances in the old days when these very dons themselves traversed their quadrangles with such hopes and fears in respect to the issue of an examination, as the destruction of the world or its salvation would scarcely rouse in them now; but what was it likely they could know about a man who at sixty-five was only a curate, who had never asked for anything, never tried for anything; but had kept himself out of sight and knowledge for a lifetime? Those of them who had a dim recollection that 'old St. John' was Chester's curate in charge, naturally thought that he held that precarious and unprofitable place for so long, because of some personal connection with the locality, or preference for it, which he was well off enough to be able to indulge. He had been poor in his youth, but probably his wife had had money, or something had fallen to him. What so likely as that something good should fall by inheritance to a man with such a patrician name? Therefore let nobody blame the dons. They might have been capable (though I don't know whether they would have had any right to exercise their patronage so) of a great act of poetic justice, and might have given to the undistinguished but old member of their college the reward of his long exertions, had they known. But as they did not know, what could these good men do but allot it to the excellent young Fellow – already the winner of all kinds of honours – who condescended to be willing to accept the

humble rectory? Everybody said it was not worth Mildmay's
while to shelve himself in an obscure place like Brentburn; that
it was a strange thing for him to do; that he would hate it as
poor Chester – also an extremely accomplished man and
fellow of his college – had done. Gossips – and such beings
exist in the most classical places – feared that he must want the
money; though some thought he was merely disinclined to let
a tolerable small living, not far from town, and in a good
county, where there were many 'nice families,' pass him; but
very few people, so far as I am aware, thought of any higher
motive which a popular young don could have for such a
fancy.

Mr Mildmay was quite one of the advanced rank of young
Oxford men. I have never been able to understand how it was
that he continued more or less orthodox, but he had done so
by special constitution of mind, I suppose, which in some
tends to belief as much as in some others it tends to unbelief.
He was not one of those uncomfortable people who are always
following out 'truth' to some bitter end or other, and refusing
all compromise. Perhaps he was not so profound as are those
troublesome spirits, but he was a great deal happier, and a
great deal more agreeable. It is quite possible that some young
reader may object to this as a shameful begging of the question
whether it is not best to follow 'truth' with bosom bare into
whatsoever wintry lands that oft-bewildered power may lead.
I don't know; some minds have little inclination towards the
sombre guesses of science, new or old; and perhaps some may
prefer Roger Mildmay for the mere fact that he did not feel
himself to have outgrown Christianity; which, I confess, is
my own feeling on the subject. However, if it is any satisfaction to the said young reader, I may as well avow that though
nature kept him from being sceptical, that kindly nurse did not
hinder him from throwing himself into much semi-intellectual
foolishness in other ways. To hear him talk of art was enough
to make all the Academy dance with fury, and drive the
ordinary learner, however little attached to the Academy, into
absolute imbecility; and his rooms were as good as a show,
with all the last fantastical delights of the day – more like a
museum of china and knick-knacks than rooms to live in. His
floors were littered with rugs, over which, in the aesthetic

dimness, unwary visitors tumbled; his walls were toned into olive greens or peacock blues, dark enough to have defied all the sunshine of the Indies to light them up. He had few pictures; but his rooms were hung with photographs 'taken direct,' and a collection of old china plates, which perhaps, in their primitive colours and broad effect 'came' better than pictures in the subdued and melancholy light. But why insist upon these details? A great many highly-cultured persons have the same kind of rooms, and Mildmay was something more than a highly-cultured person. All this amused and occupied him very much – for indeed collecting is a very amusing occupation; and when he had found something 'really good' in an old curiosity shop, it exhilarated him greatly to bring it home, and find a place for it among his precious stores, and to make it 'compose' with the other curiosities around it. As sheer play, I don't know any play more pleasant; and when he looked round upon the dim world of *objets d'art* that covered all his walls, shelves and tables, and marked the fine pictorial effect of the one brilliant spot of light which the green shade of his reading-lamp prevented from too great diffusion – when, I say, looking up from his studies, Mr Mildmay looked round upon all this, and felt that only very fine taste, and much patient labour, supported by a tolerably well-filled purse, could have brought it all together, and arranged everything into one harmonious whole, there came a glow of gentle satisfaction to the heart of the young don.

But then he sighed. All perfection is melancholy. When you have finally arranged your last acquisition, and look round upon a completeness which, even for the introduction of additional beauty, it seems wicked to disturb, what can you do but sigh? And there was more than this in the breath of melancholy – the long-drawn utterance of an unsatisfied soul in Mildmay's sigh. After all, a man cannot live for china, for aesthetic arrangement, for furniture, however exquisite; or even for art, when he is merely a critic, commentator, and amateur – not a worker in the same. You may suppose that he was weary of his loneliness; that he wanted a companion, or those domestic joys which are supposed to be so infinitely prized in England. I am sorry to say this was not the case. The class to which Mildmay belongs are rather in the way of scouting domestic joys. A man who makes a goddess of his room, who adores china, and decks his mantleshelf with lace, seldom (in theory) wants a wife, or sighs for a companion of his joys and sorrows. For why? He does not deal much in sorrows or in joys. The deepest delight which can thrill the soul in the discovery of old Worcester or royal Dresden, scarcely reaches to the height of passion; and even if a matchless cup of *Henri Deux* were to be shivered to pieces in your hand, your despair would not appeal to human sympathy as would the loss of a very much commoner piece of flesh and blood. And then young ladies as a class are not, I fear, great in the marks of china, and even in the feminine speciality of lace require years to mellow them into admiration of those archaeological morsels which cannot be worn. Besides, the very aspect of such rooms as those I have indicated (not being bold enough to attempt to describe them) is inimical to all conjoint and common existence. Solitude is taken for granted in all those dainty arrangements; in the dim air, the dusky walls, the subdued tone. A child in the place, ye heavens! imagination shivers, and dares not contemplate what might follow.

And then Mr Mildmay had exhausted this delight. I believe his rooms were papered with three different kinds of the choicest paper that ever came out of Mr Morris's hands. His curtains had been embroidered in the art school of needlework on cloth woven and dyed expressly for him. An ancient piece of lovely Italian tapestry hung over one door, and another was veiled by a glorious bit of eastern work from Damascus or Constantinople. His Italian cabinets were enough to make you faint with envy; his Venice glass – but why should I go on? The rugs which tripped you up as you threaded your way through the delicate artificial twilight were as valuable as had they had been woven in gold; and no sooner was it known that Mildmay had accepted a living than all the superior classes in the southern half of England pricked up their ears. Would there be a sale? About a thousand connoisseurs from all parts of the country balanced themselves metaphorically on one foot like Raphael's St. Michael, ready to swoop down at the first note of warning. I am not sure that among railway authorities there were not preparations for a special train.

Mr Mildmay had got tired of it all. Suddenly in that dainty dimness of high culture it had occurred to him that studies of old art and accumulations of the loveliest furniture were not life. What was life? There are so many that ask that question, and the replies are so feeble. The commonest rendering is that which Faust in sheer disgust of intellectualism plunged into – pleasure; with what results the reader knows. Pleasure in its coarser meaning, in the Faust sense, and in the vulgar sensual sense, was only a disgust to such a man as Roger Mildmay. What could he have done with his fine tastes and pure habits in the *coulisses* or the casinos? He would only have recoiled with the sickening sensations of physical loathing as well as mental. What then? Should he marry and have a family, which is the virtuous and respectable answer to his question? He had no inclination that way. The woman whom he was to marry had not yet risen on his firmament, and he was not the kind of man to determine on marriage in the abstract, dissociated from any individual. How then was he to know life, and have it? Should he go off into the distant world and travel, and discover new treasures of art in unsuspected places, and bring home his trophies from all quarters of the world? But he had done this so often already that even the idea almost fatigued him. Besides, all these expedients, pleasure, domesticity, travel, would all have been ways of pleasing himself only, and he had already done a great deal to please himself. Life must have something in it surely of sharper, more pungent flavour. It could not be a mere course of ordinary days one succeeding another, marked out by dinners, books, conversations, the same thing over again, never more than an hour of it at a time in a man's possession, nothing in it that could not be foreseen and mapped out. This could not be life. How was he to get life? He sat and wondered over this problem among his beautiful collections. He had nothing to do, you will say; and yet you can't imagine how busy he was. In short, he was never without something to do. He had edited a Greek play, he had written magazine articles, he had read papers before literary societies, he had delivered lectures. Few, very few, were his unoccupied moments. He knew a great many people in the highest classes of society, and kept up a lively intercourse with the most intelligent, the most cultivated minds of his time. He was, indeed, himself one of the most highly cultured persons of his standing; yet here he sat in the most delightful rooms in his college, sighing for life, life!

What is life? Digging, ploughing, one can understand that; but unfortunately one cannot dig, and 'to beg I am ashamed.' These familiar words suggested themselves by the merest trick of the ear to his mind unawares. To beg, the Franciscans he had seen in old Italy had not been at all ashamed; neither were the people who now and then penetrated into college rooms with – if not the Franciscan's wallet, or the penitent's rattling money-box – lists of subscriptions with which to beguile the unwary. For what? For hospitals, schools, missions, churches; the grand deduction to be drawn from all this being that there were a great many people in the world, by their own fault or that of others, miserable, sick, ignorant, wicked; and that a great many more people, from good or indifferent motives, on true or on false pretences, were making a great fuss about helping them. This fuss was in a general way annoying, and even revolting to the *dilettanti*, whose object is to see and hear only things that are beautiful, to encourage in themselves and others delightful sensations; but yet when you came to think of it, it could not be denied that the whole system of public charity had a meaning. In some cases a false, foolish, wrong meaning, no doubt; but yet —

If I were to tell you all the fancies that passed through Roger Mildmay's head on the subject, it would require volumes; and many of his thoughts were fantastic enough. The fact that he had taken orders and was the man he was, made it his proper business to teach others; but he would much rather, he thought, have reclaimed waste land, or something of that practical sort. Yes, to reclaim a bit of useless moorland and make it grow oats or even potatoes – that would be something; but then unfortunately the ludicrous side of the matter would come over him. What could he do on his bit of moorland with those white hands of his? Would it not be much more sensible to pay honest wages to some poor honest man out of work, and let him do the digging? and then where was Roger Mildmay? still left, stranded, high and dry, upon the useless ground of his present existence. Such a man in such a self-discussion is as many women are. If he works, what is the good of it? It is to occupy, to please himself, not because the work is necessary to others; indeed, it is taking bread out of the mouths of others to do badly himself that which another man, probably lounging sadly out of work, and seeing his children starve, would do well. Let him, then, go back to his own profession; and what was he to do? A clergyman must preach, and he did not feel at all at his ease in the pulpit. A clergyman must teach, and his prevailing mood was a desire to learn. A clergyman must care for the poor, and he knew nothing about the poor. The result of all these confused and unsatisfactory reasonings with himself was that when the living of Brentburn was offered to him half in joke, he made a plunge at it, and accepted. 'Let us try!' he said to himself. Anything was better than this perplexity. At the worst he could but fail.

Now, Mr St. John, as I have said, was a member of the same college, and had served the parish of Brentburn for twenty years, and what was to Roger Mildmay an adventure, a very doubtful experiment, would have been to him life and living; and next on the list of eligible persons after Mr Mildmay was the Rev. John Ruffhead, who was very anxious to marry and settle, and was a clergyman's son well trained to his work. Such injustices are everywhere around us; they are nobody's fault, we say – they are the fault of the system; but what system would mend them is hard to tell. And, on the other hand, perhaps neither Mr St. John nor Mr Ruffhead had the same high object before them as Roger had. The old man would have gone on in his gentle routine just as he had done all those years, always kind, soothing the poor folk more than he taught them; the young man would, though sure to do his duty, have thought perhaps more of the future Mrs Ruffhead, and the settling down, than any kind of heroic effort to realize life and serve the world. So that on the whole, ideally my *dilettante* had the highest ideal; though the practical effect of him no one could venture to foretell.

He had decided to accept the living of Brentburn at once, feeling the offer to be a kind of answer of the oracle – for there was a certain heathenism mingling with his Christianity – to his long-smouldering and unexpressed desires; but before concluding formally he went, by the advice of one of his friends, to look at the place, 'to see how he would like it?' 'Like it! do I want to like it?' he said to himself. Must this always be the first question? Was it not rather the first possibility held out to him in the world – of duty, and a real, necessary, and certain work which should not be to please himself?

He did not want to like it. Now, men of Mildmay's turn of mind are seldom deeply devoted to nature. They admire a fine landscape or fine sunset, no doubt, but it is chiefly for the composition, the effects of light and shade, the combination of colours. In the loveliest country they sigh for picture galleries and fine architecture, and cannot please themselves with the mists and the clouds, the woods and the waters, the warm, sweet, boundless atmosphere itself, in which others find beauty and mystery unceasing. Yet on this occasion a different result took place; although it was contrary to his own principles, when he first came out of the prosaic little railway at Brentburn and saw at his right hand, one rich cloud of foliage rounding upon another, and all the wealth of princely trees standing up in their battalions under the full warm August sky; and on the other the sweet wild common bursting forth in a purple blaze of heather, all belted and broken with the monastic gloom of the pine-woods and ineffable blue distances of the wilder country – there suddenly fell upon him a love at first sight for this insignificant rural place, which I cannot account for any more than he could. I should be disposed to say that the scent of the fir-trees went to his head, as it does to mine; but then the very soul within him melted to the great, broad, delicious greenness of shadows in the forest; and the two between them held him in an ecstasy, in that sweet lapse of all sense and thought into which nature sometimes surprises us, when all at once, without any suspicion on our part of what she is about, she throws herself open to us, and holds out her tender arms. Mildmay stood in this partial trance, not knowing what he was doing, for – two full minutes, then he picked himself up, slightly ashamed of his ecstasy, and asked his way to the church, and said to himself (as I think Mr Ruskin says somewhere) that mere nature without art to back her up is little, but that he might indeed permit himself to feel those indescribable sensations if he could look at all this as a background to a beautiful piece of ancient architecture in the shape of a church. Alas, poor Mr Mildmay! I don't know why it had never been broken to him. Ignorant persons had said 'a very nice church,' perhaps out of sheer ignorance, perhaps from the commercial point of view that a new church in perfect repair is much more delightful, to a young rector's pocket at least, than the most picturesque old one in perpetual need of restorations. But anyhow, when the church of Brentburn did burst upon him in all its newness, poor Roger put out his hand to the first support he could find, and felt disposed to swoon. The support which he found to lean on was the wooden rail, round a rather nasty duck-pond which lay between two cottages, skirting the garden hedge of one of them. Perhaps it was the odour of this very undelightful feature in the scene that made him feel like fainting, rather than the sight of the church; but he did not think so in the horror of the moment. He who had hoped to see the distant landscape all enhanced and glorified, by looking at it from among the ancestral elms or solemn yew-trees about a venerable village spire, and old grey, mossy Saxon walls – or beside the lovely tracery of some decorated window with perhaps broken pieces of old glass glimmering out like emeralds and rubies! The church, I have already said, was painfully new; it was in the most perfect good order; the stones might have been scrubbed with scrubbing-brushes that very morning; and, worse than all, it was good Gothic, quite correct and unobjectionable. The poor young don's head drooped upon his breast, his foot slipped on the edge of the duck-pond. Never was a more delicate distress; and yet but for the despairing grasp he gave to the paling, the result might have been grotesque enough.

'Be you poorly, sir?' said old Mrs Joel, who was standing, as she generally was, at her cottage door.

'No, no, I thank you,' said the new rector faintly; 'I suppose it is the sun.'

'Come in a bit and rest, bless you,' said Mrs Joel; 'you do look overcome. It is a bit strong is that water of hot days. Many a one comes to look at our cheuch. There's a power of old cheuches about, and ours is the only one I know of as is new, sir, and sweet and clean – though I says it as shouldn't,' said the old woman, smoothing her apron and curtsying with a conscious smile.

'You are the sexton's wife? you who have the charge of it?' said Mr Mildmay.

'Thank my stars! I ain't no man's wife,' said Mrs Joel. 'I be old John Joel's widow – and a queer one he was; and the curate he say as I was to keep the place, though there's a deal of jealousy about. I never see in all my born days a jealouser place than Brentburn.'

'Who is the curate?' asked Mr Mildmay.

'Bless your soul, sir, he'll be as pleased as Punch to see you. You go up bold to the big door and ask for Mr St. John; he would always have the hartis-gentlemen and that sort in, to take a cup of tea with him. The Missis didn't hold with it in her time. She had a deal of pride, though you wouldn't have thought it at first. But since she's dead and gone, Mr St. John he do have his way; and two pretty young ladies just come from school,' said Mrs Joel with a smirk. She was herself very curious about the stranger, who was evidently not a 'hartis-gentleman.' 'Maybe you was looking for lodgings, like?' she said after a pause.

'No, no,' said Mildmay, with unnecessary explanatoriness; 'I was only struck by the church, in passing, and wished to know who was the clergyman — '

'Between ourselves, sir,' said Mrs Joel, approaching closer than was pleasant, for her dinner had been highly seasoned, 'I don't know as Mr St. John is what you call the clergyman. He ain't but the curate, and I do hear as there is a real right clergyman a-coming. But you won't name it, not as coming from me? for I can't say but he's always been a good friend.'

'Oh no, I shall not name it. Good morning,' cried Mildmay hurriedly. A new church, a horrible duck-pond, an old woman who smelt of onions. He hurried along, scarcely aware in his haste until he arrived in front of it that the house beyond the church was the rectory, his future home.

CHAPTER NINE

THE ENEMY

The girls I need not say had been engaged in calculations long and weary during these intervening days. Cicely, who had at once taken possession of all the details of housekeeping, had by this time made a discovery of the most overwhelming character; which was that the curate was in arrears with all the tradespeople in the parish, and that the 'books,' instead of having the trim appearance she remembered, were full of long lists of things supplied, broken by no safe measure of weeks, but running on from month to month and from year to year, with here and there a melancholy payment 'to account' set down against it. Cicely was young and she had no money, and knew by her own experience how hard it was to make it; and she was overwhelmed by this discovery. She took the books in her lap and crept into the drawing-room beside Mab, who was making a study of the children in the dreary stillness of the afternoon. The two little boys were posed against the big sofa, on the carpet. The young artist had pulled off their shoes and stockings, and, indeed, left very little clothes at all upon Charley, who let her do as she pleased with him without remonstrance, sucking his thumb and gazing at her with his pale blue eyes. Harry had protested, but had to submit to the taking away of his shoes, and now sat gloomily regarding his toes, and trying to keep awake with supernatural lurches and recoveries; Charley, more placid, had dropped off. He had still his thumb in his mouth, his round cheek lying flushed against the cushion, his round white limbs huddled up in a motionless stillness of sleep. Harry sat upright, as upright as possible, and nodded. Mab had got them both outlined on her paper, and was working with great energy and absorption when Cicely came in with the books in her lap. 'Oh, go away, go away,' cried Mab,

79

'whoever you are! Don't disturb them! If you wake them all is lost!'

Cicely stood at the door watching the group. Mab had improvised an easel, she had put on a linen blouse over her black and white muslin dress. She had closed the shutters of two windows, leaving the light from the middle one to fall upon the children. In the cool shade, moving now and then a step backwards to see the effect of her drawing, her light figure, full of purpose and energy, her pretty white hand a little stained with the charcoal with which she was working, she was a picture in herself. Cicely, her eyes very red and heavy – for indeed she had been crying – and the bundle of grocery books in her apron, paused and looked at her sister with a gush of admiration, a sharp pinch of something like envy. Mab could do this which looked like witchcraft, while she could only count, and count, and cry over these hopeless books. What good would crying do? If she cried her eyes out it would not pay a sixpence. Cicely knew she had more 'sense' than Mab, It was natural. She was nineteen, Mab only eighteen, and a year is so much at that age! But Mab was clever. She could do something which Cicely could not even understand; and she would be able to make money, which Cicely could scarcely hope to do. It was envy, but of a generous kind. Cicely went across the room quite humbly behind backs, not to disturb her sister's work, and sat down by the darkened window, through which a fresh little breeze from the garden was coming in. It distracted her for a moment from her more serious cares to watch the work going on. She thought how pretty Mab looked, lighting up the poetical darkness, working away so vigorously and pleasantly with only that pucker of anxiety in her white forehead, lest her sitters should move. 'Oh, quiet, quiet!' she said, almost breathless. 'He must not either go to sleep or wake right up, till I have put them in. Roll the ball to him softly, Cicely, quite softly as if he were a kitten.' Cicely put away the terrible books and knelt down on the carpet and rolled the big ball, which Mab had been moving with her foot towards little dozing Harry, who watched it with eyes glazing over with sleep. The light and the warmth and the stillness were too much for him. Just as the ball arrived at his soft little pink toes he tumbled over all in a heap, with his head upon Charley. Mab gave a cry of vexation. 'But never mind, it was not your fault,' she said, to make up for her impatience. And indeed Cicely felt it was rather hard to be blamed.

'After all it does not matter,' said Mab. 'I have done enough – but I shall never get them to look like that again. How pretty children are even when they are ugly! What pictures such things make! how anybody can help making pictures all the day long I can't imagine. It is only that you will not try.'

'I would try if I had any hope,' said Cicely; 'I would do anything. Oh, I wonder if there is anything I could do!'

'Why, of course you can teach,' said Mab, consoling her, 'a great deal better than I can. I get impatient; but you shan't teach; I am the brother and you are the sister, and you are to keep my house.'

'That was all very well,' said Cicely, 'so long as there was only us two; but now look,' she cried pointing to the two children lying over one another in the light, asleep, 'there is *them* – and papa – '

'They are delightful like that,' cried Mab starting up; 'oh, quick, give me that portfolio with the paper! I must try them again. Just look at all those legs and arms! – and yet they are not a bit pretty in real life,' cried Mab in the fervour of her art, making a fine natural distinction.

Cicely handed her all she wanted, and looked on with wondering admiration for a moment; but then she shook her head slightly and sighed. 'You live in another world,' she said, 'you artists. Oh, Mab, I don't want to disturb you, but if you knew how unhappy I am — '

'What is the matter? and why should you be more anxious than papa is?' cried Mab busy with her charcoal. 'Don't make yourself unhappy, dear. Things always come right somehow. I think so as well as papa.'

'You don't mind either of you so long as you have — Oh, you don't know how bad things are. Mab! we are in debt.'

Mab stopped her work, appalled, and looked her sister in the face. This was a terrible word to the two girls, who never had known what it was to have any money. 'In debt!' she said.

'Yes, in debt – do you wonder now that I am wretched? I don't know even if papa knows; and now he has lost even the little income he had, and we have given up our situations. Oh, Mab! Mab! think a little; what are we to do?'

Mab let her chalk fall out of her hand. She went and knelt down by Cicely's side, and put one soft cheek against another as if that would do any good. 'Oh, how can I tell?' she said with tears in her eyes. 'I never was any good to think. Is it much – is it very bad? is there anything we can do?'

Cicely shed a few tears over the butcher's book which was uppermost. 'if we were staying here for ever,' she said, 'as we were all foolish enough to think when we came – we might have paid it with a struggle. I should have sent away those two maids, and tried to do everything myself.'

'Everything, Cicely?' Mab was as much appalled at the thought of life without a Betsy, as a fine lady would be denuded of her establishment. The want of a maid-of-all-work represents a dreadful coming down in life, almost more than a greater apparent loss does. Her countenance fell, the corners of her mouth took a downward curve, and her pride received a crushing blow. Yet if you consider what Betsy was, the loss was not deadly. But as usual it was not the actual but the sentimental view of the case which struck the girls.

'Yes,' said Cicely, with a solemn paleness on her face. She felt the humiliation too. 'I shouldn't mind *doing* things,' she said, her voice breaking a little; 'it is what people will think. Us, a clergyman's daughters! but what is the use even of that?' she cried; 'it will do no good now. Papa must leave Brentburn, and we may have not a shilling, not a penny now, to pay those things with. I think and think – but I cannot tell what we are to do.'

The two clung together in an agony of silence for a moment; how many wringings of the heart have been caused by a little money! and so often those who suffer are not those who are to blame. The ruin that seemed to be involved was unspeakable to the two girls; they did not know what the butcher and the baker might be able to do to them; nor did they know of any way of escape.

'If there was any hope,' said Cicely after a pause, 'of staying here – I would go round to them all, and ask them to take pity on us; to let us begin again paying every week, and wait till we could scrape some money together for what is past. That, I think, would be quite possible, if we were to stay; and we might take pupils — '

'To be sure,' cried Mab, relieved, springing up with the easy hope of a sanguine disposition, 'and I might get something to do. In the meantime I can finish my drawing. They have not stirred a bit, look, Cicely. They are like two little white statues. It may be a pity that they were ever born, as Aunt Jane says – but they are delightful models. I almost think,' Mab went on piously, working with bold and rapid fingers, 'that in all this that has happened there must have been a special providence for me.'

Cicely looked up with surprise at this speech, but she made no reply. She was too full of thought to see the humour of the suggestion. Mab's art furnished a delightful way of escape for her out of all perplexity; but Cicely could only go back to the butcher's book. 'What could we do, I wonder,' she said half to herself, for she did not expect any advice from her sister, 'about the living? Very likely they don't know anything about poor papa. It may be very highminded never to ask for anything,' said poor Cicely, 'but then how can we expect that other people will come and thrust bread into our mouths? It is better to ask than to starve. As a matter of fact we cannot starve quietly, because if we are found dead of hunger, there is sure to be a business in the papers, and everything exposed. "Death from starvation, of a clergyman's family!" That would make a great deal more fuss than quietly going and asking for something for papa. I am not a bold girl – at least I don't think so,' she cried, her soft face growing crimson at the thought, 'but I would not mind going to any one, if it was the Head of the College, or the Lord Chancellor, or even the Queen!'

'I wonder,' said Mab, 'if we met the Queen driving in the forest – as one does sometimes – whether we might not ask her, as people used to do long ago? I don't think she would mind. Why should she mind? She could not be frightened, or even angry, with two girls.'

Cicely shook her head. 'The Queen has nothing to do with Brentburn; and why should she be troubled with us any more than any other lady? No! that sort of thing has to be done in a business way,' said the elder sister seriously. 'If I could find out who was the chief man, the Head of the College — '

They had been so much absorbed that they had not heard any sound outside; and at this moment the door was suddenly thrown open, admitting a flood of cross light, and revealing suddenly the figures of the curate and some one who followed him.

'My dears!' began Mr St. John, surprised.

'Oh, papa! you have woke them up. You have spoiled my light!' cried Mab, in despair.

Cicely started to her feet, letting the account books tumble on the floor; and the two little boys raised a simultaneous howl of sleepy woe. 'Harry wants his tea,' they both piped piteously. Mr Mildmay, whom the curate had met at the gate, looked with a surprise I cannot describe on this extraordinary scene. The white babies in the light had seemed to him at first an exquisite little 'composition,' which went to his very heart; and the two other figures, half lit up by the stream of unwelcome light from the door, bewildered the young man. Who were they, or what? One indignant, holding her charcoal with artistic energy; the other, startled, gazing at himself with a hostile sentiment, which he could not understand, in her eyes.

'My love,' said the gentle curate, 'you should not make a studio of the drawing-room.' Mr St. John was not disturbed by the wailing of the little boys, to which, I suppose, he was used. 'Cicely, this is Mr Mildmay, from Oxford, who has come — to look at the parish.' he added, with a gentle sigh. 'Let us have tea.'

Why did the girl look at him with that paleness of anger in her face? Mr Mildmay's attention was distracted from the drawing and the artist, who, naturally, would have interested him most, by the gleam of hostility, the resentment and defiance in Cicely's eyes.

'Yes, papa,' she said shortly; and with merely an inclination of her head to acknowledge his introduction to her, she took up the children, Charley in one arm, who was half dressed; Harry under the other, whose feet were bare, and carried them out of the room. She had divined the first moment she saw him, a dark figure against the light, who he was; and I cannot describe the bitterness that swelled like a flood through poor Cicely's heart. It was all over, then! There was no further hope, however fantastical, from College or Chancellor, or Queen! Fantastic, indeed, the hope had been; but Cicely was young, and had been more buoyed up by this delusion, even in her despair, than she was aware of. She felt herself fall down, down into unspeakable depths, and the very heart within her seemed to feel the physical pain of it, lying crushed and sore, throbbing all over with sudden suffering. The passionate force of the shock gave her strength, or I do not think she could have carried the two children away as she did, one in each arm, while the stranger looked on amazed. Little Charley, always peaceable, held her fast round the neck, with his head against her cheek, but Harry, whom she carried under her other arm, lifted his head a little from that horizontal position, and kept up his melancholy whine. She was not fond of the children; how could she be? and I think would gladly have 'given them a shake' in the excitement and misery of her feelings. It was so hard upon the girl, that I think she might be forgiven for feeling that thus her young arms were to be hampered all her life; and, meanwhile, she felt that her father and sister would be perfectly amiable to the stranger, who was about to supplant them, and turn them out of their house. This, I am afraid, exasperated Cicely as much as anything else. 'These two' would have no *arrière pensée;* they would be perfectly kind to him, as though he were acting the part of their best friend.

And, indeed, this was how it turned out. When she went back, having disposed of the children, to make the tea, Cicely found Mab and Mr Mildmay in great amity over the uncompleted drawing. He had been criticizing, but he had been praising as well; and Mab was flushed with pleasure and interest. She ran off laughing, to take off her blouse and wash her hands, when Cicely came in, and the elder sister, who felt that her eyes were still red, felt at the same time that her ungenial and constrained reception of him had struck the new-comer. She went and gathered up the account books from the floor with a sigh. Despair was in her heart. How could she talk and smile as the others had been doing? As for Mr St. John, he was as pleased with his visitor as if he had brought him something, instead of taking all hope from him. It was rarely the good man saw any but heavy parish people –

the rural souls with whom indeed he was friendly, but who had nothing to say to him except about their crops and local gossip. The gossip of Oxford was much sweeter to his ears. He liked to tell of the aspect of things 'in my time,' as I suppose we all do; and how different this and that was now-a-days. 'I knew him when he was a curate like myself,' he said, with a soft sigh, talking of the dean, that lofty dignitary. 'We were at school together, and I used to be the better man;' and this was spoken of the vice-chancellor himself; and he enjoyed and wondered to hear of all their grandeurs. He had met Mildmay on the road, looking through the gate at the rectory, and had addressed him in his suave old-world way as a stranger. Then they had talked of the church, that most natural of subjects between two clergymen; and then, half reluctantly, half with a sense of compulsion, the stranger had told him who he was. Mr St. John, though he was poor, had all the hospitable instincts of a prince. He insisted that his new acquaintance should come in and see the house, and hear about everything. He would have given the same invitation, he said afterwards, to any probable new resident in the parish, and why not to the new rector? for in Mr St. John's mind there was no gall.

But to describe Mildmay's feelings when he was suddenly introduced into this novel world is more difficult. He was taken entirely by surprise. He did not know anything about the curate in charge. If he thought of his predecessor at all it was the late rector he thought of, who died on the shores of the Bay of Naples after a life-long banishment from England. He could understand all that; to go away altogether after art, antiquity, Pompeii, classic editings, and aesthetic delights was perfectly comprehensible to the young Oxford man. But this – what was this? The old man before him, so gentle, so suave, so smiling, his own inferior in position for was he not rector elect, while Mr St. John was but curate? Yet so far above him in years and experience, and all that constitutes superiority among gentlemen of equal breeding. Why was he here as curate? and why did *that* girl look at himself with so much suppressed passion in her eyes? and where had the other been trained to draw so well? and what was the meaning of the two children, so unlike all the others, whom his young enemy had carried off impetuously, instead of ringing the bell for their nurse as any one else would have done? Mildmay felt a thrilling sensation of newness as he sat down at the tea-table, and looked on, an interested spectator, at all that was proceeding under his eyes. This in its way was evidently *life*; there was no mistaking the passion that existed underneath this quiet surface, the something more than met the eye. Was it a skeleton in the closet, as the domestic cynic says? But these were not words that seemed to apply to this calm old man and these young girls. It was life, not the quiet of books, and learned talk, and superficial discussion, but a quiet full of possibilities, full of hidden struggle and feeling. Mildmay felt as if he had come out of his den in the dark like an owl, and half blinking in the unusual light, was placed as spectator of some strange drama, some episode full of interest, to the character of which he had as yet no clue.

'You are looking at the furniture; it is not mine,' said Mr St. John, 'except the carpets, which, as you say, are much worn. The other things are all Mr Chester's. I am expecting every day to hear what is to be done with them. Most likely they will sell it; if you wanted anything — '

Mildmay made a gesture of horror in spite of himself, and Mab laughed.

'You do not think Mr Mildmay wants all that mahogany, papa? The catafalque there, Cicely and I agreed it was more like a tomb in Westminster Abbey than anything else.'

'What is amiss with it?' said Mr St. John. 'I always understood it was very good. I am told they don't make things nearly so strong or so substantial now. Poor Chester! He was a man of very fine taste, Mr Mildmay. But why do you laugh, my dear? That was why he was so fond of Italy; shattered health, you know. Those men who are so fond of art are generally excitable; a little thing has an effect upon them. Cicely, give Mr Mildmay some tea.'

'Yes, papa,' said Cicely; and gave the stranger a look which made him think his tea might be poisoned. Mr St. John went maundering kindly —

'You said you were going to London, and had left your things at the station? Why shouldn't you stay all night here instead? There are a great many things that I would like to

show you – the church and the school for instance, and I
should like to take you to see some of my poor people. Cicely,
we can give Mr Mildmay a bed?'

Cicely looked up at her father quickly. There was a
half-entreaty, a pathetic wonder, mingled with anger, in her
eyes. 'How can you?' she seemed to say. Then she answered
hesitating, 'There are plenty of beds, but I don't know if they
are aired – if they are comfortable.' Strangely enough, the
more reluctant she was to have him, the more inclined
Mildmay felt to stay.

'It is very kind,' he said. 'I cannot think how it is possible
that I can have had the assurance to thrust myself upon you
like this. I am afraid Miss St. John thinks it would be very
troublesome.'

'Troublesome! There is no trouble at all. Cicely is not so
foolish and inhospitable,' said the curate in full current of his
open-heartedness. 'My dear, it is fine warm weather, and Mr
Mildmay is a young man. He is not afraid of rheumatics like
the old people in the parish. He and I will walk up to the
station after tea and fetch his bag, and I will show him several
things on the way. You will tell Betsy?'

'I will see that everything is ready,' she said, with so much
more meaning in the words than was natural or necessary. Her
eyes were a little dilated with crying, and slightly red at the
edges; there was surprise and remonstrance in them, and she
did not condescend by a single word to second her father's
invitation. This settled the question. Had she asked him,
Mildmay might have been indifferent; but as she did not ask
him, he made up his mind it was quite necessary he should
stay.

'I shall perhaps see you finish that group,' he said to Mab,
who was interested and amused by the novelty of his
appearance, as her father was.

'Ah, but I shall never get them into the same *pose*! If papa
had not come in so suddenly, waking them – besides spoiling
my light — '

'I am afraid it was partly my fault,' he said; 'but I did not
expect to be brought into the presence of an artist.'

The colour rose on Mab's cheeks. 'Please don't flatter me,'
she said. 'I want so much to be an artist. Shall I ever be able to

do anything, do you think? for you seem to know.'

Cicely looked at her sister, her eyes sparkling with offence
and reproach. 'The people who know you best think so,' she
said. 'It is not right to ask a stranger. How can Mr Mildmay
know?'

How hostile she was! between her smiling pretty sister, who
was ready to talk as much as he pleased, and her kind old suave
father, what a rugged implacable young woman! What could
he have done to her? Mildmay felt as much aggrieved when
she called him a stranger, as if it had been a downright injury.
'I know a little about art,' he said quite humbly; 'enough to
perceive that your sister has a great deal of real talent, Miss St.
John.'

'Yes, yes, she is clever,' said the curate. 'I hope it will be of
some use to you, my poor Mab. Now, Mr Mildmay, let us
go. I want to show you the rectory fields, and the real village,
which is some way off. You must not think this cluster of
houses is Brentburn. It is pleasant walking in the cool of the
afternoon, and, my dears, a walk will be good for you too.
Come down by the common and meet us. Cicely,' he added in
a half-whisper, standing aside to let his guest pass, 'my dear,
you are not so polite as I hoped. I wish you would look more
kind and more pleased.

'But I am not pleased. Oh, papa, why did you ask him? I
cannot bear the sight of him,' she cried.

'My love!' said the astonished curate. He was so much
surprised by this outburst that he did not know how to reply.
Then he put his hand softly upon her forehead, and looked
into her eyes. 'I see what it is. You are a little feverish: you are
not well. It is the hot weather, no doubt,' he said.

'Oh, papa! I am well enough; but I am very wretched. Let
me speak to you when we have got rid of this man – before
you go to bed.'&&'Surely, my dear,' he said soothingly, and
kissed her forehead. 'I should advise you to lie down for a
little, and keep quiet, and the fever may pass off. But I must
not keep my guest waiting,' and with this Mr St. John went
away, talking cheerfully in the hall to his companion as he
rejoined him. 'It is trying weather,' they heard him saying. 'I
stopped behind for a moment to speak to my eldest daughter.
I do not think she is well,'

'Will papa discuss your health with this new man?' cried Mab. 'How funny he is! But don't be so savage, Ciss. If it must be, let us make the best of it. Mr Mildmay is very nice to talk to. Let us take whatever amusement is thrown in our way.'

'Oh, amusement!' said Cicely, 'You are like papa; you don't think what is involved. This is an end of everything. What are we to do? Where are we to go? His name is not Mildmay; it is Ruin and Destruction. It is all I can do not to burst out upon him and ask him, oh! how has he the heart – how has he the heart to come here!'

'If you did I think he would not come,' said Mab calmly. 'What a pity people cannot say exactly what they think. But if he gave it up, there would be someone else. We must make up our minds to it. And how beautifully poor papa behaves through it all.'

'I wish he were not so beautiful!' cried Cicely in her despair, almost grinding her white teeth. 'I think you will drive me mad between you – papa and you.'

CHAPTER TEN

IN THE PARISH

Mr Mildmay had a very pleasant walk. He went through Brentburn proper, which was a mile from the church on the rich woodland side of the parish, an ordinary little village, a mixture of old picturesque Berkshire cottages, with high sloping roofs and aged harmonious mossy brick walls, and very new square houses in the bilious brick of modern use – mean and clean and angular. The cottages, with their wild old gardens and mossed apple-trees delighted him; but the curate shook his head, 'They will be the curse of your life,' he said solemnly, at which the young Oxford man was disposed to laugh.

A few people were standing about their doors enjoying the cool evening, at whom the new rector looked with curiosity. They were very commonplace people, with the set hard faces so common among the rural poor, half caused by exposure to the open air, and half by the dull routine in which their life is spent. Mildmay looked at them wistfully. Were they the kind of people among whom he could find the life he sought? A few of the women were gossiping, the men stared blankly at him as he passed, saluting the curate gruffly; and evidently the wag among them made some rough joke, received with loud laughter, upon the two black coats.

'Yes,' said the curate mildly, 'that fellow Joe Endley is one of the worst in the parish. It was at us, no doubt, they were laughing. Anything above their own level, except money, they don't understand; and they know I have no money. Good evening Mr Wilkins. What a sweet evening it is.'

'Good evening, sir,' said the grocer, coming, with his apron round him from his shop-door. 'I thought perhaps as you was comin' to see me , sir, along o' the letter I sent you.'

'I did not get any letter,' said Mr St. John, looking at the grocer in a helpless, pitiful way, which his companion remarked wonderingly. The curate seemed to shrink somehow: a painful look came upon his face.

'I sent up this afternoon with my cart,' said Wilkins, 'to say as , if it was quite convenient — '

'My daughter will see to it – my daughter will see to it,' said the curate anxiously. 'I am occupied at present, as you perceive, and in a hurry. She will see you, or I, to-morrow.'

And he shuffled on through the dust of the highroad, quickening his pace. His step had been the long, firm, manly step, of a man still young, till they met with this interruption. But poor Mr St John fell into a shuffle when he met the grocer. His cheek got a hectic flush; he shrank visibly; his knees and his elbows grew prominent. He did not speak again till they had got beyond the village. Then he drew breath, and his natural outline came slowly back. 'You will find much hardness among the people,' he said; 'Heaven forbid that I should blame them, poor souls; they live hardly, and have hardness to bear from others; but when any question arises between them and one who has unfortunately the niceties – the feelings – that we are brought up to — ' (the curate stopped); 'and I never was used to it,' he said, as if to himself, in a low voice.

What did it all mean? the new rector said to himself. I think it was easy enough to divine, for my part; but then the rector was young, and had always been well off, and it did not occur to him that a grocer, simply as grocer, could have any power over a clergyman; more and more he felt convinced that some drama, some domestic tragedy, must be connected with the St. Johns, and he felt more and more eager to find out. They went to the station, and sent a boy to the rectory with Mildmay's portmanteau, and then they strayed home by the common, across which the setting sun threw its very last slanting arrow of gold.

'This is delightful!' said Mildmay. 'What freedom! what breadth of atmosphere! One feels oneself on the moors, in the great ample world, not shut in by walls and houses.'

'No, there is little of these,' said the curate; 'and it is very healthy, I have always understood: the common is what my girls love. But I don't see them coming.' He arched his hand over his eyes as a defence against the light, as he looked along the road for his daughters. Mr St. John had quite recovered himself. I don't think that even the name of Wilkins would have discouraged him now. In the warm and balmy air he took off his hat, holding up his venerable bare head to the sky. It was a head which might have served for that of an old saint. His white hair was still thick and abundant, his eyes full of soft light, his expression tranquil as the evening. 'I have come here in many troubles,' he said, 'and I have always been refreshed. I don't pretend to know much about art, Mr Mildmay, but nature is always soothing. Greenness cools the eyes whether it is study or tears that have fevered them. But I wonder what has become of the girls.'

Mildmay was charmed by the meditative turn his companion's remarks had taken, but the question about the girls embarrassed him.

'I am afraid,' he said, 'that my intrusion has perhaps given Miss St. John some trouble.'

'No; there is the servant, you know, a very good sort of girl, and Cicely is like her dear mother – never taken by surprise. If you are here as long as I have been you will know how pleasant it is to see a new face. We country folks rust; we fall into a fixed routine. I myself, see, was about to take this little byway unconsciously, a path I often take, forgetting there was any one with me — '

The curate looked wistfully along the thread of path; it had been worn by his own feet, and he seldom concluded his evening walk otherwise. Mildmay followed the narrow line with his eyes.

'It leads to the churchyard,' he said. 'I like a country churchyard. May we go there before we go in? What a pity the church is so new! and this part of Berkshire is rich in old churches, I understand?'

'It is in good repair, and much more wholesome than the old ones,' said Mr St. John. 'They may be more picturesque. Here you can see into the rectory garden, the ground slopes so much; the church is very much higher than the common. It used to be sweet to me, looking back at the lights in the girls' rooms, when I stood — there they are on the lawn now, Mr Mildmay. They have not gone out, after all.'

Mildmay looking down from the churchyard path, felt that it was dishonourable to spy upon the two girls unaware of his scrutiny, whom he could just see within the wall of the rectory garden; but he could not help feeling that this was more and more like a drama which was being played before him. He followed Mr St. John along the narrow path to the little white stile which admitted to the churchyard. The curate ceased his tranquil talk as they entered that inclosure. He turned mechanically as it seemed, to the left hand, and went round to a white cross upon a grave turned towards the common. It was of common stone, grey with years. The curate took off his hat again, and stood by it quite simply and calmly.

'It used to be sweet to me, standing here, to see the lights in the girls' rooms,' he said once more. The soft tranquillity of his tone suited the still twilight, the pensive silent plain. It was too still for sorrow, nor was there any touch of unhappiness in the gentle voice. Young Mildmay uncovered too, and stood wondering, reverent, with a swell of sympathy in his heart. Some men would have felt with anguish the unspeakable separation between the mother under the dews and the twinkle of the lights in her children's windows; but Mr St. John was not of that mind. Yet, somehow, to have this stranger here made his loss seem fresher to him. 'Cicely is very like her mother,' he said, and touched the cross softly with his hand as if caressing it, and turned away. Mr Mildmay could see that there were two paths up the mound to the white gate, and the meaning of them struck him vividly – one was that by which they had just come from the common, the other led down straight to the rectory. His heart was more touched than I can say, by the gentle fidelity, consoled and calm, yet always tender, which had worn that double line through the grass.

Mr St. John, however, made a hesitating pause at a corner before he took this second way home. 'My other poor wife, poor Mrs St. John, lies there; but that I can show you to-morrow,' he said, in his gentle unchanged voice, and quietly went on to the gate, leading the way. 'Supper will be ready,' the curate continued, when they emerged again upon the turf. We live a very simple primitive life here; our meals are not arranged quite as yours are, but it comes to the same thing. In short, whatever seeming differences there are, all ways of living come to much the same thing.'

Did they so? Mr St. John's meaning was of the simplest. He meant that whether you called your latest meal dinner or supper did not matter much; but his companion gave it a broader sense. With a jar of laughter in his mind that broke up the reverential respect of the previous moment, he followed his simple host into the house, which by-and-by was to be his own house. Poor Mrs St. John, who was not the mother of the girls; whose grave could be shown to-morrow; for whose sake these paths had not been worn across the grass; the stranger gave her her little meed of human notice in that smothered laugh! Poor Miss Brown!

The supper was homely enough – cold meat and salad, and bread and cheese and jam – and would have been cheerful and pleasant, Mr Mildmay thought, but for the absorbed looks of that elder daughter, who was still somewhat unfriendly to him. He went upstairs to his room, where a large mahogany four-post bed, with heavy moreen hangings, awaited him, before the night was very far advanced. When he had been there for a short time, he saw that his door was not shut, and went to close it. As he did so, he caught a glimpse of Cicely going downstairs. She had retired some time before he did, so that her reappearance struck him all the more; and she was quite unconscious that he saw her. She carried a candle in one hand, and a pile of tradesmen's books in the other. She was pale, her look fixed, her nostrils a little dilated, like someone going to a painful task he thought. As she moved down the dark staircase, a speck of light, with her candle shining on the whiteness of her face and dress, the walls, by which she flitted, looked more and more like the scenery of a drama to the young man. If they only would have opened, as in the *real* theatre, and shown him where she was going, what she was about to do! But this was very mean curiosity on Mr Mildmay's part. He shut his door humbly, that she might not be disturbed by the sound, and after a while went meekly to bed, trying to say to himself that he had no right to pry into the business of these good people, who had been so kind to him; though, indeed, she had not been kind to him, he

reflected, by way of lessening his own sense of guilt. He heard
subdued voices below for some time after, and wished more
than ever that the scenery would open, and reveal this scene to
him; but the substantial walls stood fast, and the moreen
curtains hung grimly about him, shutting out everything.
There was no compromise about the furniture at the rectory;
the pillared bedposts stood square, and stern, and strong, till
poor Mildmay, dozing within them in the warm August
night, thought them Samson's pillars in the house of Dagon,
or the pillars of the earth.

Cicely went down to her father very resolute with her
books. She had intended to day very little to him, but he had
exasperated her, and she felt that she could not let him off. But
her courage sank a little when she got into the study, and saw
his white head in the light of the solitary candle. There were
two candles on the table, but faithful to an old frugal habit, Mr
St. John had put out one of them when his guest left him. The
room was good-sized, and full of huge mahogany bookcases;
and as the table was at one end of it, there is no telling how full
of gloom it was. One of the windows was open, and a great
solid piece of darkness seemed to have taken its place, and to be
pouring in. Mr St. John was looking over some old sermons,
bending his head over the papers, with spectacles upon his
nose, which he took off when Cicely came in. He did not
usually sit up for so long, and he was rather aggrieved at the
late interview she had asked for. He did not like to be disturbed
out of his usual way, and he felt that she was going to speak to
him about Wilkins, the most painful subject which could be
suggested. Cicely, too, when he raised his head, and took off
his spectacles, found the interview a great deal more difficult
than in her excited feelings she had supposed.

'Well, my dear.' he said gently; 'you wanted to speak to me.'
He gave a little shiver when he saw the books in her hand.

'Yes. papa,' she said, laying them down on the table; and
then there was a pause. The soft night air came in, and crept
wistfully about the room, moving the curtains. When it
approaches midnight, even in August, there is always
something chill and mournful in the night wind.

'I wanted to speak to you,' said Cicely, catching her breath a
little; 'it was about the books. I don't know if you have looked

at them lately. Oh, papa! do you know that we are – in debt? I don't know how to say it – a great deal in debt!'

'Not a great deal, my dear.' he said faintly; 'something, I know. Wilkins spoke to me to-day – almost before Mr Mildmay.'

'It is not Wilkins alone,' said Cicely solemnly; 'it is everybody. The butcher, too; and, oh! so many little people. How are they ever to be paid? When I looked over the books to-day, not knowing – Oh! do you know how it has happened? Can they be cheating? It is my only hope.'

'My dear,' said the curate, faltering, 'better that one should have done wrong than that a great many should have done wrong. Poor Mrs St. John – nay, I should say both of us, Cicely; for I was also to, blame. We were not like your mother, my dear; it all came natural to your mother; but she, or rather we — ' Mr St. John's voice sank into an indistinct confusion. He was too good to blame the poor woman who was dead, and he did not know how to meet the eyes thus shining upon him, youthful, inexorable, of Hester's child. But even Cicely was moved by her father's wistful looks and the humility of his tone.

'If only one could see any way of paying them,' she said; 'if even we had been staying here! I had a plan and we might have done it. And it brings it all so near, and makes it so certain to see this man.'

'My love,' said the curate remonstrating, 'we knew that some one must come. It is not his fault. Why should we be unkind to him'

'Unkind! Oh papa!' cried Cicely in her exasperation, 'what had we to do with him? It was not our business to feast him and pet him. But that is nothing,' she said, trembling with excitement; 'I will not blame you, papa, for that or anything, if only you will say now what you are going to do, or where you think we can go, or what I must say to these poor people. We cannot stay here and starve, or till they put us in prison – only tell me what we must do.'

'How can I tell you, Cicely,' said the curate, 'when I do not know myself? I must advertise or something,' he said helplessly. 'I am old, my dear. Few people want a curate of my age; I suppose it almost looks like a stigma on a man to be a curate at my age.'

'Papa!' Cicely stopped short in what she was going to say, and looked at him with strained and anxious eyes. She had meant to assail him for still being a curate, but his self-condemnation closed the girl's lips, or rather roused her in defence.

'Yes.' said Mr St. John, 'you may say I ought to have thought of that sooner; but when things go on for a long time one asks one's self why should not they go on for ever? "He said, There will be peace in my time." That was selfish of Hezekiah, my dear, very selfish, when you come to think of it. But I dare say it never seemed so to him, and neither did it to me.'

Cicely was utterly overpowered by this; her anger and impatience died out of her, and compunction and remorse rose in her heart. 'That is not the right way to look at it,' she said. 'It is a shame that a man like you should only be a curate – oh, a shame to the Church and every one! Mr Chester, who never was here, never did anything, what right had he to be the rector? – and this other person — ' It was so necessary for poor Cicely in the disturbance of her mind to be angry with some one that naturally her wrath grew wild and bitter when she was free to pour it out upon strangers.

'Hush! hush! my dear,' said the curate, with a half smile at her vehemence; for indeed he was deeply relieved to have the tide of indignation turned away from himself.

'Why should I hush, papa? It is your own college, you say; but they never take the trouble to ask who is at Brentburn, who has been taking the duty, who has looked after the people when the rector has been so long away. When people have the patronage of a parish in their hands, ought they not to know about it? And how did they dare, how did they venture, to give it to anybody but you?'

'You don't understand,' said Mr St. John. 'The livings are given to the Fellows, Cicely, to people who have distinguished themselves. The dons have no right to alienate a living, as it were, to put it away from those who have a right to it, and give it to one like me.'

'What have they distinguished themselves in, papa? In Latin and Greek – which will do a great deal in the parish, don't you

think? whereas you have distinguished yourself in Brentburn
— '

'I have not done very much , my dear,' said the curate,
shaking his head.

'You have done all that has been done, papa; what are those
college people worth? This fine gentleman!' cried Cicely, with
scorn. (I wonder poor Mildmay did not feel himself shrink
even within his four pillars and moreen curtains.) 'He knows
about art if you please, and shudders at the sight of Mr
Chester's mahogany. Poor old things,' the girl cried, turning
round to look at the old bookcases with her eyes streaming, 'I
only know how fond I am of them now!'

'I cannot tell how thankful her father was that the conversation had taken this turn. *He* too felt tenderly towards the old
unlovely walls which had sheltered him so long, and in the
circumstances he felt it no harm to speak a little more strongly
than he felt. He looked round upon the ghostly room so dark
in all its corners. 'A great many things have happened to us
here,' he said, 'this was the first room we sat in, your mother
and I. What changes it has seen! I don't know how to make up
my mind to leave it.'

This brought back the girl to the original question. 'But
now,' she said, drying her eyes, 'there is no choice – we must
leave it. I suppose that is what this Mr Mildmay has really
come about? He will give you some little time, I suppose. But
papa, papa!' said Cicely, with a stamp of her foot to emphasize
her words, 'don't you see you *must* decide something – make
up your mind to something? Hoping on till the last day will do
no good to any one. And to think we should be so deep in
debt! Oh, papa, what are we to do?'

'My dear, do not be hard upon me,' said poor St. John; 'I
acknowledge, indeed, that it was my fault.'

'It was not your fault – but I don't blame anybody. There
was illness and weakness, and some people can and some
people can't,' said Cicely, with that mercy and toleration
which are always, I fear, more or less, the offspring of
contempt. 'Let us not go back upon that – but, oh, tell me,
what is to be done now?'

Mr St. John shook his venerable head piteously. 'What do
you think, Cicely?' he said.

This was all she could get from him; and, oh, how glad he was when he was permitted to go to bed, and be done with it! He could not tell what to do – anything he had ever done had been done for him (if it is not a bull to say so), and he had no more idea what independent step to take in this emergency, than one of the little boys had, to whose room he paid a half-surreptitious visit on his way to his own. Poor little souls! they were surreptitious altogether; even their father felt they had no right to be there in his daughters' way. He went in, shading his candle with his hand, not to disturb the slumbers of Annie, the little nursemaid, and approached the two little cots on tip-toe, and looked at the two little white faces on the pillows. 'Poor little things,' he said to himself. Miss Brown was well out of it; she had escaped all this trouble, and could not be called to account, either for the babies, or those debts, which thus rose up against her in judgement. A dim giddiness of despair had made Mr St. John's head swim while his daughter was questioning him; but now that the pressure was removed he was relieved. He sighed softly as he left the subject altogether, and said his prayers, and slept soundly enough. Neither the debts nor the babies weighed upon him – at least 'no more than reason;' he was quite able to sleep and to forget.

When Mr Mildmay came downstairs next morning, and looked in at the open door of the dining-room, he saw Cicely 'laying the cloth' there, putting down the white cups and saucers, and preparing the breakfast-table with her own hands. He was so much surprised at this, that he withdrew hastily, before she perceived him, with an uneasy sense that she might not like to be caught in such an occupation, and went to the garden, where, however, he could still see her through the open windows. He was not used to anything of the kind, and it surprised him much. But when he got outside he began to reflect, why should she be ashamed of it? There was nothing in the action which was not graceful or seemly. He saw her moving about, arranging one thing after another, and the sight made somehow a revolution in his mind. He had been in the habit of thinking it rather dreadful, that a man should expose his wife – a lady – to be debased into such ignoble offices, or that any gentlewoman should have such things to do. This was the first time he had ever seen domestic business of a homely kind done by a lady, and my *dilettante* was utterly annoyed at himself, when he found that, instead of being hurt and wounded by the sight, he liked it! Terrible confession! He went up and down the garden walks, pretending to himself that he was enjoying the fresh air of the morning, but actually peeping, spying, at the windows, watching Miss St. John arrange the breakfast. She had not seen him, but, quite unconscious of observation, absorbed in her own thoughts, she went on with her occupation. There were more things to do than to put the table to rights, for Betsy's work was manifold, and did not admit of very careful housemaid work. Mr Mildmay watched her for some time, coming and going; and then he became aware of another little scene which was going on still nearer to himself. Out from a side door came the two little boys, hand in hand, with their hats tied on, and overshadowing the little pallid faces like two mushrooms. They were followed out by their little nurse, who watched their decorous exit with approval. 'Now, take your walk, till I come and fetch you,' said this small guardian; upon which the two little urchins, tottering, but solemn, began a serious promenade, so far along the gravel walk, so far back again, turning at each end as on an imaginary quarterdeck. The little boys tottered now and then, but recovered themselves, and went on steadily up and down, backward and forward, without a break. Mildmay was fond of children (so long as they did not bore him), and he was more amused than he could say. He made a few steps across the lawn to meet them, and held out his hands. 'Come along here,' he said; 'come on the grass.' The solemn babies paused and looked at him, but were not to be beguiled from their steady promenade. Their portentous gravity amazed him – even the children were mysterious in this romantic rectory. He went up to meet them on their next turn.

'Come, little ones,' he said, 'let us be friends. What are your names?'

They stood and looked at him with their big blue eyes, holding fast by each other. They were unprepared for this emergency, as their father was unprepared for the bigger emergency in which he found himself. At last one small piping voice responded 'Harry!' the other instinctively began to suck his thumb.

'Harry – and what else? – come, tell me,' said the new rector; 'you are not both Harry.' He stood looking at them, and they stood and looked at him; and the two babies, three years old, understood as much about that quintessence of Oxford, and education and culture, as he did of them; they gazed at him with their four blue eyes exactly in a row. 'Come, speak,' he said, laughing; 'you have lost your tongues.' This reproach roused Charlie, who took his thumb out of his mouth and put his whole hand in, to search for the tongue which was not lost.

The sound of Mildmay's voice roused Cicely. She came to the window, and looking out saw him there, standing in front of the children. Many schemes had been throbbing in her head all night. She had not slept tranquilly, like her father. She had been pondering plans till her brain felt like a honeycomb, each cell holding some active notion. She paused a moment, all the pulses in her beginning to throb, and looked out upon the opportunity before her. Then, after a moment's hesitation, she put down the little brush she held in her hand, threw up the window a little higher and stepped out – to try one other throw, though the game seemed played out, with Fortune and Fate!

CHAPTER ELEVEN

CICELY'S APPEAL

Cicely St. John was not in the least beautiful. The chief charm
she had, except her youthful freshness, was the air of life,
activity, and animation which breathed about her. Dulness,
idleness, weariness, langour were almost impossible to the girl
– impossible, at least, except for the moment. To be doing
something was a necessity of her nature, and she did that
something so heartily, that there was nothing irritating in her
activity. Life (but for bills and debts, and the inaction of
others) was a pleasure to her. Her perpetual motion was so
easy and pleasant and harmonious, that it jarred upon nobody.
When she came out, suddenly stepping from the dining-room
window, all the sweetness of the morning seemed to concent-
rate in this one figure, so bright, so living, so full of simple
power; and this, after the sombre agitation and distress in
which she had been enveloped on the previous night, was the
most extraordinary revelation to the stranger, who did not
know Cicely. He could scarcely believe it was the same, any
more than a man could believe a sunshiny, brilliant summer
morning to be the same as the pallid, rainy troubled dawn
which preceded the sun-rising. Cicely had been entirely cast
down in the evening; every way of escape seemed to have
closed upon her; she was in despair. But the night had brought
counsel, as it so often does; and to-day she had risen full of
plans and resolutions and hopes, and was herself again, as
much as if there were no debts in her way, as if her father's
position was as sure and stable as they had all foolishly
thought it. The moment she came into this little group in the
garden its character changed. Two poor little startled babies
gazing at a man who understood nothing about them, and
gazed back at them with a wonder as great as their own,
without any possible point on which they could come into

contact: this is what the curious encounter had been. Mild-may, as thinking himself much the most advanced being, smiled at the children, and experienced a certain amusement in their bewildered, helpless looks; yet he was not a bit wiser in knowledge of them, in power to help them, in understanding of their incomplete natures, than they were in respect to him. But when Cicely stepped out, the group grew human. Whatever was going to be done, whatever was necessary to be done, or said, she was the one capable of doing or saying. Her light, firm step rang on the gravel with a meaning in it; she comprehended both the previously helpless sides of the ques-tion, and made them into a whole. Her very appearance had brightness and relief in it. The children (as was natural and proper) were swathed in black woollen frocks, trimmed with crape, and looked under their black hats like two little black mushrooms, with their heads tilted back. Cicely, too, poss-essed decorous mourning for poor Mrs St. John; but at home, in the morning, Mab and she considered it sufficient in the circumstances to wear black and white prints, in which white predominated, with black ribbons; so that her very appearance agreed with the sunshine. May would have suited her perhaps better than August, but still she was like the morning, ready for whatever day might bring. Mildmay saluted her with a curious sensation of surprise and pleasure; for this was the one, he perceived at once, who had looked at him with so much hostility – and the change in her was very agreeable. Even the children were moved a little. Charley's mouth widened over his thumb with a feeble smile, and Harry took his gaze from Mildmay to fix it upon her, and murmured 'Zat's Cicely,' getting over her name with a run, and feeling that he had achieved a triumph. Little Annie, the nursemaid, however, who was jealous of the sisters, appeared at this moment, and led her charges away.

'Funny little souls!' Mildmay said, looking after them; then fearing he might have offended his hostess, and run the risk of driving her back into her former hostility, he said something hastily about the garden, which, of course, was the safest thing to do.

'Yes, it is a nice garden,' said Cicely; at least, you will be able to make it very nice. We have never taken enough trouble with it, or spent enough money upon it, which means the same thing. You are very fond of the country, Mr Mildmay?'

'Am I?' he said. 'I really did not know.'

'Of country amusements, then – riding, and that sort of thing? We are quite near the race-ground, and this, I believe, is a very good hunting country.'

'But these are not clerical amusements, are they?' he said, laughing; 'not the things one would choose a parish for?'

'No; certainly papa takes no interest in them: but then he is old; he does not care for amusement at all.'

'And why should you think amusement is my great object? Do I look so utterly frivolous?' said Mildmay, piqued.

'Nay,' said Cicely, 'I don't know you well enough to tell how you look. I only thought perhaps you had some reason for choosing Brentburn out of all the world; perhaps love of the country, as I said; or love for – something. It could not be croquet – which is the chief thing in summer – for that you could have anywhere,' she added, with a nervous little laugh.

'I hope, Miss St. John, there are other motives — '

'Oh yes, many others. You might be going to be married, which people say is a very common reason; but indeed you must not think I am prying. It was only – curiosity. If you had not some object,' said Cicely, looking at him with a wistful glance, 'you would never leave Oxford, where there is society and books and everything any one can desire, to come here.'

'You think that is everything any one could desire?' he said smiling, with a flattered sense of his superiority – having found all these desirable things too little to content him – over this inexperienced creature. 'But, Miss St. John, you forget the only motive worth discussing. There is a great deal that is very pleasant in Oxford – society, as you say, and books, and art, and much besides; but I am of no use to any one there. All the other people are just as well educated, as well off, as good, or better than I am. I live only to enjoy myself. Now, one wants more than that. Work, something to exercise one's highest faculties. I want to do something for my fellow-creatures; to be of a little use. There must be much to do, much to improve, much to amend in a parish like this — '

A rapid rush of colour came to Cicely's face. 'To improve and amend!' she said quickly. 'Ah! you speak at your ease, Mr

Mildmay – in a parish where papa has been working for twenty years!'

Mildmay gave her a startled, wondering look. To be thus interrupted while you are riding, full tilt, your favourite hobby, is very confusing. He scarcely took in the meaning of the words 'working for twenty years.'

'Twenty years – all my lifetime and more; and you think you can mend it all at once like an old shoe!' cried Cicely, her cheeks flaming. Then she said, subduing herself, 'I beg your pardon. What you say is quite right, I know.'

But by this time her words began to take their proper meaning to his mind. 'Has Mr St. John been here so long?' he said. 'I hope you don't think I undervalue his work. I am sure it must have been better than anything I with my inexperience can do; but yet — '

'Ah! you will learn; you are young; and we always think we can do better than the old people. I do myself often,' said Cicely,, under her breath.

'I did not mean anything so presumptuous,' he said; 'indeed, I did not know. I thought of myself, as one does so often without being aware – I hope you will not form a bad opinion of me, Miss St. John. I accepted the living for the sake of the work, not for any smaller motive. Books and society are not life. It seemed to me that to instruct one's fellow-creatures so far as one can, to help them as far as one can, to bring a higher ideal into their existence — '

Cicely was bewildered by this manner of speech. She did not quite understand it. No one had ever spoken to her of a high ideal; a great deal had been said to her one time and another about doing her duty, but nothing of this. She was dazzled, and yet half contemptuous, as ignorance so often is. 'A high ideal for the poor folk in the village, and Wilkins the grocer, and old Mrs Joel with her pigs?' she cried mocking; yet while she said it she blushed for herself.

Mildmay blushed too. He was young enough to be sensitive to ridicule, and to know that high ideals should not be rashly spoken of except to sympathetic souls. 'Why not,' he said, 'for them as well as for others?' then stopped between disappointment and offence.

'Ah!' said Cicely, 'you don't know the village people. If you

spoke to them of high ideals, they would only open their
mouths and stare. If it was something to make a little money
by, poor souls! or to get new boots for their children, or even
to fatten the pigs. Now you are disgusted, Mr, Mildmay; but
you don't know how poor the people are, and how little time
they have for anything but just what is indispensable for
living.' As she said this, Cicely's eyes grew wistful, and filled
with moisture. The young man thought it was an angelical
pity for the poverty and sufferings of others; but I fear the girl
was at that moment thinking of what lay before herself.

'Miss St. John,' he said, 'when you feel for them so deeply,
you must sympathize with me too. The harder life is, has it
not the more need of some clear perception of all the higher
meanings in it? If it is worth while to be a clergyman at all, this
is the use, it seems to me, to which we should put ourselves;
and for that reason — '

'You are coming to Brentburn!' cried Cicely. The tears
disappeared from her eyes, dried by the flush of girlish
impatience and indignation that followed. 'As if they were all
heathens; as if no one else had ever taught them – and spent his
time and strength for them! Out of your Latin and Greek, and
your philosophy, and your art, and all those fine things, you
are coming to set a high ideal before poor Sally Gillows,
whose husband beats her, and the Hodges, with their hundreds of children, and the hard farmers and the hard
shopkeepers that grind the others to the ground. Well!' she
said, coming rapidly down from this indignant height to a half
disdainful calm, 'I hope you will find it answer, Mr Mildmay.
Perhaps it will do better than papa's system. He has only told
them to try and do their best, poor souls! to put up with their
troubles as well as they could, and to hope that some time or
other God would send them something better either in this
world or another. I don't think papa's way has been very
successful. after all,' said Cicely, with a faint laugh; 'perhaps
yours may be the best.'

'I think you do me injustice,' said Mildmay, feeling the
attack so unprovoked that he could afford to be magnanimous. 'I have never thought of setting up my way in opposition
to Mr St. John's way. Pray do not think so. Indeed, I did not
know, and could not think — '

'Of papa at all!' cried Cicely, interrupting him as usual. 'Why should you? No, no, it was not you who ought to have thought of him. You never heard his name before, I suppose. No one could expect it of you.'

'And if I have entered into this question,' he continued, 'it was to show you that I had not at least mere petty personal motives.'

'Oh, I beg your pardon, Mr Mildmay, I had no right to inquire into your motives at all.'

Mildmay was not vain; but he was a young man, and this was a young woman by his side, and it was she who had begun a conversation much too personal for so slight an acquaintance. When he thought of it, it was scarcely possible to avoid a touch of amiable complacency in the evident interest he had excited. 'Nay,' he said, with that smile of gratified vanity which is always irritating to a woman, 'your interest in them can be nothing but flattering to me – though perhaps I may have a difficulty in understanding — '

'Why, I am so much interested! Mr Mildmay!' cried Cicely, with her eyes flashing, 'don't you think if anyone came to you to take your place, to turn you out of your home, to banish you from everything you have ever known or cared for, and send you desolate into the world – don't you think you would be interested too? Don't you think you would wonder over him, and try to find out what he meant, and why this thing was going to be done, and why — oh, what am I saying?' cried Cicely, stopping short suddenly, and casting a terrified look at him. 'I must be going out of my senses. It is not that, it is not that I mean!'

Poor Mildmay looked at her aghast. The flash of her eyes, the energy of her words, the sudden change to paleness and horror when she saw how far she had gone, made every syllable she uttered so real, that to pass it over as a mere ebullition of girlish temper or feeling was impossible; and there was something in this sudden torrent of reproach – which, bitter as it was, implied nothing like personal, intentional wrong on his part – which softened as well as appalled him. The very denunciation was an appeal. He stood thunderstruck, looking at her, but not with any resentment in his eyes. 'Miss St. John,' he said, almost tremulously, 'I don't understand. This is all strange – all new to me.'

'Forget it,' she said hastily. 'Forgive me, Mr Mildmay, when I ask your pardon! I did not think what I was saying. Oh, don't think of it any more!'

'There is nothing to forgive,' he said; 'but you will tell me more? Indeed, I am not angry – how could I be angry? – but most anxious to know.'

'Cicely,' said the curate's gentle voice from the window, 'it is time for prayers, and we are all waiting for you. Come in, my dear.' Mr St. John stood looking out with a large prayer-book in his hand. His tall figure, with a slight wavering of constitutional feebleness and age in it, filled up one side of the window, and at his feet stood the two babies, side by side as usual, their hats taken off, and little white pinafores put on over their black frocks, looking out with round blue eyes. There was no agitation about that placid group. The little boys were almost too passive to wonder, and it had not occurred to Mr St. John as possible that anything calculated to ruffle the countenance or the mind could have been talked of between his daughter and his guest. He went in when he had called them, and took his seat at his usual table. Betsy and Annie stood by the great sideboard waiting for the family devotions, which Betsy, at least, having much to do, was somewhat impatient of; and Mab was making the tea, in order that it might be 'drawn' by the time that prayers were over. The aspect of everything was so absolutely peaceful, that when Mr Mildmay stepped into the room he could not but look at Cicely with a question in his eyes. She, her face flushed and her mouth quivering, avoided his eye, and stole away to her place at the breakfast-table behind. Mildmay, I am afraid, got little benefit by Mr St. John's prayer. He could not even hear it for thinking. Was this true? and if it was true, what must he do? A perfect tempest raged in the new rector's bosom, while the old curate read so calmly, unmoved by anything but the mild every-day devotion which was habitual to him. Secular things did not interfere with sacred in the old man's gentle soul, though they might well have done so, Heaven knows, had human necessities anything to do with human character. And when they rose from their knees, and

took their places round the breakfast-table, Mildmay's sensations became more uncomfortable still. The girl who had
denounced him as about to drive her from her home, made tea
for him, and asked him if he took cream and sugar. The old
man whom he was about to supplant placed a chair for him,
and bade him take his place with genial kindness. Mr Mildmay
had been in the habit for the greater part of his life of thinking
rather well of himself; and it is inconceivable how unpleasant
it is when a man accustomed to this view of the subject, feels
himself suddenly as small and pitiful as he did now. Mr St.
John had some letters, which he read slowly as he ate his egg,
and Mabel also had one, which occupied her. Only Cicely and
the stranger, the two who were not at ease with each other,
were free to talk, and I don't know what either of them could
have found to say.

The curate looked up from his letter with a faint sigh, and
pushed away the second egg which he had taken upon his plate
unconsciously. 'Cicely,' he said, 'this is a startling letter,
though perhaps I might have been prepared for something of
the kind, Mr Chester's relations, my dear, write to say that
they wish to sell off the furniture.' Mr St. John gave a glance
round, and for a moment his heart failed him. 'It is sudden;
but it is best, I suppose, that we should be prepared.'

'It was to be expected,' said Cicely, with a little gasp. She
grew paler, but exerted all her power to keep all signs of
emotion out of her face.

'Sell the furniture?' said Mab, with a laugh. 'Poor old
things! But who will they find to buy them?' Mab did not
think at all of the inevitable departure which must take place
before Mr Chester's mahogany could be carried away.

'You will think it very weak,' said poor Mr St. John, 'but I
have been here so long that even the dispersion of the furniture
will be something in the shape of a trial. It has seen so much.
Of course, such a grievance is merely sentimental – but it
affects one more than many greater things.'

'I did not know that you had been here so long,' said
Mildmay.

'A long time – twenty years. That is a great slice out of one's
life,' said Mr St. John. (He here thought better of a too hasty
determination, and took back his egg.) 'Almost all that has

happened to me has happened here. Here I brought your mother home, my dears. Cicely is very like what her mother was; and here you were born, and here — '

'Oh, papa, don't go on like that odious Jessica and her lover, "On such a night!" said Cicely, with a forced laugh.

'I did not mean to go on, my dear,' said the curate, half aggrieved, half submissive; and he finished his egg with a sigh.

'But I wonder very much,' said Mildmay, 'if you will pardon me for saying so, why, you did not take some steps to secure the living. You must like the place, or you would not have stayed; and nobody would have been appointed over your head; it is impossible, if the circumstances had been known.'

'My dear sir,' said the curate, with his kind smile, 'you don't think I mean to imply any grudge against you? That would shut my mouth effectually. No, there are a great many reasons why I could not do anything. First, I did not know till a few days ago that the rector was dead; he should have sent me word. Then I have grown out of acquaintance with all my friends. I have not budged out of Brentburn, except now and then to town for a day, these twenty years; and, besides all this,' he said, raising his head with simple grandeur, 'I have never asked anything from anybody, and I hope I shall end my life so. A beggar for place or living I could never be.'

Cicely, with her eyes fixed upon him with the most curious mixture of pride, wonder, humiliation, satisfaction, and shame, raised her head too, sharing this little lyrical outburst of the humble old man's self-consequence.

But Mab burst lightly in from the midst of her letter. 'Don't boast of that, papa, please,' she said. 'I wish you had asked something and got it. I am sure it would have been much better for Cicely and me.'

'My dear!' said Mr St. John, with a half smile, shaking his head. It was all the reply he made to this light interruption. Then he resumed the former subject. 'Take the letter, Cicely, and read it, and tell me what you think. It is grievous to think of a sale here, disturbing old associations. We must consult afterwards what is best to do.'

'Papa,' said Cicely, in a low voice full of agitation, 'the best thing of all would be to settle now, while Mr Mildmay is here;

to find out when he wishes to come; and then there need be no more to put up with than is absolutely necessary. It is better to know exactly when we must go.'

The curate turned his mild eyes to the young man's face. There was a look of pain and reluctance in them, but of submission; and then he smiled to save the stranger's feelings. 'It is hard upon Mr Mildmay,' he said, 'to be asked this, as if we were putting a pistol to his head; but you will understand that we wish you every good, though we may be grieved to leave our old home.'

Mildmay had been making a pretence of eating, feeling as if every morsel choked him. Now he looked up flushed and nervous. 'I am afraid I have said more than I meant,' he said. 'I don't think I have made up my mind beyond the possibility of change. It is not settled. as you think.'

'Dear me,' said Mr St. John, concerned, 'I am very sorry; I hope it is not anything you have heard here that has turned you against Brentburn? It is not a model parish, but it is no worse than other places. Cicely has been telling you about my troubles with those cottages; but, indeed, there is no parish in England where you will not have troubles of some kind – unwholesome cottages or other things.'

'I said nothing about the cottages,' said Cicely, with downcast looks. 'I hope Mr Mildmay does not mind anything I said. I say many things without thinking. It is very foolish, but it would be more foolish to pay any attention. I am sure you have often said so, papa.'

'I?' said the curate, looking at her disturbed countenance with some surprise. 'No, I do not think you are one of the foolish talkers, my dear. It is a long story about these cottages; and perhaps, I let myself be more worried than I ought. I will tell you all about it on the way to the Heath, for I think you ought to call on the Ascotts, if you will permit me to advise. They are the chief people about here. If you are ready, perhaps we should start soon; and you will come back and have some of our early dinner before you go?'

'I am ashamed to give so much trouble, to – receive so much kindness,' said Mildmay, confused. He rose when Mr St. John did, but he kept his eyes fixed upon Cicely, who kept her seat, and would not look at him. The curate had various things to do before he was ready to start. He had his scattered memoranda to collect, and to get his note-book from his study, and yesterday's newspaper to carry to an old man in the village, and a book for a sick child, and I don't know how many trifles besides. 'Papa's things are always all over the house,' Mab cried, running from one room to another in search of them. Cicely generally knew exactly where to find all these properties which Mr St. John searched for habitually with unfounded yet unalterable confidence in the large pockets of his long clerical coat. But Cicely still kept her seat, and left her duties to her sister, her mind being full of other things.

'What is the matter with Cicely?' said Mab, running back with her hands full. 'I have found them, but I don't know which of your pockets they belong to. This is the one for the note-book, and this is the one for the newspaper; but what does Cicely mean, sitting there like a log, and leaving everything to me?'

'Miss St. John,' said Mildmay, in this interval, 'may I come back as your father says? May we finish the conversation we began this morning? or is the very sight of me disagreeable to you? There are so many things I want to know.'

Cicely got up suddenly, half impatient, half sad. 'We are always glad to see any one whom papa asks,' she said; 'you must call it luncheon, Mr Mildmay, but to us it is dinner; that makes the difference between rector and curate,' she added, with a laugh.

CHAPTER TWELVE

THE PARSON'S ROUND

How brilliant was that August morning when the two men went out! the sky so blue and warm and full of sunshine, bending with friendly tenderness toward the luxuriant earth which it embraced, lost everywhere in soft distances, limits that were of the eye and not of the infinite melting space – showing through the foliage, opening out sweet and full over the breezy purpled common. The red cottage roofs, with all their lichens, shone and basked in the light; the apples reddened moment by moment, the yellow corn rustled and waved in every breath of air, conscious of the coming sickle. Everything was at its fullest blaze of colour; the trees more deeply green than usual, the sky of more profound and dazzling blue, the heather purple-royal, showing in its moorland flush against the russet-golden fields burning in the sun which gave them their last perfection of ripeness; and even the flowers in the gardens blazing their brightest to hide the fact from all men that the sweetness and hope of the year were almost lost in that harvest and climax which touches upon decay, as everything does which is perfect. The sun was too fierce for anything but red burning geraniums, and gaudy hollyhocks and rank dahlias. But the red old cottages at Brentburn were of themselves like growths of nature, with all their stains of moss, red and grey and yellow, relieved and thrown up by the waving greyness of the willows, that marked every spot of special dampness, and by the wealthy green woods that rolled away into the distance, into the sky. Everything is musical in such a morning; the very cackle of the ducks in that brown pond – how cool it looks to the dusty wayfarer! – takes a tone from the golden air; the slow roll of the leisurely cart along the country road; the voices from the cottages calling in full Berkshire drawl to Jyain and Jeo outside. A harmonious world it seemed, with nothing in it to jar or wound; the very air caressing every mother's son it met, blowing about the rags as if it loved them, conveying never a chill to the most poorly clad. How different was that broad outdoor satisfaction and fullness to the complainings and troubles enclosed by every set of four walls in the parish! Mildmay, as was natural, knew nothing about these or suspected them; his spirits rose when he came out into the summer air – to walk along the cool side of the road in the shade, and watch the triumphant sunshine blazing over everything, leaving not an inch even of the common high road unglorified, brought a swell of pleasure to his heart he could not tell why.

'You must not come to a country parish with the idea that it is Arcadia,' said Mr St. John; 'such ideas lead to a great deal of disappointment; but you must not let yourself be discouraged either. I don't think Cicely knows all the outs and ins of the story about the cottages.'

'Miss St. John said nothing about the cottages.'

'Ah! I thought she had put you out of spirits; that would be foolish,' said the curate kindly. 'You see, Mr Mildmay, everybody here thinks a great deal of a little money; it is so, I believe, in every small place; they have little, very little, Heaven knows; and somehow, when one is very poor, that gets to look of more importance than anything else. I don't say so from personal experience, though I have always been poor enough. My way, I am afraid, is to think too little of the money, not too much – which is, perhaps, as great a mistake the other way; but it is much easier, you know, to condemn those faults we have no mind to,' Mr St. John added with a smile. The visit of an intelligent stranger had quite brightened the good man up, though it ought to have depressed him, according to all principles of good sense. The curate forgot how much he himself must suffer from the change that was coming. Mildmay pleased him; he was deferential to his own grey hairs and long experience; he was willing to hear and apparently to take, his predecessor's opinion, and Mr St. John liked the novelty, the new companion, the attentive listener. He walked on quite briskly, with the easy steps of a man to whom the way is so familiar that he does not need to pause to look where he is going. Now and then he would stop to point out a view, a glimpse of the distant forest, a slope opening down upon the lower level of the common, or even a pretty cottage; and one of them, a most picturesque refuge of misery, with tiny little casement windows, bulging anyhow from the ruddy old wall, and a high roof of the most indescribable and beautiful mixture of tints, set him easily afloat again upon the subject of which his mind was full.

'Look at it!' he said; 'it is a picture. If one could only clear them out and shut them up – or rather throw them open, that the winds of heaven might enter, but not our fellow-creatures, Mr Mildmay! As I was saying, they are all poor here. The people think you do them an injury when you speak of anything that has to be paid for. Because I have tried to get the cottages put into good repair, the arrangements made a little more decent, and the places fit to live in, more than two or three of the people have left the parish church. Yes, that is quite true – I thought Cicely must have told you – well-to-do people, who might have spared a few pounds well enough. It was a trial; but what of that? I have outlived it, and perhaps done a little good.'

'The cottagers, at least must have been grateful to you,' said Mildmay; but the curate shook his head.

'The cottagers thought I was only trying to get them turned out,' he said. 'They almost mobbed me once. I told them they should not take lodgers and lodgers till every room was crowded. They are as bad as the landlords; but poor souls! it was easy to forgive them, for the shilling or two they gained was such an object to them. I thought it best to tell you; but there was really nothing in it, nothing to be annoyed about. It was soon over. You, a young man, need not be discouraged by any such episode as that.'

'Mr St. John, there is something which discourages me much more,' said Mildmay. 'When I came yesterday to see Brentburn, I did not know you at all. I had heard your name; that was all. I thought you were most likely a man of my own standing, or younger — '

'As a curate ought to be,' said Mr St. John, once more shaking his head. 'Yes; I was saying to Cicely, it is almost a stigma upon a man to be a curate at my age; but so it is, and I cannot help it. Perhaps if I had not settled down so completely when I was young, if I had been more energetic; I feel that now – but what good does it do? it is too late now to change my nature. The children are the worst,' he said, with a sigh, 'for they must come upon the girls.' Then recovering himself with a faint smile, 'I beg your pardon, Mr Mildmay, for going off with my own thoughts. You said it discouraged you. Do you mean my example? You must take it as a lesson and a warning, not as an example. I am very sensible it is my own fault.'

'I came to supplant you, to take your place, to turn you out of your home,' said Mildmay, finding it a kind of relief to his feelings to employ Cicely's words, 'and you received me like a friend, took me into your house, made me sit at your table —'

The curate was startled by his vehemence. He laughed, then looked at him half alarmed. 'What should I have done else?' he said. 'I hope you are a friend. Supplant me! I have been here a great deal longer than I had any right to expect. Of course, we all knew a new rector would come. The girls, indeed, had vague notions about something that might be done – they did not know what, poor things! how should they? But of course from the first I was aware what must happen. No, no; you must not let *that* trouble you. I am glad, on the contrary, very glad, that the people are going to fall into hands like yours.'

'Poor hands,' said Mildmay. 'Mr St. John, you may think it strange that I should say this; but it is you who ought to be the rector, not me. You ought to stay here; I feel it. If I come after all, I shall be doing a wrong to the people and to you, and even to the Church, where such things should not be.'

Once more Mr St. John slowly shook his head; a smile came over his face; he held out his hand. 'It is pleasant to hear you say it; somehow it is pleasant to hear you say it. I felt sure Cicely had been saying something to you this morning. But no, no; they would never have given me the living, and I should never have asked for it. As for a wrong, nobody will feel it a wrong; not myself, nor the Church, and the people here last of all.'

'They must look upon you as their father,' said Mildmay warmly. 'Nothing else is possible. To them it is the greatest wrong of all.'

'You speak like a – boy,' said the curate. 'Yes, you speak like a kind, warm-hearted boy. The girls say the same kind of things. You are all young, and think of what ought to be, not of what is. The people! The Church does not give them any voice in the matter, and it is just as well. Mr Mildmay, I've been a long time among them. I've tried to do what I could for them. Some of them like me well enough; but the people have never forgotten that I was only curate – not rector. They have remembered it all these twenty years, when sometimes I was half tempted to forget it myself.'

'Oh, sir, do not think so badly of human nature!' said Mildmay, almost with a recoil from so hard a judgement.

'Do I think badly of human nature? I don't feel that I do; and why should this be thinking badly? Which is best for them to have, a man who is well off, who is a real authority in the parish, whom the farmers and masters will stand in awe of, and who will be able to help them in trouble – or a poor man who has to struggle for himself, who has nothing to spare, and no great influence with any one? I shall feel it, perhaps, a little,' said Mr St. John, with a smile; 'but it will be quite unreasonable to feel it. In a month you will be twice as popular in the parish as I am after twenty years.'

'It is not possible!' said the young man.

'Ah, my dear Mr Mildmay, a great many things are possible! The girls think like you. I suppose it is natural; but when you come to take everything into account – the only thing to have been desired was that I should have died before Mr Chester; or, let us say that he should have outlived me, which sounds more cheerful. Come,' said the curate with an effort, 'don't let us think of this. I hope you are a friend, Mr Mildmay, as I said; but, as you say yourself, you are only a friend of yesterday, so why you should take my burden on your shoulders I don't know. I think we may venture to call on the Ascotts now. He is a little rough, or rather bluff, but a good man; and she is a little – fanciful,' said the curate, searching for a pleasant word, 'but a kind woman. If you take to them, and they to you — '

'On what pretence should I go to see them, unsettled as I am about my future?' said Mildmay, hesitating.

The curate looked at him with a smile. He rang the bell, then opened the door, which, like most innocent country doors, opened from the outside. Then he fixed his mild eyes upon the young man. He had some gentle insight in his way by right of his years and experience of life, simple-minded as he was. 'You go as the new rector – the best of introductions,' he said, and led the way smiling. It was not difficult, perhaps, to see through the struggle in Mildmay's mind between his own wish and determination, and his sympathetic sense of the hardship involved to others. I think the curate was quite right in believing that it was the personal inclination which would gain the day, and not the generous impulse; as, indeed, Mr St. John fully recognized it ought to be.

Mr Ascott was in his library, reading the newspaper, but with such an array of papers about him, as made that indulgence look momentary and accidental. He was not the squire of the parish, but he had a considerable landed property in the neighbourhood, and liked to be considered as holding that position. He received Mr Mildmay, boldly introduced by the curate as the new rector, with the greatest cordiality. 'I had not seen the appointment,' he said, 'but I am most happy to welcome you to the parish. I hope you like what you have seen of it? This is quite an agreeable surprise.'

Mildmay found it very difficult to reply, for was not every word of congratulation addressed to him an injury to his companion, whose star must set as his rose? The curate, however, showed no such feeling. His *amour propre* was quite satisfied by being the first to know and to present to the parish its new rector. 'Yes, I thought you would be pleased to hear at once,' he said, with gentle complacency. 'I would not let him pass your door.'

'Poor Chester! This reminds me of him,' said Mr Ascott. 'He came to Brentburn in my father's time, when I was a young fellow at home fresh from the university. He was a very accomplished man. It was a pity he had such bad health. A parish gets out of order when it is without the proper authorities. Even a good deputy – and St. John, I am sure, has been the best of deputies – is never like the man himself.'

'That is just what I have been saying,' said Mr St. John; but though he took it with great equanimity, it was less pleasant to him to hear this, than to say it himself. 'I think I will leave you now,' he added. 'I have a great deal to do this morning. Mr

Ascott will tell you many things that will be really valuable,
and at two o'clock or sooner we will expect you at the
rectory.'

'It is a pity to trouble you and your girls, St. John. He can
have some luncheon here. Mrs Ascott will be delighted to see
him.'

'I shall be at the rectory without fail,' said Mildmay, with a
sense of partial offence. He belonged to the rectory, not to this
complacent secular person. A certain *esprit de corps* was within
him. If the rest of the world neglected the poor curate, he at
least would show that to him the old priest was the first person
in the parish. 'Or,' he added, hesitating, 'I will go with you
now.'

Mr St. John did not wish this. He felt that he would be less
at his ease with his poor people if conscious of this new man
fresh from Oxford at his elbow. There might be, for anything
he knew to the contrary, newfangled ways even of visiting the
sick. To talk to them cheerily, kindly, as he had always done,
might not fall in with the ideas of duty held by 'high' schools
of doctrine, of whatever kind. He went away plodding along
the high road in the sultry noon, with a smile still upon his
face, which faded, however, when the stimulus of Mildmay's
company, and the gratification of presenting the stranger to
the great people of the parish, had subsided. These
circumstances were less exhilarating when the curate was
alone, and had to remember Wilkins and all the outstanding
bills, and the fact that the furniture in the rectory was to be
sold, and that Cicely that very night would ask him once more
what he had made up his mind to do? What could he make up
his mind to do? The very question, when he put it to himself
merely, and when it was not backed up by an eager young
face, and a pair of eyes blazing into him, was bewildering
enough; it made the curate's head go round and round. Even
when he came to Brentburn twenty years ago it was not his
own doing. Friends had found the appointment for him, and
arranged all the preliminaries. Nothing had been left for him
but to accept it, and he had accepted. And at that time he had
Hester to fall back on. But now to 'look out for something,' to
apply for another curacy, to advertise and answer advertise-
ments, describing himself and his capabilities – how was he to

do it? He was quite ready to consent to anything, to let Cicely manage for him if she would; but to take the initiative himself! The very thought of this produced a nervous confusion in his mind which seemed to make an end of all his powers.

'You must come upstairs and see my wife,' said Mr Ascott. 'She will be delighted to make your acquaintance. She has been a great deal in society, and I don't doubt you and she will find many people to talk about. As for me, I am but a country fellow, I don't go much into the world. When your interests are all in the country, why, stick to the country is my maxim; but my wife is fond of fine people. You and she will find a hundred mutual acquaintances in half-an-hour, you will see.'

'But I am not fond of fine people – nor have I so many acquaintances.'

'Oh, you Oxford dons know everybody. They all pass through your hands. Come along, it will be quite a pleasure for my wife to see you. Adelaide, I am bringing you some one who will be a surprise to you as well as a pleasure. Mr Mildmay, our new rector, my dear.'

'Our new rector!' Mrs Ascott said, with a subdued outcry of surprise. She was seated in a corner of a large light room with three or four large windows looking out upon a charming lawn and garden, beyond which appeared the tufted undulations of the common, and the smooth green turf and white posts of the race-ground. With a house like this, looking out upon so interesting a spot, no one need be surprised that Mrs Ascott's fine friends 'kept her up,' and that for at least one week in the year she was as popular and sought after as any queen. Though it was only one week in the year, it had a certain influence upon her manners. She lived all the year through in a state of reflected glory from this brief but ever-recurring climax of existence. The air of conferring a favour, the look of gracious politeness, yet preoccupation, which suited a woman overbalanced by the claims of many candidates for her hospitality, never departed from her. She gave that little cry of surprise just as she would have done had her husband brought a stranger to her to see if she could give him a bed for the race week. 'I am delighted to make Mr Mildmay's acquaintance,' she said; 'but, my dear, I thought there was going to be an effort made for poor Mr St. John?'

This was in a lower tone, as she might have said, 'But there is only one spare room, and that I have promised to Mr St. John.' Her husband laughed.

'I told you, my dear, that was nonsense. What do ladies know of such matters? They talked of some foolish petition or other to the Lord Chancellor, as if the Lord Chancellor had anything to do with it! You may be very thankful you had me behind you, my dear, to keep you from such a foolish mistake. No; Mr Mildmay has it, and I am very glad. The dons have done themselves credit by their choice, and we are in great luck. I hope you will not be like your predecessor, Mr Mildmay, and take a dislike to the parish. We must do our best, Adelaide, to prevent that.'

'Indeed, I hope so,' said the lady. I am sure I am delighted. I think I have met some relations of yours, Mr Mildmay – the Hamptons of Thornbury? Yes; I felt sure I had heard them mention you. You recollect, Henry, they lunched with us here the year before last, on the cup day? They came with Lady Teddington – charming people. And you know all the Teddingtons, of course? What a nice family they are! We see a great deal of Lord Charles, who is often in this neighbourhood. His dear mother is often rather anxious about him. I fear – I fear he is just a little disposed to be what you gentlemen call fast.'

'We gentlemen don't mince our words,' said her husband; 'rowdy young scamp, that is what I call him; bad lot.'

'You are very severe, Henry – very severe – except when it is a favourite of your own. How glad I am we are getting some one we know to the rectory. When do you take possession, Mr Mildmay? We shall be quite near neighbours, and will see a great deal of you, I hope.'

'I do not feel quite sure, since I have been here, whether I will come to the rectory at all,' said Mildmay. 'Mr St. John was so hasty in his announcement, that I feel myself a swindler coming here under false pretences. I have not made up my mind whether I will accept the living or not.'

'Since you have been here? Then you don't like the place,' said Mr Ascott. 'I must say I am surprised. I think you are hasty, as well as St. John. Poor Chester, to be sure, did not like it, but that was because he thought it did not agree with him. The greatest nonsense! it is as healthy a place as any in

England; it has a hundred advantages. Perhaps this sort of thing mayn't suit you as a clergyman,' he said, waving his hand towards the distant race-course; 'but it gives a great deal of life to the place.'

'And so near town,' said Mrs Ascott; 'and such nice people in the neighbourhood! Indeed, Mr Mildmay, you must let us persuade you; you must really stay.'

'Come, now,' cried her husband, 'let's talk it over. What's your objection? Depend upon it, Adelaide, it is those pets of yours, the St. John's who have been putting nonsense into his head.'

'Poor things, what do they know!' said Mrs Ascott, with a sigh. 'But indeed, Mr Mildmay, now that we have seen you, and have a chance of some one we can like, with such nice connections, we cannot let you go.'

This was all very flattering and pleasant. 'You are extremely kind,' said Mildmay. 'I must put it to the credit of my relations, for I have no right to such kindness. No, it is not any objection to the place. It is a still stronger objection. I heard Mrs Ascott herself speak of some effort to be made for Mr St. John — '

'I – what did I say?' cried the lady. 'Mr St. John? Yes. I was sorry, of course; very sorry.'

'It was all nonsense,' said the husband. 'I told her so. She never meant it; only what could one say to the girls when they appealed top her? She is a soft-hearted goose – eh, Adelaide? One prefers women to be so. But as for old St. John, it is sheer nonsense. Poor old fellow! yes, I am sorry for him. But whose fault is it? He knew Chester's life was not worth *that*; yet he has hung on, taking no trouble, doing nothing for himself. It is not your part or our part to bother our minds for a man who does nothing for himself.'

'That is true enough,' said Mildmay; 'but his long services to the parish, his age, his devotion to his work – it does not seem right. I don't say for you or for me, but in the abstract — '

'Devotion?' said Mr Ascott. 'Oh, yes; he has done his work well enough, I suppose. That's what is called devotion when a man dies or goes away. Yes, oh yes, we may allow him the credit of that, the poor old fogey, but – yes, oh yes, a good old fellow enough. When you have said that, there's no more to say. Perhaps in the abstract it was a shame that Chester should have the lion's share of the income, and St. John all the work, but that's all over; and as for any hesitation of yours on his account — '

'It may be foolish,' said the young man, 'but I do hesitate – I cannot help feeling that there is a great wrong involved – to Mr St. John, of course, in the first place – but without even thinking of any individual, it is a sort of thing that must injure the Church; and I don't like to be the instrument of injuring the Church.'

'Tut – tut – tut!' said Mr Ascott; 'your conscience is too tender by far.'

'Mr Mildmay,' said the lady sweetly, 'you must not expect me to follow such deep reasoning. I leave that to superior minds; but you ought to think what a great thing it is for a parish to have some one to look up to – some one the poor people can feel to be really their superior.'

'Not a poor beggar of a curate,' cried her husband. 'There, Adelaide! you have hit the right nail on the head. That's the true way to look at the subject. Poor old St. John! I don't say he's been well treated by destiny. He has had a deal of hard work, and he has stuck to it; but, bless you! how is a man like that to be distinguished from a Dissenting preacher, for instance? Of course, he's a clergyman, in orders and all that, as good as the Archbishop of Canterbury; but he has no position – no means – nothing to make him the centre of the parish, as the clergyman ought to be. Why, the poorest ;labourer in the parish looks down upon the curate. "Parson's just as poor as we is." they say. I've hear them. He has got to run up bills in the little shops, and all that, just as they have. He has no money to relieve them with when they're out of work. The farmers look down upon him. They think nothing of a man that's poor; and as for the gentry — '

'Stop, Henry,' said Mrs Ascott; 'the gentry have always been very kind to the St. Johns. We were always sorry for the girls. Poor things! their mother was really quite a lady, though I never heard that she had anything. We were all grieved about this last sad affair, when he married the governess; and I should always have made a point of being kind to the girls.

That is a very different thing, however, Mr Mildmay,' she added, with a sweet smile, 'from having a clergyman whom one can really look up to, and who will be a friend and neighbour as well as a clergyman. You will stay to luncheon? I think I hear the bell.'

CHAPTER THIRTEEN

WHAT THE GIRLS COULD DO

Mildmay left the house of the Ascotts hurriedly at this intimation. He thought them pleasant people enough – for who does not think those people pleasant who flatter and praise him? – but he would not allow himself to be persuaded out of his determination to return to the rectory. I must add however that his mind was in a more confused state than ever as he skirted the common by the way the curate had taken him on the previous night. There were two sides to every question; that could not be gainsaid. To leave Brentburn after passing twenty years here in arduous discharge of all the rector's duties, but with the rank and remuneration only of the curate, was an injury too hard to contemplate to Mr St. John; but then it was not Mildmay's fault that he should interfere at his own cost to put it right. It was not even the fault of the parish. It was nobody's fault but his own, foolish as he was, neglecting all chances of 'bettering himself.' If a man would do nothing for himself, how could it be the duty of others, of people no way connected with him, scarcely knowing him, to do it for him? This argument was unanswerable; nothing could be more reasonable, more certain; and yet – Mildmay felt that he himself was young, that the rectory of Brentburn was not much to him one way or the other. He had wanted it as the means of living a more real life than that which was possible to him in his college rooms; but he had no stronger reason, no special choice of the place, no conviction that he could do absolute good here; and why should he then take so lightly what it would cost him nothing to reject, but which was everything to the curate? Then, on the other hand, there was the parish to consider. What if – extraordinary as that seemed – it did not want Mr St. John? What if really his very poverty, his very gentleness, made him unsuitable for it? The argument

126

seemed a miserable one, so far as the money went; but it might
be true. The Ascotts, for instance, were the curate's friends;
but this was their opinion. Altogether Mr Mildmay was very
much perplexed on the subject. He wished he had not come to
see for himself, just as an artist has sometimes been sorry for
having consulted that very troublesome reality, Nature, who
will not lend herself to any theory. If he had come without any
previous inspection of the place, without any knowledge of
the circumstances, how much better it would have been!
Whereas now he was weighed down by the consideration of
things with which he had really nothing to do. As he went
along, full of these thoughts, he met the old woman whom he
had first spoken to by the duck-pond on the day before, and
who had invited him to sit down in her cottage. To his
surprise – for he did not at first recollect who she was – she
made him a curtsy, and stopped short to speak to him. As it
was in the full blaze of the midday sunshine, Mildmay would
very gladly have escaped – not to say that he was anxious to
get back to the rectory, and to finish, as he persuaded himself
was quite necessary, his conversation with Cicely. Old Mrs
Joel, however, stood her ground. She had an old-fashioned
large straw bonnet on her head, which protected her from the
sun; and besides, was more tolerant of the sunshine, and more
used to exposure than he was.

'Sir,' she said, 'I hear as you're the new gentleman as is
coming to our parish. I am a poor woman, sir, the widow o'
Job Joel, as was about Brentburn church, man and boy, for
more than forty year. He began in the choir, he did, and
played the fiddle in the old times; and then, when that was
done away with, my husband he was promoted to be clerk,
and died in it. They could not ezacktly make me clerk, seeing
as I'm nothing but a woman; but Dick Williams, as is the
sexton, ain't married, and I've got the cleaning of the church,
and the pew-opening, if you please, sir; and I hope, sir, as you
won't think it's nothing but justice to an old servant, to let me
stay?'

'What do you think of Mr St. John going away?' asked
Mildmay abruptly.

The old woman stared, half alarmed, and made him another
curtsy, to occupy the time till she could think how to answer.

'Mr St. John, sir? He's a dear good gentleman, sir; as innocent as a baby. When he's gone, sir, they will find the miss of him,' she said, examining his face keenly to see how he meant her to answer, which is one of the highest arts of the poor.

'If he goes away, after being here so long, why shouldn't you be sent away, too?' said Mildmay. He felt how absurd was this questioning, as of an oracle, which came from the confused state of his own mind, not from any expectation of an answer; and then he could not but smile to himself at the idea of thus offering up a victim to the curate's *manes*.

Mrs Joel was much startled. 'Lord bless us!' she said, making a step backwards. Then commanding herself, 'It weren't Mr St. John, sir, as gave me my place; but the rector hisself. Mr St. John is as good as gold, but he ain't not to say my master. Besides, there's a many as can do the parson's work, but there ain't many, not in this parish, as could do mine. Mr St. John would be a loss – but me, sir — '

Here she made another curtsy, and Mildmay laughed in spite of himself. 'You – would be a greater loss?' he said. 'Well, perhaps so; but if there are any good reasons why he should leave, there must be the same for you.'

'I don't see it, sir,' said Mrs Joel promptly. 'The parson's old, and he's a bit past his work; but I defy any one in the parish to say as the church ain't as neat as a new pin. Mr St. John's getting a bit feeble in the legs; he can't go long walks now like once he could. Me! I may be old, but as for my mop and my duster, I ain't behind nobody. Lord bless you! it's a very different thing with Mr St. John from what it is with me. He's got those girls of his to think upon, and those little children. What's he got to do with little children at his age? But I've nobody but myself to go troubling *my* brains about. I thinks o' my work, and nought else. You won't get another woman in the parish as will do it as cheap and as comfortable as me.'

'But don't you think,' said Mildmay – whose conduct I cannot excuse, and whose only apology is that his mind was entirely occupied with one subject – 'don't you think it is very hard upon Mr St. John at his age, to go away?'

Mrs Joel found herself in a dilemma. She had no desire to speak ill of the curate, but if she spoke too well of him, might not that annoy the new rector, and endanger her own cause? She eyed him very keenly, never taking her eyes off his face, to be guided by its changes. 'Between gentlefolks and poor folks,' she said at last, philosophically, 'there's a great gulf fixed, as is said in the Bible. They can't judge for us, nor us for them. He's a great deal abler to speak for hisself, and settle for hisself, than the likes o' me; and I reckon as he could stay on if he'd a mind to; but me, sir, it's your pleasure as I've got to look to,' said the old woman, with another curtsy. This oracle, it was clear, had no response or guidance to give.

'Well,' he said, carelessly. 'I will speak to Miss St. John – for I don't know about the parish; and if she approves — '

A gleam of intelligence came into the keen old eyes which regarded him so closely; the old face lighted up with a twinkle of mingled pleasure, and malice, and kindness. 'If that's so, the Lord be praised!' she cried; 'and I hope, sir, it's Miss Cicely; for if ever there was a good wife, it's her dear mother as is dead and gone; and Miss Cicely's her very breathing image. Good morning to you, and God bless you, sir, and I hope as I haven't made too bold.'

What does the old woman mean? Mildmay said to himself bewildered. He repeated the question over and over again as he pursued his way to the rectory. What was it to him that Cicely St. John was like her mother? The curate, too, had insisted upon this fact as if it was of some importance. What interest do they suppose me to take in the late Mrs St. John? he said, with great surprise and confusion to himself.

Meanwhile, the girls in the rectory had been fully occupied. When their father went out, they held a council of war together, at which indeed Mab did not do much more than question and assent, for her mind was not inventive or full of resources as Cicely's was. It was she, however, who opened the consultation. 'What were you saying to Mr Mildmay in the garden?' said Mab. 'You told him something. He did not look the same to-day as he did last night.'

'I told him nothing,' said Cicely. 'I was so foolish as to let him see that we felt it very much. No, I must not say foolish. How could we help but feel it? It is injustice, if it was the

Queen herself who did it. But perhaps papa is right – if he does
not come, some one else would come. And he has a heart. I do
not hate him so much as I did last night.'

'Hate him! I do not hate him at all. He knows how to draw,
and said some things that were sense – really sense – and so
few people do that,' said Mab, thinking of her sketch. 'I must
have those mites again when the light is about the same as last
time, and finish it. Cicely, what are you thinking of now?'

'So many things,' said the girl, with a sigh. 'Oh, what a
change, what a change, since we came! How foolish we have
been, thinking we were to stay here always! Now, in six
weeks or so, we must go – I don't know where; and we must
pay our debts – I don't know how; and we must live without
anything to live on. Mab, help me! Papa won't do anything;
we must settle it all, you and I.'

'You need not say you and I, Cicely. I never was clever at
plans. It must be all yourself. What a good thing you are like
mamma! Don't you think we might go to Aunt Jane?'

Aunt Jane kept us at school for three years,' said Cicely.
'She has not very much herself. How can I ask her for more? If
it were not so dreadful to lose you, I should say, Go, Mab –
she would be glad to have *you* – and work at your drawing,
and learn all you can, while I stay with papa here.'

Cicely's eyes filled with tears, and her steady voice faltered.
Mab threw her arms round her sister's neck. 'I will never leave
you. I will never go away from you. What is drawing or
anything if we must be parted? – we never were parted all our
lives.'

'That is very true,' said Cicely, drying her eyes. 'But we
can't do as we like now. I suppose people never can do what
they like in this world. We used to think it was only till we
grew up. Mab, listen – now is the time when we must settle
what to do. Papa is no good. I don't mean to blame him; but
he has been spoiled; he has always had things done for him. I
saw that last night. To ask him only makes him unhappy; I
have been thinking and thinking, and I see what to do.'

Mab raised her head from her sister's shoulder, and looked
at Cicely with great tender believing eyes. The two forlorn
young creatures had nobody to help them; but the one trusted
in the other, which was a safeguard for the weaker soul; and

she who had nobody to trust in except God, felt that inspiration of the burden which was laid upon her, which sometimes is the strongest of all supports to the strong. Her voice still faltered a little, and her eyes glistened, but she put what was worse first, as a brave soul naturally does.

'Mab, you must go – it is the best – you are always happy with your work, and Aunt Jane will be very kind to you; and the sooner you can make money, don't you see? It would not do to go back to school, even if Miss Blandy would have us, for all we could do there was to keep ourselves. Mab, you are so clever, you will soon now be able to help; and you know, even if papa gets something, there will always be the little boys.'

'Yes, I know,' said Mab, subdued. 'Oh Cicely, don't be vexed! I should like it – I know I should like it – but for leaving you.'

Cicely's bosom heaved with a suppressed sob. 'You must not mind me. I shall have so much to do, I shall have no time to think; and so long as one can keep one's self from thinking! – There now, that is settled. I wanted to say it, and I dared not. After that – Mab, don't ask me my plans! I am going round this very day,' cried Cicely, springing to her feet, 'to all those people we owe money to.' This sudden movement was half the impulse of her vivacious nature, which could not continue in one tone, whatever happened, and, half an artifice to conceal the emotion which was too deep for her sister to share. Cicely felt the idea of the separation much more than Mab did, though it was Mab who was crying over it; and the elder sister dared not dwell upon the thought. 'I must go round to them all,' said Cicely, taking the opportunity to get rid of her tears, 'and ask them to have a little patience. There will be another half-year's income before we leave, and they shall have all, all I can give them. I hope they will be reasonable. Mab, I ought to go now.'

'Oh, what will you say to them? Oh, how have you the courage to do it? Oh Cicely! when it is not your fault. It is papa who ought to do it!' cried Mab.

'It does not matter so much who ought to do it,' said Cicely, with composure. 'Some one *must* do it, and I don't know who will but me. Then I think there ought to be an advertisement written for the *Guardian*.'

'Cicely, you said you were to stay with papa!'

'It is not for me; it is for papa himself. Poor papa! Oh, what a shame, what a shame, at his age! And a young man, *that* young man, with nothing to recommend him, coming in to everything, and turning us out! I can't talk about it,' cried Cicely. 'The best thing for us is to go and do something. I can make up the advertisement on the way.'

And in the heat of this, she put on her hat and went out, leaving Mab half stupefied by the suddenness of all those settlements. Mab had not the courage to offer to go to Wilkins and the rest with her sister. She cried over all that Cicely had to do; but she knew very well that she had not the strength to do it. She went and arranged her easel, and set to work very diligently. That was always something; and to make money, would not that be best of all, as well as the pleasantest? Mab did not care for tiring herself, nor did she think of her own enjoyment. That she should be the brother working for both, and Cicely the sister keeping her house, had always been the girl's ideal, which was far from a selfish one. But she could not do what Cicely was doing. She could not steer the poor little ship of the family fortunes or misfortunes through this dangerous passage. Though she was, she hoped, to take the man's part of breadwinner, for the moment she shrank into that woman's part which women too often are not permitted to hold. To keep quiet at home, wondering and working in obscurity – wondering how the brave adventurer was faring who had to fight for bare life outside in the world.

I dare not follow Cicely through her morning's work; it would take up so much time; and it would not be pleasant for us any more than it was for her. 'Don't you make yourself unhappy, Miss,' said the butcher, 'I know as you mean well by every one. A few pounds ain't much to me, the Lord be praised! and I'll wait, and welcome, for I know as you mean well.' Cicely, poor child! being only nineteen, cried when these kind words were said to her, and was taken into the hot and greasy parlour, where the butcher's wife was sitting, and petted and comforted. 'Bless you, things will turn out a deal better than you think,' Mrs Butcher said; 'they always does.

Wait till we see the handsome young gentleman as is coming through the woods for you, Miss Cicely dear: and a good wife he'll have, like your dear mother,' this kind woman added, smiling, yet wiping her eyes. But Wilkins the grocer was much more difficult to manage, and to him Cicely set her fair young face like a flint, biting her lips to keep them steady, and keeping all vestige of tears from her eyes. 'Whatever you do,' she said with those firm pale lips, 'we cannot pay you now; but you shall be paid if you have the patience;' and at last, notwithstanding the insults which wrung Cicely's heart, this savage, too, was overcome. She went home all throbbing and aching from this last conflict, her heart full of bitterness and those sharp stings of poverty which are so hard to bear. It was not her fault; no extravagance of hers had swelled those bills; an how many people threw away every day much more than would have saved all that torture of heart and mind to this helpless and guiltless girl! Mildmay himself had paid for a Palissy dish, hideous with crawling reptiles, a great deal more than would have satisfied Wilkins and relieved poor Cicely's delicate shoulders of this humiliating burden; but what of that? The young man whom she saw in the distance approaching the rectory from the other side could at that moment have paid every one of those terrible debts that were crushing Cicely, and never felt it; but I repeat, what of that? Under no pretence could he have done it; nothing in the world would have induced the proud, delicate girl to betray the pangs which cut her soul. Thus the poor and the rich walk together shoulder by shoulder every day as if they were equal, and one has to go on in hopeless labour like Sisyphus, heaving up the burden which the other could toss into space with the lifting of a finger. So it is, and so it must be, I suppose, till time and civilization come to an end.

Meanwhile these two came nearer, approaching each other from different points. And what Mildmay saw was not the brave but burdened creature we know of, dear reader, bleeding and aching from battles more bitter than Inkerman, with a whole little world of helpless beings hanging upon her, but only a fresh, bright-eyed girl, in a black and white frock, with a black hat shading her face from the sunshine, moving lightly in the animation of her youth across the white high road – a creature full of delicate strength, and variety, and brightness; like her mother! Mildmay could not help thinking that Mrs St. John must have been a pretty woman, and there came a little pang of sympathy into his heart when he thought of the grave in the twilight where the curate had led him, from which the light in the girls' windows was always visible, and to which his patient feet had worn that path across the grass. To be sure, across the pathos of this picture there would come the jar of that serio-comic reference to the other Mrs St. John, who, poor soul! lay neglected down the other turning. This made the new rector laugh within himself. But he suppressed all signs of the laugh when he came up to Cicely, who, though she gave him a smile of greeting, did not seem in a laughing mood. She was the first to speak.

'Have you left papa behind you, Mr Mildmay? He has always a great many places to go to, and parish work is not pleasant on such a hot day.'

Was there an insinuation in this that he had abandoned the unpleasant work, finding it uncongenial to him? Poor Cicely was sore and wounded, and the temptation to give a passing sting in her turn was great.

'Mr St. John did not permit me to try its pleasantness or unpleasantness,' said Mildmay. 'He took me over the parish indeed, and showed me the church and the school, and some other things; and then he left me at Mr Ascott's. I come from the Heath now.'

'Ah, from the Heath?' said Cicely, changing colour a little, and looking at him with inquiring eyes. What had they done or said, she wondered, to him? for she could not forget the projected petition to the Lord Chancellor, which had raised a fallacious hope in their hearts when she saw Mrs Ascott last.

'They have a pretty house, and they seem kind people,' said Mildmay, not knowing what to say.

'Yes, they have a pretty house,' Cicely looked at him even more eagerly, with many questions on her lips. Had they said nothing to him? Had they received him at once as the new rector without a word? Kind! what did he mean when he said they were kind? Had they, too, without an effort, without a remonstrance, gone over to the enemy?

Mr St. John somewhat rashly introduced me as the new rector,' said Mildmay, 'which was very premature; and they knew some relations of mine. Miss St. John, the Ascotts are much less interesting to me than our conversation of this morning. Since then my mind has been in a very confused state. I can no longer feel that anything is settled about the living.'

'Didn't they say anything?' said Cicely, scarcely listening to him; 'didn't they make any objection?' This was a shock of a new kind which she was not prepared for. 'I beg your pardon,' she cried; 'they had no right to make any objection; but didn't they say anything at least – about papa?'

What was Mildmay to answer? He hesitated scarcely a moment, but her quick eye saw it.

'A great deal,' he said eagerly; 'they said, as every one must, that Mr St. John's long devotion — '

'Don't try to deceive me,' said Cicely, with a smile of desperation. 'I see you do not mean it. They did not say anything sincere. They were delighted to receive a new rector, a new neighbour, young and happy and well off — '

'Miss St. John – '

'Yes, I know; it is quite natural, quite right. I have nothing to say against it. Papa has only been here for twenty years, knowing all their troubles, doing things for them which he never would have done for himself; but "Le roi est mort; vive le roi!" cried the impetuous girl in a flash of passion; in the strength of which she suddenly calmed down, and smiling, turned to him again. 'Is it not a pretty house? and Mrs Ascott is very pretty too – has been, people say, but I think it is hard to say, has been. She is not young, but she has the beauty of her age.'

'I take very little interest in Mrs Ascott,' said Mildmay, 'seeing I never saw her till to-day; but I take a great deal of interest in what you were saying this morning.'

'You never saw any of us till yesterday, Mr Mildmay.'

'I suppose that is quite true. I cannot help it – it is different. Miss St. John, I don't know what you would think of the life I have been living, but yours has had a great effect upon me. What am I to do? you have unsettled me, you have confused my mind and all my intentions. Now tell me what to do.'

'I,' said Cicely aghast. 'oh, if I could only see a little in advance, if I could tell what to do myself!'

'You cannot slide out of it like this,' he said; 'nay, pardon me, I don't mean to be unkind; but what am I to do?'

Cicely looked at him with a rapid revulsion of feeling from indignation to friendliness. 'Oh,' she cried, 'can't you fancy how a poor girl, so helpless as I am, is driven often to say a great deal more than she means? What can we do, we girls? – say out some of the things that choke us, that make our hearts bitter within us, and then be sorry for it afterwards? that is all we are good for. We cannot go and do things like you men, and we feel all the sharper, all the keener because we cannot *do*. Mr Mildmay, all that I said was quite true; but what does that matter? a thing may be wrong and false to every principle, and yet it cannot be helped. You ought not to have the living; papa ought to have it; but what then? No one will give it to papa, and if you don't take it some one else will; therefore, take it, though it is wicked and a cruel wrong. It is not your fault, it is — I don't know whose fault. One feels as if it were God's fault sometimes,' cried Cicely; 'but that must be wrong; the world is all wrong and unjust, and hard – hard; only sometimes there is somebody who is very kind, very good, who makes you feel that it is not God's fault, and you forgive even the world.'

She put up her hand to wipe the tears from those young shining eyes, which indignation and wretchedness and tears only made the brighter. Cicely was thinking of the butcher – you will say no very elevated thought. But Mildmay, wondering, and touched to the heart, asked himself, with a suppressed throb of emotion, could she mean him?

'I am going back to Oxford,' he said hastily. 'I shall not go to town. The first thing I do will be to see everybody concerned, and to tell them what you say. Yes, Miss St. John, you are right; it is wicked and wrong that I or any one should have it while your father is here. I will tell the Master so, I will tell them all so. It shall not be my fault if Mr St. John does not have his rights.'

They were close to the rectory gate, and as fire communicates to fire, the passionate impulse and fervour of Cicely's countenance had transferred themselves to Mr Mildmay, whose eyes were shining, and his cheeks flushed with purpose

like her own. Cicely was not used to this rapid transmission of
energy. She gazed at him half frightened. Usually her
interlocutor did all that was possible to calm her down –
wondered at her, blamed her a little, chilled her vehemence
with surprised or disapproving looks. This new companion
who caught fire at her was new to the girl. She was half
alarmed at what she had done.

'Will you do so, really?' she said, the tears starting to her
eyes. 'O Mr Mildmay, perhaps I am wrong! Papa would not
advise you so. He would say he never asked for anything in his
life, and that he would not be a beggar for a living now. And
think – perhaps I should not have said half so much if I could
have done anything. I am too ignorant and too inexperienced
for any one to be guided by me.'

'Yes, you are ignorant,' cried the young man. 'You don't
know the sophistries with which we blind ourselves and each
other. You dare to think what is right and what is wrong –
and, for once in my life, so shall I.'

The moisture that had been gathering dropped all at once in
two great unexpected tears out of Cicely's eyes. Her face
lighted like the sky when the sun rises, a rosy suffusion as of
dawn came over her. Her emotion was so increased by
surprise that even now she did not know what to think. In the
least likely quarter all at once, in her moment of need, she had
found sympathy and succour; and I think perhaps that even
the most strong and self-sustaining do not know how much
they have wanted sympathy and comprehension until it
comes. It made Cicely weak, not strong. She felt that she
could have sat down on the roadside and cried. She had an
idiotic impulse to tell him everything, and especially about the
butcher – how kind he had been. These impulses passed
through her mind mechanically, or, as one ought to say
nowadays, automatically; but Cicely, who had no notion of
being an automaton, crushed them in the bud. And what she
really would have said in the tumult of her feelings, beyond
what the look in her eyes said, behind the tears, I cannot tell, if
it had not been that the curate came forth, leisurely at that
moment from the rectory, making it necessary that tears and
every other evidence of emotion should be cleared away.

'Cicely, it is time for dinner,' he said. 'You should not walk, my dear, in the heat of the day; and Mr Mildmay, too, must be tired, and want something to refresh him. It is a long time since breakfast,' said the gentle curate, opening the door that his guest might precede him. Mr St. John was not a great eater, but he had a mild, regular appetite, and did not like any disrespect to the dinner hour.

CHAPTER FOURTEEN

HOW TO EXERCISE CHURCH PATRONAGE

Mildmay made his way back to Oxford without any delay. He knew that the Master of the college, who was a man with a family, had not yet set out on the inevitable autumn tour. But I must add that, though no man could have been more anxious to obtain preferment in his own person than he was to transfer his preferment to another, yet various doubts of the practicability of what he was going to attempt interfered, as he got further and further from Brentburn, with the enthusiasm which had sprung up so warmly in Cicely's presence. It would be very difficult, he felt, to convey to the Master the same clear perception of the rights of the case as had got into his own head by what he had seen and heard at the rectory; and if all he made by his hesitation was to throw the living into the hands of Ruffhead! For Brentburn was no longer an indifferent place – the same as any other in the estimation of the young don; quite the reverse; it was very interesting to him now. Notwithstanding the bran-new church, he felt that no other parish under the sun was half so attractive. The churchyard, with those two narrow threads of paths; the windows, with the lights in them, which glimmered within sight of the grave; the old-fashioned, sunny garden; the red cottages, with not one wall which was not awry, and projecting at every conceivable angle; the common, with its flush of heather – all these had come out of the unknown, and made themselves plain and apparent to him. He felt Brentburn to be in a manner his own; a thing which he would be willing to give to Mr St. John, or rather to lend him for his lifetime; but he did not feel the least inclination to let it fall into the hands of any other man. Neither did he feel inclined to do as Mr Chester, the late rector, had done – to expatriate himself, and leave the work of his parish to the curate in charge. Besides, he could not do this, for he was in perfect health; and he could neither tell the necessary lie himself, nor, he thought, get any doctor to tell it for him. As he got nearer and nearer to the moment which must decide all these uncertainties, he got more and more confused and troubled in his mind. The Master was the college, as it happened at that moment; he was by far the most influential and the most powerful person in it; and what he said was the thing that would be done. Mildmay accordingly took his way with very mingled feelings, across the quadrangle to the beautiful and picturesque old house in which this potentate dwelt. Had he any right to attempt to make such a bargain as was in his mind? It was enough that the living had been offered to him. What had he to say but yes or no.

The Master's house was in a state of confusion when Mildmay entered it. The old hall was full of trunks, the oaken staircase encumbered with servants and young people running up and down in all the bustle of a move. Eight children of all ages, and half as many servants, was the Master – brave man! – about to carry off to Switzerland. The packing was terrible, and not less terrible the feelings of the heads of the expedition, who were at that moment concluding their last calculation of expenses, and making up little bundles of circular notes. 'Here is Mr Mildmay,' said the Master's wife, 'and, thank Heaven! this reckoning up is over;' and she escaped with a relieved countenance, giving the new comer a smile of gratitude. The head of the college was slightly flustrated, if such a vulgar word can be used of such a sublime person. I hope no one will suspect me of Romanizing tendencies, but perhaps a pale ecclesiastic, worn with thought, and untroubled by children, would have been more like the typical head of a college than this comely yet careworn papa. The idea, however, flashed through Mildmay's mind, who had the greatest reverence for the Master, that these very cares, this evident partaking of human nature's most ordinary burdens, would make the great don feel for the poor curate. Does not a touch of nature make the whole world kin?

'Well, Mildmay,' said the Master, 'come to say good-bye? You are just in time. We are off to-night by the Antwerp boat, which we have decided is the best way with our enormous party.' Here the good man sighed. 'Where are you going? You young fellows don't know you're born, as people say – coming and going, whenever the fancy seizes you, as light as a bird. Ah! wait till you have eight children, my dear fellow, to drag about the world.'

'That could not be for some time at least,' said Mildmay, with a laugh; 'but I am not so disinterested in my visit as to have come merely to say good-bye. I wanted to speak to you about Brentburn.'

'Ah – oh,' said the Master, 'to be sure, your living. You have been to see it? Well! and how do you think it will feel to be an orderly rector, setting a good example, instead of enjoying yourself, and collecting crockery here?'

That was a cruel speech, and Mildmay grew red at the unworthy title crockery; but the Master's savage sentiments on the subject were known. What is a man with eight children to be expected to know about rare china?

'I believe there are much better collections than mine in some country rectories,' he said; 'but, never mind; I want to speak to you of something more interesting than crockery. I do not think I can take Brentburn.'

The Master framed his lips into that shape which in a profane and secular person would have produced a whistle of surprise. 'So!' he said, 'you don't like it? But I thought you were set upon it. All the better for poor Ruffhead, who will now be able to marry after all.'

'That is just what I wanted to speak to you about,' said Mildmay, embarrassed. 'I don't want it to fall to Ruffhead. Listen, before you say anything! I don't want to play the part of the dog in the manger. Ruffhead is young, and so am I; but, my dear Master, listen to me. The curate in charge, Mr St. John, is not young; he has been twenty years at Brentburn, a laborious excellent clergyman. Think how it would look in any other profession, if either Ruffhead or I should thus step over his head.'

'The curate in charge!' said the Master, bewildered. 'What are you talking about? What has he to do with it? I know nothing about your curate in charge.'

'Of course you don't; and therefore there seemed to be some hope in coming to tell you. He is a member of our own college; that of itself is something. He used to know you, he says, long ago, when he was an undergraduate. He has been Chester's curate at Brentburn, occupying the place of the incumbent, and doing everything for twenty years; and now that Chester is dead, there is nothing for him but to be turned out at a moment's notice, and to seek his bread, at over sixty, somewhere else – and he has children too.'

'This last sentence was added at a venture to touch the Master's sympathies; but I don't think that dignitary perceived the application; for what is there in common between the master of a college and a poor curate? He shook his head with, however, that sympathetic gravity and deference towards misfortune which no man who respects himself ever refuses to show.

'St. John, St. John?' he said. 'Yes, I think I recollect the name; very tall – stoops – a peaceable sort of being? Yes. So he's Chester's curate? Who would have thought it? I suppose he started in life as well as Chester did, or any of us. What has possessed him to stay so long there?'

'Well – he is, as you say, a peaceable, mild man; not one to push himself — '

'*Push* himself!' cried the Master; 'not much of that, I should think. But even if you don't push yourself, you needn't stay for twenty years a curate. What does he mean by it? I am afraid there must be something wrong.'

'And I am quite sure there is nothing wrong,' cried Mild-may, warmly, 'unless devotion to thankless work, and for-getfulness of self is wrong; for that is all his worst enemy can lay to his charge.'

'You are very warm about it,' said the Master, with some surprise; 'which does you credit, Mildmay. But, my dear fellow, what do you expect me – what do you expect the college to do? We can't provide for our poor members who let themselves drop out of sight and knowledge. Perhaps if you don't take the living, and Ruffhead does, you might speak to him to keep your friend on as curate. But I have nothing to do with that kind of arrangement. And I'm sure you will excuse me when I tell you we start to-night.'

'Master,' said Mildmay solemnly, 'when you hear of a young colonel of thirty promoted over the head of an old captain of twice his age, what do you say?'

'Say, sir!' cried the Master, whose sentiments on this, as on most other subjects, were well known; 'say! why I say it's a disgrace to the country. I say it's the abominable system of purchase which keeps our best soldiers languishing. Pray, what do you mean by that smile? You know I have no patience to discuss such a question; and I cannot see what it has to do with what we were talking of,' he added, abruptly, breaking off with a look of defiance, for he suddenly saw the mistake he had made in Mildmay's face.

'Hasn't it?' said the other. 'If you will think a moment – Ruffhead and I are both as innocent of parochial knowledge as – as little Ned there.' (Ned at this moment had come to the window which opened upon the garden, and, knocking with impatient knuckles, had summoned his father out.) 'Mr St. John has some thirty years' experience, and is thoroughly known and loved by the people. What can anybody think – what can any one say – if one of us miserable subalterns is put over that veteran's head? Where but in the Church could such a thing be done – without at least such a clamour as would set half England by the ears?'

'Softly, softly,' cried the Master. '(Get away, you little imp. I'll come presently.) You mustn't abuse the Church, Mild-may. Our arrangements may be imperfect, as indeed all arrangements are which are left in human hands. But, depend upon it, the system is the best that could be devised; and there is no real analogy between the two professions. A soldier is helpless who can only buy his promotion, and has no money to buy it with. But a clergyman has a hundred ways of making his qualifications known, and as a matter of fact I think preferment is very justly distributed. I have known dozens of men, with no money and very little influence, whose talents and virtues alone – but you must know that as well as I do. In this case there must be something behind – something wrong – extreme indolence, or incapacity, or something —'

'There is nothing but extreme modesty, and a timid retiring disposition.'

'Yes, yes, yes,' cried the Master; 'these are the pretty names for it. Indolence which does nothing for itself, and hangs a dead weight upon friends. Now, tell me seriously and soberly, why do you come to, me with this story? What, in such a case, do you suppose I can do?'

'If you were a private patron,' said Mildmay, 'I should say boldly, I have come to ask you to give this living to the best man – the man who has a right to it; not a new man going to try experiments like myself, but one who knows what he is doing, who has done all that has been done there for twenty years. I would say you were bound to exercise your private judgement on behalf of the parish in preference to all promises or supposed rights; and that you should offer the living of Brentburn to Mr St. John without an hour's delay.'

'That is all very well,' said the Master, scratching his head, as if he had been a rustic clodhopper, instead of a learned and accomplished scholar, 'and very well put and perhaps true. I say, *perhaps* true, for of course this is only one side of the question. But I am not a private patron. I am only a sort of trustee of the patronage, exercising it in conjunction with various other people. Come, Mildmay, you know as well as I do, poor old St. John, though his may be a hard case, has no claim whatever upon the college; and if you don't accept it, there's Ruffhead and two or three others who have a right to their chance. You may be sure Ruffhead won't give up his chance of marriage and domestic bliss for any poor curate. Of course the case, as you state it, is hard. What does the parish say?'

'The parish! I was not there long enough to find out the opinion of the parish.'

'Ah, you hesitate. Look here, Mildmay; if I were a betting man, I'd give you odds, or whatever you call it, that the parish would prefer you.'

'It is impossible; or if they did, it would only be a double wrong.' But Mildmay's voice was not so confident as when he had been pleading Mr St. John's cause, and his eyes fell before the Master's penetrating eyes.

'A wrong if you like, but it's human nature,' said the Master, with some triumph. 'I will speak to the Dean about it, if I see him this afternoon, and I'll speak to Singleton. If they think anything of your arguments, I shan't oppose. But I warn you I don't think it the least likely. His age, if there were nothing else, is against him, rather than in his favour.

We don't want parishes hampered with an old man past work.'

'He is just as old being curate as if he were rector.'

'Yes, yes. But to give him the living now, at his age, would be to weight the parish with him till he was a hundred, and destroy the chance for young men like yourself. *You* don't mind, but I can tell you Ruffhead does. No, no. Singleton will never hear of it; and what can I do? I am going away.'

'Singleton will do whatever you tell him,' said Mildmay; 'and you could write even though are going away.'

'Hush, hush,' said the Master, with a half laugh, 'that is all a popular delusion. Singleton is the most independent-minded man I know – and the others are as obstinate as pigs. Talk of turning them as one likes! Poor old St. John, though! we might hear of another place to suit him, perhaps. He has something of his own, I suppose – some private income? How many children has he of course, being only a curate, he must have heaps of children. (Coming, you rascal! coming, Ned.)'

'He has two daughters grown up,' said Mildmay, 'and two small children; and so far as I can judge is — What is there to laugh at?' he added, with a look of the greatest surprise.

'So, so; he has *daughters?*' said the Master, with a burst of genial laughter. 'That is it? Don't blush, my dear fellow; as good men as you have been in the same predicament. Go and marry her, which will be much more sensible; and I hope Miss St. John is everything that is pretty and charming for your sake.'

Perhaps Mildmay blushed, but he was not aware of it. He felt himself grow pale in a white heat of passion. 'This is a very poor joke,' he said. 'Excuse me, Master, if I must say so. I speak to you of an injury to the Church, and a serious wrong to one of her priests and you answer me with a jest most inappropriate to the occasion. I saw Miss – I mean Mr St. John and his family for the first time two days ago. Personal feeling of any kind has not been my inducement to make this appeal to your sense of justice. But I have made a mistake, it seems. Good morning! I will not detain you more.'

'Why, Mildmay! a man may have his joke. Don't take it in this tragical way. And don't be so withering in your irony about my sense of justice,' said the Master, with a laugh, half apologetic, half angry. But he did not ask the young man to sit down again. 'Justice goes both ways,' he added; 'and I have justice to the college, and justice to its more distinguished members, and even to the parish, for whose good we are all called upon to act – to consider; as well as justice to Mr St. John, which really is not our affair. But, my dear fellow, all this is very admirable in you – and don't think I fail to see that, though you say I made a poor joke. Yes, I am in a hurry, there is no denying it; but I'll see Singleton, and leave the matter in his hands. Meet you in the Oberland, eh? My wife talks of St. Moritz, but we never can drag the children all that way. Good-bye.'

Mildmay marched out of the old house with all his pulses tingling. It seemed to him that poor Cicely, in the midst of all the anxieties that lurked in her young eyes, had been insulted. Was it that sort of folly he was thinking of, or she, poor girl, who had said nothing to him but reproaches? But yet, I will allow, that absolutely innocent as he felt of any such levity, the accusation excited him more, perhaps, than was needful. He could not forget or forgive it, as one forgives a sorry jest at one's own expense, the reason being, he said to himself, that it was an insult to her, and that this insult had come upon a young innocent creature through him, which was doubly hard. He was still tingling with this blow, when he met his second in succession, so to speak, Mr Ruffhead, who was serving a curacy near Oxford, and who had a slight unspoken, unacknowledged grudge at his brother Fellow who had been preferred before himself. Mildmay, in his excitement, laid hold upon this probable heir of his, in case he should give up Brentburn, and poured the whole story into his ears, asking with some heat and passion for his advice. 'I don't see how I can take the living over Mr St. John's head; it seems to me the most terrible injustice,' he cried.

Mr Ruffhead shook his head.

You must not ask my advice,' said that sensible person. 'If you don't take it, and it's offered to me, I shall of course. I don't know Mr St. John, and if one neglected one's own interests for every hard case one heard of, where would one be? I can't afford to play with my chances. I daresay you think I am very hard-hearted; but that is what I should do.'

This plain declaration of sentiment subdued Mildmay, and brought him back to matters of fact. 'I suppose you are right; but I have not made up my mind to decline the living,' he said coldly, and did not ask Ruffhead to dinner as he had at first intended. No man, they say, likes his heir, and this kind of inheritance was doubly disagreeable to think of. Certainly, if the only alternative was Ruffhead and his honeymooning (which somehow it disgusted Mildmay to think of, as of something almost insulting to himself), it would be better, much better, that he himself should take Brentburn. He would not give it up only to see it passed on to this commonplace fellow, to enable him, forsooth, to marry some still more commonplace woman. Good heavens! was that the way to traffic with a cure of souls? He went back to his beautiful rooms in a most disturbed state of mind, and drew up impatiently the blinds which were not intended to be drawn up. The hot August light came in scorching and broad over all his delights, and made him loathe them; he tripped upon, and kicked away to the end of the room, a rug for which you or I, dear reader, would have given one of our ears; and jerked his Italian tapestry to one side, and I think, if good sense had not restrained him, would have liked to take up his very best bit of china and smashed it into a hundred pieces. But after a while he smiled at himself, and reduced the blaze of daylight to a proper artistic tone, and tried to eat some luncheon. Yesterday at the same hour he had shared the curate's dinner, with Cicely at the head of the table, looking at him with sweet eyes, in which there was still the dewy look of past tears. She had the house and all its cares upon her delicate shoulders, that girl; and her innocent name had been made the subject of a jest – through him!

CHAPTER FIFTEEN

THE ARTIST AND THE HOUSEKEEPER

I do not suppose that Cicely St. John had really any hope in her new acquaintance, or believed, when she looked at the matter reasonably, that his self-renunciation, if he had the strength of mind to carry it out, would really secure for her father the living of Brentburn. But yet a certain amount of faith is natural at her years, and she was vaguely strengthened and exhilarated by that suppressed expectation of something pleasant that might possibly happen, which is so great an element in human happiness; and, with this comfort in her soul, went about her work, preparing for the worst, which, to be sure, notwithstanding her hope, was, she felt, inevitable. Mab, when the stranger's enthusiastic adoption of her sister's suggestion was told to her, accepted it for her part with delight, as a thing settled. A true artist has always more or less a practical mind. However strong his imagination may be, he does not confine himself to fancies, or even words, but makes something tangible and visible out of it, and this faculty more or less shapes the fashion of his thinking. Mab, who possessed in addition that delightful mixture of matter-of-factness which is peculiar to womankind, seized upon the hope and made it into reality. She went to her work as gaily as if all the clouds had been in reality dispersed from her path. This time it was little Annie, the nursemaid – Cicely having interfered to protect the babies from perpetual posing – who supplied her with the necessary 'life.' Annie did not much like it. She would have been satisfied, indeed, and even proud, had 'her picture' been taken in her best frock, with all her Sunday ribbons; but to be thrust into a torn old dingy garment, with bare feet, filled the little handmaiden with disgust and rage great enough for a full-grown woman. 'Folks will think as I ain't got no decent clothes,' she said; and Mab's injudicious consolation, to the effect that 'folks would never see the picture,' did not at all mend the matter. Cicely, however, drew up her slight person, and 'looked Miss St. John,' according to Mab's description; and Annie was cowed. There were at least twenty different representations in Mab's sketch-books of moments in which Cicely had looked Miss. St, John; and it was Mab's conviction in life as well as in art that no opponent could stand before such a demonstration. Barefooted, in her ragged frock, Annie did not look an amiable young person, which, I am ashamed to say, delighted the artist. 'She will do for the naughty little girl in the fairy tale, the one with toads and frogs dropping from her lips,' cried Mab, in high glee. 'And if it comes well I shall send it to Mr Mildmay, to show we feel how kind he is.'

'Wait till he has been kind,' said Cicely, shaking her head. 'I always liked the naughty little girl best, not that complacent smiling creature who knew she had been good, and whom everybody praised. Oh, what a pity that the world is not like a fairy tale! where the good are always rewarded, and even the naughty, when they are sorry. If we were to help any number of old women, what would it matter now?'

'But I suppose,' said Mab, somewhat wistfully, for she distrusted her sister's words, which she did not understand, and was afraid people might think Cicely Broad Church, 'I suppose whatever may happen in the meantime, it all comes right in the end?'

'Papa is not so very far from the end, and it has not come right for him.'

'O Cicely, how can you talk so! Papa is not so old. He will live years and years yet!' cried Mab, her eyes filling.

'I hope so. Oh, I hope so! I did not think of merely living. But he cannot get anything very great now, can he, to make up for so long waiting? So long – longer,' said Cicely, with a little awe, thinking of that enormous lapse of time, 'than we have been alive!'

'If he gets the living, he will not want anything more,' said Mab, blithely working away with her charcoal. 'How delightful it will be! More than double what we have now? Fancy! After all, you will be able to furnish as you said.'

'But not in amber satin,' said Cicely, beguiled into a smile.

'In soft, soft Venetian stuff, half green, half blue, half no colour at all. Ah! she has moved! Cicely, Cicely, go and talk to her for heaven's sake, or my picture will be spoilt!'

'If you please, miss, I can't stop here no longer. It's time as I was looking after the children. How is Betsy to remember in the middle of her cooking the right time to give 'em their cod-liver oil?'

'I'll go and look after the children,' said Cicely. 'What you have got to do, Annie, is to stop here.'

Upon which Annie burst into floods of tears, and fell altogether out of pose. 'There ain't no justice in it!' she said. I'm put up here to look like a gipsy or a beggar; and mother will never get over it, after all her slaving and toiling to get me decent clothes!'

Thus it will be perceived that life studies in the domestic circle are very difficult to manage. After a little interval of mingled coaxing and scolding, something like the lapsed attitude was recovered, and Annie brought back into obedience. 'If you will be good, I'll draw a picture of you in your Sunday frock to give to your mother,' said Mab – a promise which had too good an effect upon her model, driving away the clouds from her countenance; and Cicely went away to administer the cod-liver oil. It was not a very delightful office, and I think that now and then, at this crisis, it seemed to Cicely that Mab had the best of it, with her work, which was a delight to her, and which occupied both her mind and her fingers; care seemed to fly the moment she got that charcoal in her hand. There was no grudge in this sense of disadvantage. Nature had done it, against which there is no appeal. I don't think, however, that care would have weighed heavily on Mab, even if she had not been an artist. She would have hung upon Cicely all the same if her occupation had been but needlework, and looked for everything from her hands.

But it was not until Annie was released, and could throw off the ragged frock in which she had been made picturesque, and return to her charge, that Cicely could begin the more important business that waited for her. She took this quite quietly, not thinking it necessary to be on the look-out for a grievance, and took her work into the nursery, where the two babies were playing in a solemn sort of way. They had their playthings laid out upon the floor, and had some mild little squabbles over them. 'Zat's Harry's!' she heard again and again, mingled with faint sounds of resistance. The children were very mysterious to Cicely. She was half afraid of them as mystic incomprehensible creatures, to whom everybody in heaven and earth did injustice. After a while she put down her work and watched them play. They had a large box of bricks before them, playthings which Cicely herself well remembered, and the play seemed to consist in one little brother diving into the long box in search of one individual brick, which, when he produced it, the other snatched at, saying, 'Zat's Harry's.' Charley, who wanted both his hands to swim with on the edge of the box, did not have his thumb in his mouth this time; but he was silenced by the unvarying claim. They did not laugh, nor did they cry, as other children do; but sat over the box of bricks, in a dumb conflict, of which it was impossible to tell whether it was strife or play.

'Are they all Harry's?' asked Cicely, suddenly moved to interfere. The sound of the voice startled the little creatures on the floor. They turned right round, and contemplated her from the carpet with round and wondering eyes.

'Zat's Harry's,' said the small boy over again with the iteration common to children. Charley was not prepared with any reply. He put his thumb into his mouth in default of any more extended explanation. Cicely repeated her question – I fear raising her voice, for patience was not Cicely's forte; whereupon Harry's eyes, who was the boldest, got bigger and bigger, and redder and redder, with fright, and Charley began to whimper. This irritated the sister much. 'You little silly things!' she said, 'I am not scolding you. What are you crying for? Come here, Harry, and tell me why you take all the bricks? They are Charley's too.'

Children are the angels of life; but they are sometimes little demons for all that. To see these two pale little creatures sitting half dead with fright, gazing at her sunny young countenance as if she were an ogre, exasperated Cicely. She jumped up, half laughing, half furious, and at that movement the babies set up a unanimous howl of terror. This fairly daunted her, courageous as she was. She went back to her seat again, having half a mind to cry too. 'I am not going to touch you,' said Cicely piteously. 'Why are you frightened at me? If you will come here I will tell you a story.' She was too young to have the maternal instinct so warmly developed as to make her all at once, without rhyme or reason, 'fond of' her little half-brothers; but she was anxious to do her duty, and deeply wounded that they did not 'take to her.' Children, she said to herself with an internal whisper of self-pity, had always taken to her before; and she was not aware of that instinctive resistance, half defiance, half fright, which seems to repel the child-dependent from those whose duty it is to take care of it – most unreasonable, often most cruel, but yet apparently most universal of sentiments. Is it that the very idea of a benefactor, even before the mind is capable of comprehending what it is, sets nature on edge? This was rather a hard lesson for the girl, especially as, while they were still howling, little Annie burst in indignant, and threw herself down beside the children, who clung to her, sobbing, one on each side. 'You have made 'em cry, miss,' cried Annie, 'and missus's orders was as they was never to be allowed to cry. It is very dangerous for boys; it busts their little insides. Did she frighten 'em, then? the naughty lady. Never mind, never minds, my precious! Annie's here.'

To see this child spread out upon the floor with these chicks under her wings would have been amusing to a cool spectator. But Cicely did not take it in that light. She waited till the children were pacified, and had returned to their play, and then she took the little nursemaid by the arm, and led her to the door. 'You are not to enter this room again or come near the children,' she said in a still voice which made Annie tremble. 'If you make a noise I will beat you. Go downstairs to your sister, and I will see you afterwards. Not a word! I have nothing more to say to you here.'

Cicely went back again to her seat trembling with the excitement of the moment, and then said to herself, what a fool she was! but oh! what a much greater fool Miss Brown had been to leave this legacy of trouble to two girls who had never done any harm to her. 'Though, I suppose,' Cicely added to herself with a sense of justice, 'she was not thinking about us.' And indeed it was not likely that poor Mrs St. John had brought these babies into the world solely to bother her husband's daughters. Poor Cicely, who had a thousand other things to do, and who already felt that it was impolitic, though necessary, to dismiss Annie, pondered long, gazing at those pale-faced and terrible infants, how she was to win them over, which looked as hard as any of her other painful pieces of business. At last some kind fairy put it into her head to sing: at which the two turned round once more upon their bases solemnly, and stared at her, intermitting their play till the song was finished. Then an incident occurred almost unparalleled in the nursery chronicles of Brentburn. Charley took his thumb out of his mouth, and looking up at her with his pale eyes, said of his own accord, 'Adain.'

'Come here then, and sit on my lap,' said Cicely, holding out her hand. There was a momentary struggle between terror and gathering confidence, and then pushing himself up by the big box of bricks Charley approached gradually, keeping a wary eye upon her movements. Once on her lap, however, the little adventurer felt himself comfortable. She was soft and pleasant, and had a bigger shoulder to support him and a longer arm to enfold him than Annie. He leant back against her, feeling the charm of that softness and sweetness, though he did not know how. 'Adain,' said Charley; and put his thumb in his mouth with all the feelings of a connoisseur in a state of perfect bodily ease prepared to enjoy the *morceau* specially given at his desire.

Thus Cicely conquered the babies once for all. Harry, too much astounded by thus seeing his lead taken from him to make any remonstrance, followed his brother in dumb surprise, and stood against her, leaning on her knee. They made the prettiest group; for, as Mab said, even when they are ugly, how pretty children are! and they 'compose' so beautifully with a pretty young woman, making even a commonplace mother into a Madonna and Lady of Blessing. Cicely sang them a song, so very low down in the scale at once both of music and of poetry that I dare not shock the refined reader by naming it, especially after that well-worn comparison; and this time both Harry and Charley joined in the encore, the latter too happy to think of withdrawing that cherished thumb from his mouth, murmuring thickly, 'Adain.'

'But, oh, what a waste of time – what a waste of time it will be!' cried poor Cicely, when she took refuge in the garden, putting the delicate children to play upon a great rug, stretched on the grass. 'To be sure there will be one mouth less to feed, which is always something. You must help me a little while I write my letters, Mab.'

'Who are you going to write to?' said Mab, with colloquial incorrectness which would have shocked out of their senses the Miss Blandys, and all the excellent persons concerned in bringing her up. 'Oh yes, I will try to help; but won't you forgive Annie, just for this little time, and let her stay?'

'I can't be defied in my own house,' said Cicely, erecting her head with an air which frightened Mab herself; 'and I must take to it sooner or later. Wherever we go, it is I that must look after them. Well! it will be a trouble at first; but I shall like it when I get fond of them. Mab, we ought to be fond of them now.'

Mab looked at the children, and then laughed. 'I don't hate them,' she said; 'they are such funny little things, as if they had been born about a hundred years before their time. I believe, really, they are not children at all, but old, old men, that know a great deal more than we do. I am sure that Charley could say something very wonderful if he liked. He has a great deal in him, if he would but take his thumb out of his mouth.'

'Charley is my boy,' said Cicely, brightening up; 'he is the one I like best.'

'I like him best, too. He is the funniest. Are you going to write there?'

'I must keep my eye upon them,' said Cicely, with great solemnity. She was pleased with her victory, and felt it to be of the most prodigious importance that she should not lose the 'influence' she had gained; for she was silly, as became her age, as well as wise. She had brought out her little desk – a very commonplace little article, indeed, of rosewood, with brass bindings – and seated herself under the old mulberry-tree, with the wind ruffling her papers. and catching in the short curling locks about her forehead. (N.B. – Don't suppose, dear reader, that she had cut them short; those stray curls were carefully smoothed away under the long braids when she brushed her hair; but the breeze caught them in a way which vexed Cicely as being untidy.) It was as pretty a garden scene as you could see; the old mulberry bending down its heavy branches, the babies on the rug at the girl's feet; but yet, when you look over Cicely's shoulder, a shadow falls upon the pretty scene. She had two letters to write, and something still less agreeable than her letters – an advertisement for the *Guardian*. This was very difficult, and brought many a sigh from her young breast.

"'An elderly clergyman who has filled the office of curate for a very long time in one parish, finding it now necessary to make a change, desires to find a similar — "'

'Do you think that will do?' said Mab. 'It is as if poor papa were a butler, or something – "filled the office of curate for a long time in one parish" – it does not sound nice.'

'We must not be bound by what sounds nice,' said Cicely. 'It is not nice, in fact – is it? How hard it is to put even such a little thing as this as one ought! Will this do better? – "A clergyman, who has long occupied the position of curate in charge, in a small parish, wishes to hear of a similar — " What, Mab? I cannot say situation, can I? that is like a butler again. Oh, dear, dear; it is so very much like a butler altogether. Tell me a word.'

'Position,' said Mab.

'But I have just said position. "A clergyman who has long held the – an *appointment* as curate in charge" there, that is better – "wishes to hear of a similar position in a small parish." I think that will do.'

'Isn't there a Latin word? *Locum* something or other; would not that be more dignified?' said Mab.

'*Locum tenens*. I prefer English,' said Cicely; 'and now I suppose we must say something about his opinions. Poor dear papa! I am sure I do not know whether he is High, or Low, or Broad.'

'Not Broad,' said Mab, pointedly; for she was very orthodox. 'Say sound; I have often seen that, and it does not commit you to anything, – sound, but not extreme, like Miss Blandy's clergyman.'

"'Of sound, but not extreme principles,"' wrote Cicely. 'That sounds a little strange, for you might say that a man who could not tell a lie, but yet did not mind a fib, was sound, but not extreme. "Church principles" – is that better? But I don't like that either. Stop, I have it – "He is a sound, but not extreme Churchman" – that is the very thing – "and has much experience" (Ah! poor papa!) "in managing a parish. Apply" – but that is another question. Where ought they to apply? We cannot give, I suppose, the full name and address here?'

'I wonder if any one will apply? But, Cicely, suppose all comes right, as I am sure it will, you may be deceiving some one, making them think – Here is the very person I want; and then how disappointed they will be!'

'Oh, if there is only *their* disappointment to think of! Mab, you must not think there is any reliance to be put on Mr Mildmay. He meant it; yes, tears came into his eyes,' cried Cicely, with a look of gratitude and pleasure in her own. 'But when he goes back among those Oxford men, those dons, do you think they will pay any attention to him? They will laugh at him; they will say he is a Quixote; they will turn it all into fun, or think it his folly.'

'Why should Oxford dons be so much worse than other men?' said Mab, surprised. 'Papa is an Oxford man – he is not hard-hearted. Dons, I suppose, are just like other people?'

'No,' said Cicely, who was arguing against herself, struggling against the tide of fictitious hope, which sometimes threatened to carry her away. 'The live by themselves among their books; they have nobody belonging to them; their hearts dry up, and they don't care for common troubles. Oh, I know it: they are often more heathens than Christians. I have no faith in those sort of people. He will have a struggle with them, and then he will find it to be of no use. I am as sure as if it had happened already,' cried Cicely, her bright eyes sparkling indignant behind her tears.

'At least we need not think them so bad till we know,' said Mab, more charitably.

Cicely had excited herself by this impassioned statement, in which indeed the Oxford men were innocent sufferers enough, seeing that she knew nothing about them. 'I must not let myself believe it; I dare not let myself believe it,' she said in her heart; 'but, oh! if by chance things did happen *so!*' What abundant compensation, what lavish apology, did this impetuous young woman feel herself ready to offer to those maligned dons!

The advertisement was at last fairly written out, with the exception of the address to be given. 'Papa may surely tell me where they are to apply,' Cicely said, though with doubts in her mind as to whether he was good even for this; and then she wrote her letters, one of which was in Mr St. John's name to the lawyer who had written to him about the furniture, asking that the sale might not take place until the curate's half-year, which ended in the end of September, should be out. Mr St. John would not do this himself. 'Why should I ask any favour of those people who do not know me?' he said; but he had at length consented that Cicely might write 'if she liked;' and in any case the lawyer's letter had to be answered. Cicely made this appeal as business-like as possible. 'I wonder how a man would write who did not mind much – to whom this was only a little convenience,' she said to her sister. 'I don't want to go and ask as if one was asking a favour of a friend – as if we cared.'

'But we do care; and it would be a favour —'

'Never mind. I wish we knew what a man would say that was quite independent and did not care. "If it is the same to you, it would be more convenient for me not to have the furniture disturbed till the 22nd of September" — that is the kind of thing. We girls always make too much of a favour of everything,' said Cicely, writing; and she produced an admirable imitation of a business letter, to which she appended her own signature, 'Cecil St. John,' which was also her father's, with great boldness. The curate's handwriting was almost more womanlike than hers, for Cicely's generation are not taught to write Italian hands, and I do not think the lawyer suspected the sex of the production. When she had finished this, she wrote upon another sheet of paper, 'My dear Aunt, I am — ' and then she stopped sharply. 'It is cool now, let us take them out for a walk on the common,' she said, shutting up her desk. 'I can finish this to-night.'

It was not, however, the walk on the common Cicely wanted, but to hide from her sister that the letter to Aunt Jane was much less easy than even those other dolorous pieces of business. Poor Cicely looked upon the life before her with a shudder. To live alone in some new place, where nobody knew her, as nursemaid to these babies, and attendant upon her father, without her sweet companion, the little sister, who, though so near in age, had always been the protected one, the reliant dependent nature, believing in Cicely, and giving her infinite support by that belief. How could she do it? Yet she herself, who felt it most, must insist upon it; must be the one to arrange and settle it all, as so often happens. It would not be half so painful to Mab as to Cicely; yet Mab would be passive in it , and Cicely active; and she could not write under Mab's smiling eyes betraying the sacrifice it cost her. Mab laughed at her sister's impetuosity, and concluded that it was exactly like Cicely to tire of her work all in a moment, and dash into something else. And, accordingly, the children's out-door apparel was got from the nursery, and the girls put on their hats, and strayed out by the garden door upon the common, with its heathery knolls and furze bushes. Harry and Charley had never in all their small lives had such a walk as this. The girls mounted them upon their shoulders, and ran races with them, Charley against Harry, till first one twin, and them the other, was beguiled into shrill little gusts of laughter: after which they were silent – themselves frightened by the unusual sound. But when the races ended, Charley, certainly the hero of the day, opened his mouth and spoke, and said 'Adain!' and this time when they laughed the babies were not frightened. Then they were set down and rolled upon the soft grass, and throned in mossy seats among the purple fragrant heather. What an evening it was! The sky all ablaze with the sunset, with clouds of rosy flame hanging like canopies over the faint delicious openings of that celestial green which belongs to a summer evening. The curate, coming from a distant round into the parish, which had occupied him all the day, found them on the grass under the big beech-tree, watching the glow of colour in the west. He had never seen his girls 'talking to' his babies before so kindly, and the old man was glad.

'But it is quite late enough to have them out; they have been used to such early hours,' he said.

'And Harry wants his tea,' piped that small hero, with a half whimper.

Then the girls jumped up, and looked at each other, and Cicely grew crimson. Here was a beginning to make, an advantage terrible to think of, to be given to the dethroned Annie, who no doubt was enjoying it keenly. Cicely had already forgotten the children's tea!

CHAPTER SIXTEEN

REALITY

Cicely wrote her letter to her aunt that evening, dropping some tears over it when Mab was not by to see; and almost as soon as it was possible she had a very kind answer, granting her request, and more. Aunt Jane declared that she would receive Mab with great delight, and do everything that could be done to further her art-studies, which, as the British Museum was near, and 'a very good artist' lived next door to Miss Maydew, seemed likely to be something worth while. 'She shall be to me like my own child; though I have never concealed from either of you that you, Cicely, are my pet.' wrote Miss Maydew; and she added a still more liberal invitation. 'If you want to spend a few days anywhere between leaving Brentburn and going to the new place, wherever that may be, you must come here – babies and all. I can manage to find beds for you near; and it will be a nice little holiday for us all,' said the kind woman. She even added a postscript, to the effect that, if there was a little money wanting at the time of the removal, Cicely was 'not to hesitate' to apply to her: and what could woman do more? Sympathy and hospitality, and a little money, 'is wanted.' Alas! perhaps it is because the money is so sure to be wanted that so few people venture on such an offer; but Miss Maydew knew she was safe with Hester's child, who was so like her mother. Cicely's other letter was successful, too. The lawyer who represented the Chester family was quite willing to postpone the sale until Mr St. John's time was up. After all, the world is not so very bad as it is called. Nobody was cruel to the St. Johns. The tradespeople agreed to wait for their money. The Chesters would not for the world disturb the departing curate until he was ready to go; and Mrs Ascott, and all the other great people in the parish, called and made much

of the girls. The church was more full than usual every
Sunday, for a vague expectation of a farewell (or, as old Mrs
Joel called it, a funeral) sermon was in the people's minds. A
great many of them, now it came to the point, were very sorry
that Mr St. John was going. They would have signed freely
anything that had been set before them to make the curate
stay. But, nevertheless, they were all interested about his
farewell sermon, and what he would say for himself, and what
account he would give of various matters which stuck fast in
their rustic recollections. Thus the weeks stole away quite
placidly, and the harvest was got in, and August wore out
under a great blazing moon with the utmost cheerfulness. One
or two answers came to the advertisement in the *Guardian;* but
they were not of an encouraging kind. Cicely felt that it was
better to repeat it and wait; and her father was always pleased
to wait under all circumstances; and the long bright days went
away one by one in a kind of noiseless procession, which
Cicely felt herself watch with a dreary dismay and restlessness.
Nothing had happened yet to avert the calamity that was
impending. Everything, on the contrary, seemed preparing
for it – leading up to it – though still Mr St. John went 'into
the parish,' and still all went on as usual at the rectory. The
curate showed no symptom of feeling these last days different
from any other; but the girls kept looking forward, and
hoping for something, with a hope which gradually fell sick,
and grew speechless – and nothing came.

One day when Mrs Ascott called, Cicely had got into that
state of exhaustion and strained anxiety when the mind grows
desperate. She had been occupied with the children all day, not
able to get free of them – Annie having finally departed, and
Betsy, being too much displeased at the loss of her sister and
subordinate to make any offer of help. The babies had grown
more active and more loquacious under the changed *régime,*
and this, though it was her own doing, increased poor Cicely's
cares. Mab was upstairs preparing for her departure, which
was to be a few days before the general breaking up. Altogether when Mrs Ascott came in, fresh and cool out of her
carriage, Cicely was not in the best mood to receive her. She
gave the children her work-basket to play with to keep them
quiet, and cleared her own brow as best she could, as she stood

up and welcomed the great lady. How fresh her toilette was, how unwrinkled her face! a woman altogether at ease, and ready to smile upon everything. She shook hands with Cicely, and took her seat with smiling prettiness. 'I have come really on business,' she said; 'to see if we could be of any use to you, Cicely – in packing or any of your preparations; and to ask if the time is quite fixed? I suppose your papa must have heard from Mr Mildmay, and that all is settled now?'

'All – settled?' said Cicely, faintly. The words, so softly and prettily said, went into the girl's heart like a knife; and yet it was no more than she expected – no more.

'The appointment, as you would see, is in the paper to-day. I am so sorry your papa is going, my dear; but as he must go, and we cannot help it, at least we have reason to be thankful that we are getting such a good man as Mr Mildmay. It will be some little compensation to the parish for losing Mr St. John.'

'Is it – in the papers?' said Cicely, feeling suddenly hoarse and unable to speak.

'You feel it, my poor dear child! – of course you must feel it – and so do we all. There will not be a dry eye in the whole church when Mr St. John preaches his farewell sermon. To think that he should have been here so long – though it is a little consolation, Mr Ascott says, that we are getting a thorough gentleman, and so well connected – an admirable man.'

'Consolation!' cried Cicely, raising her head. 'What consolation is wanted? Papa is pretty well worn out; he has done almost as much work as a man can do. People cannot keep old things when they are worn out – the new are better; but why should any one pretend to make a moan over it? I do not see what consolation the parish can want. If you cry at the farewell sermon, Mrs Ascott, I shall laugh. Why should not your eyes be dry – as dry as the fields – as dry as people's hearts?'

'Cicely, Cicely!' cried Mrs Ascott, shocked; 'my dear, I am very sorry for it, but a misfortune like this should be borne in a better spirit. I am sure your poor dear papa would say so; and it is nobody's fault.'

'It is everybody's fault,' cried Cicely, forgetting herself, getting up in her passion, and walking about the room: 'the parish, and the Church, and all the world! Oh, you may smile! It does not touch you; you are well off; you cannot be put out of your home; you cannot have everything taken from you, and see everybody smiling pity upon you, and no one putting a hand out to help. Pity! we don't want pity,' cried Cicely; 'we want justice. How dare you all stand by and see it done? The Church, the Church! that everybody preaches about as if it was God, and yet that lets an old servant be so treated – an old servant that has worked so hard, never sparing himself! If this is the Church's doing, the Church is harder than the farmers – worse, worse than worldly people. Do you think God will be pleased because he is well connected? or is it God's fault?' Here her voice broke with a sob and shudder, and suddenly dropping from her height of passion, Cicely said faintly, 'Papa!'

'What is it?' said the curate, coming in. 'Surely I heard something very strange. Mrs Ascott, I beg your pardon; my ears must have deceived me. I thought Cicely must be repeating, to amuse herself, some speech, perhaps out of *Paradise Lost*. I have heard of some great man who was caught doing that, and frightened everybody who heard him,' said Mr St. John, shaking hands with the visitor with his friendly smile.

He sat down, weary and dusty from 'the parish,' and there was a painful pause. Cicely stole away to the corner where her little brothers were playing, her pulse bounding, her heart throbbing, her cheeks aflame, her whole being, soul and body, full of the strong pain and violent stimulus of the shock she had received. She had never expected anything else, she said to herself; she had steadily prepared for the going away, the ruin that awaited them; but, nevertheless, her heart had never believed in it, since that conversation with Mildmay at the rectory gate. Day by day she had awoke with a certainty in her mind, never put into words, that the good news would come, that all would be well. But the shock did not crush her, as it does some people; it woke her up into freshened force and life; her heart seemed to thrill and throb, not so much with pain as with activity, and energy and power.

'Cicely is very much excited,' said Mrs Ascott in a low tone. 'I fear she is very excitable; and she ought to be more careful in her position – a clergyman's daughter what she says. I think you ought to speak to her, Mr St. John. She flew at me (not that I mind that) and said such things – because I mentioned that Mr Mildmays appointment was in the paper this morning; and that since we must lose you – which nobody can be more sorry for than we are – it was well at least that we were getting so good a man.'

'Ah!' said the curate. The announcement took him by surprise, and gave him a shock too, though of a different kind. He caught his breath after it, and panted for a moment. 'Is it in the papers? I have not seen it. I have no time in the morning; and, besides, I never see the *Times.*'

'We hope you will settle to dine with us one day before you go,' said Mrs Ascott. How we shall miss you, Mr St. John! I don't like to think of it – and if we can be of any use in your preparations — I hear there is to be a sale, too?'

'Not till we move. They will not put us to any inconvenience; indeed,' said the curate, with a sigh and a smile, 'everybody is very kind.'

'I am sure everybody wishes to be kind,' said Mrs Ascott, with emphasis. 'I must not take up your time any longer, for you look very tired after your rounds. But Mr St. John, mark my words, you must hold a tight hand over Cicely. She uses expressions which a clergyman's daughter ought not to use.'

'What were you saying to her, my dear?' said Mr St. John, coming in again after he had taken the lady to her carriage; 'your voice was raised, and you still look excited. What did you say?'

'It was nothing, papa. I lost my temper – who could help it? I will never do it again. To think of *that* man calmly accepting the living and turning you out of it, after all he said.'

'What good would it have done had he refused?' said Mr St. John. 'My dear, how could he help it?'

'Help it?' cried Cicely. 'Can nobody help anything in this world? Must we stand by and see all manner of wrong done and take the advantage, and then think we are innocent and cannot help it. That is what I scorn. Let him do wrong if he will, and bear the blame – that is honest at least. But to say he cannot help it; how could he ever dare to give such a miserable excuse?'

'My dear,' said the curate, 'I am too tired to argue. I don't blame Mildmay; he has done just what was natural, and I am glad he is coming here; while in the meantime talking will do no good, but I think my tea would do me good,' he added with a smile.

Always tea, Cicely could not help thinking as she went dutifully to prepare it – or dinner, or some trifle; never any serious thought of what was coming, of what had already come. She was young and impatient and unjust, as it is so natural to be at her years. The curate put his hand over his eyes when he was left alone. He was not disappointed or surprised. He had known exactly all along how it would be; but when it thus came upon him with such obvious and unmistakable reality, he felt it sharply. Twenty years! All that part of his life in which anything to speak of had happened to him, and – what was almost as hard to bear – all the familiar things which had framed in his life – the scene, the place, the people, the surroundings he was used to. He had not even his favourite consolation, forlorn pride in never having asked anything, to sustain him, for that was no longer the case. He was asking something – a poor curacy, a priest's place for a piece of bread. The pang was momentary, but it was sharp. He got up, and stretched his long languid figure, and said to himself, 'Ah, well! what is the good of thinking? It is soon enough to make oneself wretched when the moment comes,' and then he went peacefully into the dining-room to tea. This was not how the younger people took it, but then perhaps they had more capacity for feeling left.

Next morning Cicely got a letter of a very unusual description, which affected her in no small degree. It was from Mildmay, and, perhaps, it will be best to give it in full here:-

"Dear Miss St. John,

        "I have delayed writing to you until I could make sure that you must have seen or heard of the announcement in the papers which will tell the results of my last three weeks' work. Do not think that our last conversation has been obliterated from my mind. Very far from that. I have seen the Master and all who are concerned, and have done my best to show them the step which bare justice required at their hands, but ineffectually. I made a point at the same time of ascertaining what were the views of the gentleman to whom Brentburn would be offered in case I refused it, and found him quite decided on the subject. What could I do then? Should I have declined and put myself entirely out of the way of being of any use at all?

'As a matter of simple justice, I refer the question to you. What am I to do now? My thoughts on the subject have been many, I need not say, since I saw you. May I ask your father to continue at Brentburn as my curate? I am quite inexperienced; his assistance would be of infinite advantage to me; and, in point of fact, as is natural at our respective ages, I should be his curate, not he mine. May I do this? or what else can I do? The position in which I find myself is a painful one. It would have been much easier, I assure you, to have shuffled the whole matter off upon Ruffhead, and to have withdrawn. But I felt a responsibility upon me since I met you; and I ask you now urgently, feeling that I have almost a right to your advice, what am I to do?

'Yours very truly,
'Roger Mildmay.'

This letter excited Cicely greatly. By chance it arrived before the others had come into the breakfast-room, and she was able to read it without any looker-on. She put it hurriedly into her pocket before her father and sister appeared. She did not know what answer to make, neither did she feel comfortable about making any answer, and she said nothing about it all day; though – oh, how the letter burned her pocket and her mind! She had scarcely ever known what it was to have a secret before, and not to tell Mab seemed almost wrong. She felt that there was something clandestine about her, going up and down the house with that letter in her possession which nobody knew of. And to answer it – to answer it without any one knowing? This she could not do. She bore the burden of her secret all day, and surprised Mab very much by her silence about Mr Mildmay, whom the younger sister abused roundly. 'Perhaps it was not his fault,' Cicely faltered. What had come over her? What change had happened? Mab was lost in amaze.

The difficulty, however, was solved in a very unexpected way. Next morning – no later – Mr St. John himself had a letter from Oxford; a letter which made him change colour, and bend his meek brows, and then smile – but not like himself. 'Cicely, this must be your doing.' he said. 'I never made any complaints to Mr Mildmay, nor said anything to call for his pity. He asks me to be his curate,' the old man added, after a pause, with a strange smile. No one had suspected that Mr St. John was proud, until it became apparent all at once how proud he was.

'His curate – O papa! you will stay here, and never go away at all,' cried Mab out of the fulness of her heart. Cicely knew better. She grew pale, and to stop that outcry of inconvenient delight, grasped tightly her sister's hand.

'Stay here!' said Mr St. John, smiling again. 'No, Mab, I am not fallen so low as that, I hope. There is no need of a curate at Brentburn. If I could do without one, at double his age, what should he want with a curate? It is pity, pity! Oh yes, my dear, I know, very creditable to him; but I did not expect – I never expected to be exposed. Cicely, have you that letter about the curacy in Liverpool? I should like to look at it again.'

'But, papa, we agreed that it would not do; a bad town district full of dreadful people — '

'The more dreadful people are, the more they want to be looked after,' he said. 'Write and inquire about it, my dear; I am not particular. Work! that is all I want, not idleness and charity. You all know I am old – but you don't know how much strength I have in me, nor how I like work!' he cried, with a quiver in his voice.

The shock had something of the same effect upon him now that it had previously had on Cicely. The latent pride in him rose up in arms. She had to write by that post about the Liverpool curacy; and before the week was out he had accepted this strange, uncongenial post. He was to be one of three curates in a large parish, including some of the most wretched quarters in the town; the work very hard; the people very degraded.

'Papa, you will never be able to bear it,' cried Cicely, with tears in her eyes.

'Nonsense, nonsense,' he cried, with feverish energy; 'write at once and say I accept. It will do me all the good in the world.'

CHAPTER SEVENTEEN

THE BREAKING UP

The day after Mr St. John made this abrupt decision – almost the only decision he had made for himself, without stimulation from others, all his life – he went out into the parish as usual, but came home very tired, and went to bed early, which the girls thought natural enough. During the day Cicely had told Mab of her letter from Mildmay, and had written an answer to it, thanking him for his consideration, and informing him of the step her father had taken. 'We shall never forget how kind you have been,' she wrote gratefully; 'both Mab and I feel it to the bottom of our hearts. Is that too much?' she said, reading it over. 'I don't want to say too much.'

'But we must not say too little; and if a man who is willing to sacrifice the half of his income is not to be thanked for it, I don't know who is,' cried Mab, always practical.

'It is not so much the income,' Cicely said, slightly wounded by this matter-of-fact suggestion; 'it is the feeling.'

'But the offer proves the feeling,' said her sister; and indeed she was right.

Mr St. John came home, as has been said, before his usual hour, and went very early to bed. Next morning he rang his bell – the most unusual sound – and sent word by Betsy that he thought he would not get up. When Cicely went to him – as she did at once in a fright, for the bell and the message together produced a great panic in a house quite unaccustomed (at least, so far as the girls' experience went) to illness – she found him in a partial doze, his large pale hand, looking very nerveless and feeble, lying outside the coverlet.

'No, no!' he said, when she roused him; 'not very bad; not bad at all; only tired – and lazy. I have often thought of late that I should like to lie still some morning; and to-day I have

168

done it. That's all, that's all, my dear.' He would not hear of
the doctor being sent for; and wanted nothing, he declared –
nothing but a day's rest. Cicely had to go downstairs, feigning
content with this; but she was far from satisfied. They talked it
over all the morning, but there was little enough to be made of
it. There was no harm in a day's laziness, and nothing but
good in a day's rest; but yet – the girls did not know what to
think. Had he been looking ill lately? they asked each other.
But, no! he had not been looking ill – a little fatigued, perhaps;
tired by the hot weather, as he often was; but just as usual,
doing as much as he always did; spending the whole long day
'in the parish;' ready to go out morning or night when he was
called to any one who was sick. 'And what so natural as that
he should be tired?' Mab said; 'a day's rest will do him good.'
Cicely, though she was generally the leader, accepted this
decision humbly, saying nothing for her own part, but feeling
a sense of dismay steal into her mind, she could not tell why;
for though it was quite natural that he should do this, he had
never done it before; and an innovation on habits so long
established and firmly fixed was very alarming and bewildering. But Mab had the coolest judgement of the two, she
said to herself – and no doubt Mab was right.

And next day it appeared indeed that Mab had been right.
Mr St. John came down to breakfast as usual, saying cheerfully that he was quite well, and went out 'into the parish' as
usual. The day's rest had done him 'all the good in the world;'
it had 'set him up;' nor did he say anything more again about
feeling tired. How quickly the days passed during that last
fortnight! They seemed to tumble on each other, one
following on another's heels, holding so little of all the work
they ought to see completed. It was settled that the curate was
to leave on the 25th of September, in order that the sale should
be over and everything cleared away before the quarter-day.
Mildmay wrote again a pleading note to Cicely, a guarded but
anxious one to her father, pointing out with abject civility that
it would be the greatest possible advantage to himself if Mr St.
John would consent to stay. Mr St. John only smiled and
shook his head, and handed the letter to Cicely, who was not
so confidential in return. 'Write to him for me, my dear, for I
have not time. Say how obliged I am, but that it is impos-

sible.' 'Is that all, papa?' said Cicely, faltering. 'All? What could be said more? And that everything will be ready by quarter-day – everything ready.' As he said this he gave a strange bewildered look round him at the solid mahogany furniture, which stood steadfast against the walls, looking as if it never could be changed or taken away. This look was still in his eyes when he went out to the parish, and when he came back – a sort of dreamy wonder and confusion. Cicely thought he had the same look next morning, and the next and next, as if he had somehow got astray from his moorings in life, and could not make out what was going to happen to him, or why it was going to happen. Mab said, 'Nonsense, you are getting fanciful. Papa looks exactly as he has always looked;' and indeed everything went on just the same as usual, showing no other difference except this look, if there was a difference at all. He went about just as usual, preached his two little sermons on the Sunday, went to the schools, kept up all the occupations he had been used to for twenty years; but nevertheless continued to have that dazed look in his eyes, sometimes only bewildered, sometimes startled, like the look of an animal who dumbly foresees something approaching which it knows to be malign, but can neither avert nor understand. This, at least, was what Cicely saw in her father's eyes; no one else dreamt of looking at his eyes particularly, or cared what they meant. Perhaps his usually tranquil manners were disturbed a little, but how natural that was! In the evening when they were sitting together he would grow quite talkative, telling the girls little stories of his first coming here, and of their mother's trials in the new parish, and would even laugh softly over them, saying, 'Poor Hester! You grow more and more like her, Cicely, my dear!' and then he would drop into long silence, never taking a book or the newspaper which came in the evening, but sitting quite still looking round him. The girls did not know, however, that his parish rounds got shorter; that in several of the cottages he had been compelled to wait and rest, and that here and there, he had seemed to forget everything around him, falling into a half faint or harmless trance, from which he would rouse up, and smile upon them, and go on. This, however, they were not told till long after, when it seemed to them, that, if they had but known; – but if they had, I don't know what they could have done.

On the 22nd Mab went to London to Aunt Jane. It was not to be a parting, for it was arranged that Mr St. John and the rest of the family were to go there also on the 25th, and rest for the night, and afterwards start on their journey to Liverpool; but still the girls were sad enough as they walked to the station together, Mab's boxes having been sent on before by Farmer Dent's cart. Their eyes were dim with tears as they went through the faded heather on the common. 'You will have plenty to fret about,' said Mab, 'with all you have got to do; and, oh, Cicely, I beg of you, don't be silly and fret about papa! He feels it, of course – but he is quite well, as well as you or me.' 'I hope so, dear,' said Cicely, meekly, with a tremor in her voice; and when they got to the station they looked through all the carriages till they saw in one a middle-aged homely woman, whose box, labelled for 'London' was being put in, under the seat. Then Cicely established Mab in the opposite corner. It was the best that could be done for her, for no one could be spared to go with her, even could they have afforded the expense. Cicely walked home alone, feeling as if the world had suddenly grown dark and lonely round her. Mab had set out upon life, and she for her part was returning to hers – to the tradespeople, who were all to be paid so much, out of the fifty pounds which the curate had to receive, and to the babies, who had no one to look after them but herself, and to her father with that bewildered look in his eyes. Next morning the auctioneer was coming to begin his inventory, and arrange the business of the sale, though the actual auction did not commence until twelve o'clock on Thursday, the day they were to leave.

On Tuesday morning, however, before he went out to the parish, Mr St. John suddenly stumbled upon the auctioneer, who had gone quietly into the study as soon as its temporary master left, and was kneeling before the large old-fashioned writing table, which Mr St. John had used for so long, examining it, and tapping it with his knuckles to see where the drawers were. He had his back to the door, and did not see the surprised spectator, who stood and looked at him for a whole minute in silence. The curate went back to the hall where

Cicely stood waiting for him with his hat in her hand. 'Who is that? – who is that man?' he said, with his eyes more cloudy and wild than they had ever been, ands a sort of palsied trembling all over him.

'No harm, papa,' said Cicely, trying to be cheerful; 'only the auctioneer.'

'Yes, yes, I remember,' he said, taking his hat from her. 'It was stupid of me not to remember.'

'But, papa, you are trembling. You are not well. Come back and rest a little,' she cried.

'No, no; it is nothing. Go back where? I suppose he is going through all the rooms?' said Mr St. John. 'No, no; it gave me a little shock, foolishly, but the air will blow it all away,' he said, with a smile, recovering himself.

What terrors were in Cicely's mind all that day! but fortunately for her she had not much time to indulge them. She had to do all her packing, to take care of the children, to separate the few things her father possessed from Mr Chester's furniture, to see after everything and everybody, providing something even (though she had so little) for the auctioneer and his men. And it was a relief to her when her father came back a little earlier than usual, and looking no worse. She said to herself that Mab was right; that he felt it, of course – which was to be expected – but otherwise was as well as usual. He had a little colour in his cheeks, and ate very well, and afterwards fell asleep in his chair. How natural it was that he should fall asleep! It was the very best thing for him. Notwithstanding, in her anxiety, Cicely went out into the garden to look at him through the open window, and make sure that all was right. How white his venerable head looked lying against the dark corner of the chair, his face like ivory but for the little pink in his cheeks, but he looked well, although he was wearied out, evidently; and no wonder! It was the most natural thing in the world.

Next day he was stronger and more cheerful in the morning. He went out, and made a round of all the poor people, saying good-bye to them; and half the people in Brentburn came crying to the doors of the cottages, and said 'Goodbye, sir!' and 'God bless you, sir!' curtsying and wiping their eyes with their aprons. All the last sixpences he had went that day to the old women and the children, to buy a little tea or some sweets in the little shop. He was very heavy about the eyes when he came home, and took his tea eagerly. Then he went out for an evening stroll, as he had been used to do before all these troubles came. He did not ask Cicely to go with him, but no doubt he knew how busy she was. When, however, she had put the children to bed, and packed everything but the last box, which was left till to-morrow morning, Cicely perceived that daylight was over, and that it was getting late. Her father was not in any of the rooms. Frightened, she ran out, and gazed about her looking for him; then, seeing no one up or down, in a sudden passion of terror, hurried up the bank to the white churchyard stile. There she found him at once, standing close by the cross on her mother's grave. He had one arm round it, and with his other hand was picking away the yellow mosses that crept over the stone; but he stopped when she called him, and picked up his hat which lay at his feet, and came with her quite submissively.

'It is late, papa,' said Cicely, with quivering lips.

'Yes, yes, my dear; yes, you are quite right,' he said, and walked towards the rectory – but like a blind man, as if he did not see where he was going. Two or three times she had to guide him to keep him from stumbling over the humble graves, for which usually he had so much reverence. He went into the house in the same way, going straight before him, as if he did not know where the door were; and, instead of going into the dining-room, where supper was laid as usual, he took up a candle which stood on the hall-table, and went to his study. Cicely followed him, alarmed; but he did nothing more than seat himself at his writing-table.

'Are you not coming to supper, papa?' she said.

'Did any one speak?' he asked, looking up eagerly as if he did not see.

'O papa, dear, come to supper!' she cried. Then his vacant face seemed to brighten.

'Yes, my love, yes. I am coming; I am coming — '

Cicely did not know what to say or to think. Was it to her he was speaking? She went away, her heart beating loud, to see that all was ready, hoping he would follow. But as he did not come in about ten minutes after, she went back. The room was dark, one corner only of it lighted by the candle, which threw all its light on his pale face and white hair. He was turning over some papers, apparently absorbed. He did not seem to observe her entrance. She went up to him softly, and put her hand upon her shoulder. 'Come, please, papa, I am waiting,' she said.

He turned to her, a great light shining over his face. 'Ah! yes, my darling, you are waiting. How long you have been waiting! But I'm ready – ready. – I knew you would come, Hester, I knew you would come when I wanted you most — '

'Papa!' cried Cicely, in a voice shrill with terror.

He started, the light went out of his face, his eyes grew cloudy and bewildered, 'What were you saying, Cicely? I am getting – a littler hard of hearing. I don't think I heard what you said.'

'Come in to supper, papa.'

'Yes, yes; but you need not trouble; there is nothing the matter,' he said, recovering himself. And he went with her and ate something dutifully, not without appetite. Then he returned to his study. When Cicely went to him there to say good-night he was smiling to himself. I am coming; I am coming,' he said. 'No need to tell me twice; I know when I am in good hands.'

'Good night, papa – you are going to bed? – we must be early to-morrow,' said Cicely.

'Yes, early – early,' he said, still smiling. 'Directly, Hester – before you have reached the gate —'

'Papa! don't you know me?' cried Cicely, trembling from head to foot.

Again he turned to her with his old face all lighted up and shining. 'Know you! my darling!' he said.

CHAPTER EIGHTEEN

THE CURATE LEAVES BRENTBURN

Cicely went to her room that night in a very nervous and disturbed condition. It was her last night, too, in the house in which she had been born; but she had no leisure to think of that, or to indulge in any natural sentiments on the subject. She was very much alarmed about her father, whose looks were so strange, but did not know what to do. That he should take her for her mother was perhaps not wonderful at such a moment of agitation; but it frightened her more than words can say. What could she do? It was night, and there was no one in the house with her but Betsy, who had for hours been buried in deepest slumbers; and even if she had been able to send for the doctor, what advance would that have made? – for he was not ill, only strange, and it was so natural that he should be strange; – and the good steady-going country doctor, acquainted with honest practical fevers and rheumatism, what help could he bring to a mind diseased? Cicely had changed her room in her new office of nurse, and now occupied a small inner chamber communicating with that of the two children. She was sitting there pondering and thinking when she heard her father come upstairs. Then he appeared suddenly bending over the children's little cots. He had a candle in his hand, and stooping feebly, kissed the little boys. He was talking to himself all the time; but she could not make out what he said, except, as he stood looking at the children, 'Poor things, poor things! God bless you.' Cicely did not show herself, anxiously as she watched, and he went out again and on to his own room. He was going to bed quietly, and after all it might turn out to be nothing; perhaps he had been dozing when he had called her Hester, and was scarcely awake. After this she intended to go to bed herself; for she was sadly worn out with her long day's work and many cares, and fell dead asleep, as youth unaccustomed to watching ever will do in the face of all trouble. The house was perfectly still so long as she was awake; not a sound disturbed the quiet except the breathing of Harry and Charley, and the tap of the jessamine branches against her windows. There was one last blossom at the end of a branch, late and long after its neighbours, which shed some of its peculiar sweetness through the open window. The relief was so great to hear her father come upstairs, and to know that he was safe in his room, that her previous fright seemed folly. She said her prayers, poor child! in her loneliness, giving tearful thanks for this blessing, and fell asleep without time to think of any bothers or sorrow of her own. Thus sometimes, perhaps, those who have other people to carry on their shoulders avoid occasionally the sharp sting of personal feeling – at least, of all the sentiments which are of secondary kind.

The morning was less warm and bright than usual, with a true autumnal haze over the trees. This soothed Cicely when she looked out. She was very early, for there were still various last things to do. She had finished her own individual concerns, and locked her box ready for removal, before it was time to call the children, who slept later and more quietly than usual by another happy dispensation of providence. Cicely heard the auctioneer arrive, and the sound of chatter and laughter with which Betsy received the men, with whom already she had made acquaintance. Why not? Shall everybody be sad because we are in trouble? Cicely asked herself; and she leant out of the window which overlooked the garden, and took a deep draught of the dewy freshness of the morning before she proceeded to wake the children and begin the day's work. Her eyes, poor child! were as dewy as the morning; but she did not give herself time to cry, or waste her strength by such an indulgence. A knock at her door disturbed her , and she shut the window hastily, and shaking off those stray drops from her eyelashes, went to see what Betsy wanted so early. Betsy stood outside, looking pale and excited. 'The men says, please, miss, will you come downstairs?' said Betsy, making an effort at a curtsy, which was so very unusual that Cicely was half amused.

'What do they want? I have to dress the children, Betsy. Could not you do instead?'

'If you please, miss, I'll dress the children. Do go — go, please Miss Cicely. I'm too frightened. O miss, your poor papa!'

'Papa?' Cicely gave the girl one frightened beseeching look, and then flew downstairs, her feet scarcely touching the steps. Why was he up so early? Why was he vexing himself with those men, and their preparations, making himself miserable about nothing, when there were so many real troubles to bear? The men were standing in a little knot by the study door, which was half open. 'What do you want with me? What is it?'

They were confused; one of them put forward another to speak to her, and there was a little rustling, and shuffling, and changing of position, which permitted her to see, as she thought, Mr St. John sitting, facing the door in his usual chair. 'Ah! it is papa who has come down, I see – thank you for not wishing to disturb him. I will tell him,' said Cicely, passing through the midst of them with swift light youthful steps.

'Don't let her go! Stop her, for God's sake!' cried one of the men, in subdued confused tones. She heard them, for she remembered them afterwards; but at that moment the words conveyed no meaning to her. She went in as any child would go up to any father. The chair was pushed away from the writing-table, facing towards the door, as if he had been expecting some one. What surprised Cicely more than the aspect of his countenance, in which at the first glance she saw no particular difference, was that he had upon his knees, folded neatly, a woman's cloak and hat – her mother's cloak and hat – which had remained in his room by his particular desire ever since Hester died.

'Papa, what are you doing with these?' she said.

There was no reply. 'Papa, are you asleep?' cried Cicely. She was getting very much frightened, her heart beating against her breast. For the moment some impulse of terror drove her back upon the men at the door. 'He has gone to sleep,' she said, hurriedly; 'he was tired, very much tired last night.'

'We have sent for the doctor, miss,' said one of the men.

'Papa, papa!' said Cicely. She had gone back to him paying no attention to them; and then she gave a low cry, and threw herself on her knees by his side, gazing up into his face, trembling. 'What is the matter?' said the girl, speaking low; 'what is it, papa? Where were you going with that hat and cloak? Speak to me, don't sit there and doze. We are to go away – to go away – don't you remember, to-day?'

Some one else came in just then, though she did not hear. It was the doctor, who came and took her by the arm to raise her.

'Run away, my dear; run upstairs till I see what is to be done,' he said. 'Somebody take her away.'

Cicely rose up quickly. 'I cannot awake him,' she said. 'Doctor, I am so glad you have come, though he would not let me send yesterday. I think he must be in a faint.'

'Go away, go away, my dear.'

It neither occurred to the poor girl to obey him nor to think what he meant. She stood by breathless while he looked at the motionless figure in the chair, and took into his own the grey cold hand which hung helpless by Mr St. John's side. Cicely did not look at her father, but at the doctor, to know what it was; and round the door the group of men gazed too awestricken, with Betsy, whom curiosity and the attraction of terror had brought downstairs, and one or two labourers from the village passing to their morning's work, who had come in, drawn by the strange fascination of *what had happened,* and staring too.

'Hours ago,' said the doctor to himself, shaking his head; 'he is quite cold; who saw him last?'

' O doctor, do something!' cried Cicely, clasping her hands; 'don't lose time; don't let him be like this; do something – oh, do something, doctor! Don't you know that we are going to-day?'

He turned round upon her very gently, and the group at the door moved with a rustling movement of sympathy. Betsy fell a crying loudly, and some of the men put their hands to their eyes. The doctor took Cicely by the arm, and turned her away with gentle force.

'My dear, you must come with me. I want to speak to you in the next room.'

'But papa?' she cried.

'My poor child,' said the compassionate doctor, 'we can do nothing for him now.'

Cicely stood quite still for a moment, then the hot blood flushed into her face, followed by sudden paleness. She drew herself out of the kind doctor's hold, and went back and knelt down again by her father's side. Do nothing more for him – while still he sat there, just as he always did, in his own chair?

'Papa, what is it?' she said, trembling, while they all stood round. Suddenly the roughest of all the men, one of the labourers, broke forth into loud sobs.

'Don't you, miss – don't, for the love of God!' cried the man.

She could not hear it. All this came fresh to her word for word a little later, but just then she heard nothing. She took the hand the doctor had taken, and put her warm cheek and young lips to it.

'He is cold because he has been sleeping in his chair.' she cried, appealing to them. 'Nothing else – what could it be else? and we are going away to-day!'

The doctor grasped at her arm, almost hurting her. 'Come,' he said, 'Cicely, this is not like you. We must carry him to bed. Come with me to another room. I want to ask you how he was last night.'

This argument subdued her, and she went meekly out of the room, trying to think that her father was to be carried to his bed, and that all might still be well. Trying to think so; though a chill had fallen upon her, and she knew, in spite of herself.

The men shut the door reverently as the doctor took her away, leaving him there whom no one dared to touch, while they stood outside talking in whispers. Mr St. John, still and cold, kept possession of the place. He had gone last night, when Cicely saw him, to fetch those relics of his Hester, which he had kept for so many years in his room; but, in his feeble state, had been so long searching before he could find them, that sleep had overtaken Cicely, and she had not heard him stumbling downstairs again with his candle. Heaven knows what fancy it was that had sent him to seek his wife's cloak and hat; his mind had got confused altogether with trouble and weakness, and the shock of uprootal; and then he had sat down again with a smile, with her familiar garments ready for her, to wait through the night till Hester came. What hour or moment it was no one could tell; but Hester, or some other angel, had come for him according to his expectation, and left nothing but the case and husk of him sitting, as he had sat waiting for her, with her cloak upon his knees.

'I am going to telegraph for her sister,' said the doctor, coming out with red eyes after all was done that could be done, both for the living and the dead. 'Of course you will send and stop the people coming; there can be no sale to-day.'

'Of course,' said the auctioneer. The young lady wouldn't believe it, my man tells me. I must get them off at once, or they'll get drinking. They're all upset like a parcel of women – what with finding him, and what with seeing the young lady. Poor thing! and, so far as I can learn, very badly left?'

'Left!' cried the doctor; there was derision in the very word. 'They are not *left* at all; they have not a penny in the world. Poor St. John, we must not say a word now against him, and there is not much to say. He got on with everybody. He did his duty by rich and poor. There was never a better cler-gyman, always ready when you called him, early or late; more ready for nothing,' the doctor added remorsefully, 'than I am for my best paying patients. We might have done more to smooth his way for him, perhaps, but he never could take care of money or do anything to help himself; and now they'll have to pay for it, these two poor girls.'

Thus the curate's record was made. The news went through the parish like the wind, in all its details; dozens of people were stopped in the village going to the sale, and a little comforted for their disappointment by the exciting story. Some of the people thought it was poor Miss Brown, the *other* Mrs St. John, whom he was looking for. Some felt it a strange heathenish sort of thing of him, a clergyman, that he should be thinking at that last moment of anything but the golden city with the gates of pearl; and thought there was a dreadful materialism in the cloak and hat. But most people felt a thrill of real emotion, and the moment he was dead, mourned Mr St. John truly, declaring that Brentburn would never see the like of him again. Mrs Ascott cried so that she got a very bad headache, and was obliged to go and lie down. But she sent her maid to ask if they could do anything, and even postponed a dinner-party which was to have been that evening, which

was a very gratifying token of respect. Mrs Joel, who was
perhaps at the other extremity of the social scale, cried too, but
had no headache, and went off at once to the rectory to make
herself useful, pulling all the blinds down, which Betsy had
neglected, and telling all the callers that poor Miss Cicely was
as well as could be expected, though 'it have given her a
dreadful shock.' The trunks stood all ready packed and
corded, with Mr St. John's name upon them. But he had no
need of them, though he had kept his word and left Brentburn
on the appointed day. After a while people began to think that
perhaps it was the best thing that could have happened – best
for him certainly – he could never have borne the rooting up,
they said – he could never have borne Liverpool, so noisy and
quarrelsome. 'Why, it would have killed him in a fortnight,
such a place,' said Mr Ascott, who had not, however, lent a
hand in any way to help him in his struggle against fate.

Mab, it is needless to say, came down at once with Aunt
Jane, utterly crushed and helpless with sorrow. Poor Cicely,
who was only beginning to realize what it was, and to make
sure that her father absolutely was dead, and beyond the reach
of all bringing back, had to rouse herself, and take her sister
into her arms and console her. Mab sobbed quietly when she
was in her sister's arms, feeling a sense of strong protection in
them.

'I have still you, Cicely,' she said, clinging to her.

'But Cicely has no one,' said Aunt Jane, kissing the pale girl
with that compassionate insight which age sometimes brings
even to those who do not possess it by nature. 'But it is best
for you to have them all to look after, if you could but see it,
my poor child!'

'I do see it,' said Cicely – and then she had to disentangle
herself from Mab's clinging, and to go out of the room where
they had shut themselves up, to see somebody about the
'arrangements,' though indeed everybody was very kind and
spared her as much as they could.

After the first shock was over it may well be supposed what
consultations there were within the darkened rooms. The
funeral did not take place till the following Tuesday, as
English custom demands, and the days were very slow and
terrible to the two girls, hedged round by all the prejudices of

decorum, who could do nothing but dwell with their grief in the gloomy house which crushed their young spirits with its veiled windows and changeless dimness. That, and far more, they were ready to do for their father and the love they bore him; but to feel life arrested and stopped short by that shadow of death is hard upon the young. Miss Maydew, whose grief naturally was of a much lighter description than that of the girls, and with whom decorum was stronger than grief, kept them upstairs in their rooms, and treated them as invalids, which was the right thing to do in the circumstances. Only at dusk would she let them go even into the garden, to get the breath of air which nature demanded. She knew all the proper ceremonials which ought to be observed when there was 'a death in the house,' and was not quite sure even now how far it was right to let them discuss what they were going to do. To make up for this, she carried to them the scraps of parish gossip which she gleaned from Mrs Joel and from Betsy in the kitchen. There had, it appeared, been a double tragedy in the parish. A few days after the death of the curate, the village schoolmistress, a young widow with several babies, had 'dropped down' and died of heart disease in the midst of the frightened children. 'It is a terrible warning to the parish,' said Miss Maydew, 'two such events in one week. But your dear papa, everybody knows, was ready to go, and I hope Mrs Jones was too. They tell me she was a good woman.'

'And what is to become of the children?' said Cicely, thinking of her own burden.

'Oh, my dear, the children will be provided for; they always are somehow. There are so many institutions for orphans, and people are very good if you know how to get at them. No doubt somebody will take them up. I don't doubt Mr Ascott has votes for the British Orphans' or St. Ann's Society, or some of these. Speaking of that, my dears, I have been thinking that we ought to try for something of the same kind ourselves. Cicely, hear first what I have got to say before you speak. It is no disgrace. How are Mab and you to maintain these two little boys? Of course you shall have all that I can give you, but I have so little; and if girls can maintain themselves, it is all they are likely to do. There is a society, I am sure, for the orphans of clergymen—'

'Aunt Jane! Papa's sons shall never be charity boys – never! if I should work my fingers to the bone, as people say.'

'Your fingers to the bone – what good would that do? Listen to me, girls. Both of you can make a fair enough living for yourselves. You will easily get a good governess's place, Cicely; for, though you are not very accomplished, you are so thorough – and Mab, perhaps, if she succeeds, may do still better. But consider what that is: fifty pounds a year at the ourside; and at first you could not look for that; and you are always expected to dress well and look nice, and Mab would have all sorts of expenses for her materials and models and so forth. The cheapest good school for boys I ever heard of was forty pounds without clothes, and at present they are too young for school. It is a woman's work to look after two little things like that. What can you do with them? If you stay and take care of them, you will all three starve. It would be far better to get them into some asylum where they would be well looked after; and then,' said Aunt Jane, insinuatingly, 'if you got on very well, or of anything fortunate happened, you could take them back, don't you see, whenever you liked.'

Mab, moved by this, turned her eyes to Cicely for her cue; for there was a great deal of reason in what Aunt Jane said.

'Don't say anything more about it, please,' said Cicely. 'We must not say too much, for I may break down, or any one may break down; but they shall not go upon charity if I can help it. Oh, charity is very good, I know; we may be glad of it, all of us, if we get sick or can't find anything to do; but I must try first – I must try!'

'O Cicely, this is pride, the same sort of pride that prevented your poor papa from asking for anything — '

'Hush, Aunt Jane! Whatever he did was right; but I am not like papa. I don't mind asking so long as it is for work. I have an idea now. Poor Mrs Jones! I am very sorry for her, leaving her children desolate. But some one will have to come in her place. Why should it not be me? There is a little house quite comfortable and pleasant where I could have the children; and I think the parish would not refuse me, if it was only for papa's sake.'

'Cicely! my dear child, of what are you thinking?' said Miss Maydew, in dismay. 'A parish schoolmistress! you are dreaming. All this has been too much for you. My dear, my dear, you must never think of such a thing again!'

'O Cicely, it is not a place for a lady, surely,' cried Mab.

'Look here,' said Cicely, the colour mounting to her face. 'I'd take in washing if it was necessary, and if I knew how. A lady! there's nothing about ladies that I know of in the Bible. Whatever a woman can do I'm ready to try, and I don't care, not the worth of a pin, whether it's a place for a lady or not. O Aunt Jane, I beg your pardon. I know how good you are – but charity! I can't bear the thought of charity. I must try my own way.'

'Cicely, listen to me,' cried Aunt Jane, with tears. 'I held back, for the children are not my flesh and blood as you are. Perhaps it was mean of me to hold back. O Cicely, I wanted to save what I had for you; but, my dear, if it comes to that, better, far better, that you should bring them to London. I don't say I'm fond of children,' said Miss Maydew; 'it's so long since I had anything to do with them. I don't say but what they'd worry me sometimes; but bring them, Cicely, and we'll do what we can to get on, and when you find a situation, I'll – I'll – try — '

Her voice sank into quavering hesitation, a sob interrupted her. She was ready to do almost all they wanted of her, but this was hard; still, sooner than sacrifice her niece's gentility, the standing of the family – Cicely had good sense enough to perceive that enough had been said. She kissed her aunt heartily with tender thanks, but she did not accept her offer or say anything further about her own plans. For the moment nothing could be done, whatever the decision might be.

CHAPTER NINETEEN

THE RECTOR'S BEGINNING

Mr Mildmay came to Brentburn the Saturday after the curate's death. The Ascotts invited him to their house, and he went there feeling more like a culprit than an innocent man has any right to do. He fairly broke down in the pulpit next day, in the little address he made to the people. 'God knows,' he said to them, 'that I would give everything I have in the world to bring back to you the familiar voice which you have heard here so long, and which had the teachings of a long experience to give you, teachings more precious than anything a new beginner can say. When I think that but for my appointment this tragedy might not have happened, my heart sinks within me; and yet I am blameless, though all who loved him have a right to blame me.' His voice quivered, his eyes filled with tears, and all the Brentburn folks, who were not struck dumb with wonder, wept. But many of them were struck dumb with wonder, and Mr Ascott, who was his host, and felt responsible for him, did more than wonder. He interfered energetically when the service was over. 'Mildmay,' he said solemnly, 'mark my words, this will never do. You are no more to blame for poor St. John's death than I am or any one, and nobody has a right to blame you. Good heavens, if you had never heard of the poor fellow, don't you think it would have happened all the same? You did a great deal more than any one else would have done – is that why you think it is your fault?'

Mildmay did not make any reply to this remonstrance. Perhaps after he had said it, he felt, as so may impulsive men are apt to do, a hot nervous shame for having said it, and betraying his feelings; but he would not discuss the question with the Ascotts, who had no self-reproach in the matter, no idea that any one could have helped it. They discussed the

question now, the first shock being over, and a comfortable
Sunday put between them and the event, with great calm.

'He was just the sort of man that would not even have his
life insured,' said Mr Ascott. 'What those poor girls are to do,
I do not know. Go out for governesses, I suppose, poor
things! the common expedient; but then there are those babies.
There ought to be an Act of Parliament against second
families. I never had any patience with that marriage; and Miss
Brown, I suppose, had no friends that could take them up?'

'None that I know of,' his wife replied. 'It is a dreadful
burden for those girls. It will hamper them in their situations,
if they get situations, and keep them from marrying — '

'They are pretty girls,' said Mr Ascott. 'I don't see why they
shouldn't marry.'

'That is all very well, Henry,' she replied; 'but what man, in
his senses, would marry a girl with a couple of children
dependent on her?'

'A ready-made family,' he said with a laugh.

This was on the Sunday evening after dinner. It was dusk,
and they could not see their guest's face, who took no part in
the conversation. To hear such a discussion as this, touching
the spoiling of a girl's marriage, is quite a commonplace
matter, which the greater part of the world would think it
foolishly fastidious to object to, and probably Mr Mildmay
had heard such talk upon other occasions quite unmoved; but
it is astonishing the difference it makes when you know the
girl thus discussed, and have, let us say, 'a respect' for her. He
felt the blood come hot to his face; he dared not say anything,
lest he should say too much. Was it mere poverty that exposed
those forlorn young creatures, whose case surely was sad
enough to put all laughter out of court, to such comment? Mrs
Ascott thought it quite possible that Mr Mildmay, fresh from
Oxford, might consider female society frivolous, and was
reserving himself for loftier conversation with her husband,
and that this was the reason of his silence, so she went away
smiling, rustling her silken skirts to the drawing-room, in the
humility which becomes the weaker vessel, not feeling herself
equal to that loftier strain, to make the gentlemen's tea.

Her husband, however, came upstairs after her, by himself.
Mildmay had gone out for a stroll, he said, and seemed to

prefer being alone; he was afraid, after all, he was a morose sort of fellow, with very little 'go' in him. As for the new rector, he was very glad to get out into the stillness of the dewy common after the hot room and the fumes of Mr Ascott's excellent port, which he disliked, being altogether a man of the new school. He skirted the common under the soft light of some stars, and the incipient radiance of the moon, which had not yet risen, but showed that she was rising. He went even as far as the back of the rectory, and that little path which the curate's feet had worn, which he followed reverently to the grey cross upon Hester's grave. Here a flood of peaceful and friendly thoughts came over the young man, bringing the tears to his eyes. He had only known Mr St. John for about twenty-four hours, yet how much this short acquaintance had affected him! He seemed to be thinking of a dear old friend when he remembered the few moments he had stood here, six weeks before, listening to the curate's simple talk. 'The lights in the girls' windows;' there they were, the only lights in the dark house, a glimmer through the half-closed shutters. Then he thought of the old man, bewildered with death and death's weakness, sitting with his wife's cloak and hat ready, waiting for her to come who had been waiting all these years under the sod for him to come. 'I shall go to her, but she will not come to me,' said the new rector to himself, letting a tear fall upon the cross where the curate's hand had rested so tenderly. His heart was full of that swelling sensation of sympathetic sorrow which is both sweet and painful. And *she* was, they all said, so like her mother. Would any one, he wondered, think of *her* sometimes as Mr St. John had done of his Hester? Or would nobody, in his senses, marry a girl burdened with two babies dependent on her? When those words came back to his mind, his cheeks reddened, his pace quickened in a sudden flash of anger. And it was a woman who had said it a woman whose heart, it might have been thought, would have bled for the orphans, not much more than children any of them, who were thus left in the world to struggle for themselves.

It was Mildmay who took all the trouble about the funeral, and read the service himself, with a voice full of emotion. The people had scarcely known before how much they felt the loss of Mr St. John. If the new parson was thus affected, how much more ought they to be! Everybody wept in the churchyard, and Mr Mildmay laid that day the foundation of a popularity far beyond that which any clergyman of Brentburn, within the memory of man, had enjoyed before. 'He was so feelin' hearted,' the poor people said; they shed tears for the old curate who was gone, but they became suddenly enthusiasts for the new rector. The one was past, and had got a beautiful funeral, carriages coming from all parts of the county; and what could man desire more? The other was the present, cheerful and full of promise. A thrill of friendliness ran through every corner of the parish. The tragedy which preceded his arrival, strangely enough, made the most favourable preface possible to the commencement of the new reign.

'Do you think I might call upon Miss St. John?' Mildmay asked, the second day after the funeral. 'I would not intrude upon her for the world; but they will be going away, I suppose – and if you think I might venture —'

He addressed Mrs Ascott, but her husband replied. 'Venture? to be sure you may venture,' said that cheerful person. 'Of course you must want to ascertain when they go and all that. Come, I'll go with you myself if you have any scruples. I should like to see Cicely, poor thing! to tell her if I can be of any use — We are not much in the governessing line; but you, Adelaide, with all your fine friends — '

'Tell her I should have gone to her before now, but that my nerves have been upset with all that has happened,' said Mrs Ascott. 'Of course I have written and told her how much I feel for her; but say *everything* for me, Henry. I will make an effort to go to-morrow, though I know that to enter that house will unhinge me quite. If she is able to talk of business, tell her to refer any one to me. Of course we shall do everything we possibly can.'

'Of course; yes, yes, I'll say *everything*,' said her husband; but on the way, when MIldmay reluctantly followed him, feeling his purpose defeated, Mr Ascott gave forth his individual sentiments. 'Cicely St. John will never answer as a governess,' he said; 'she is far too independent, and proud – very proud. So was her father before her. He prided himself, I believe, on never having asked for anything. God bless us! a nice sort of world this would be if nobody asked for anything.

That girl spoke to me once about the living as if it was *my* business to do something in respect to what she thought her father's rights! Ridiculous! but women are very absurd in their notions. She was always what is called a high-spirited girl; the very worst recommendation I think that any girl can have.'

Mildmay made no reply; he was not disposed to criticise Cicely, or to discuss her with Mr Ascott. The rectory was all open again, the shutters put back, the blinds drawn up. In the faded old drawing-room, where the gentlemen were put by Betsy to wait for Miss St. John, everything looked as usual, except a scrap of paper here and there marked Lot –. This had been done by the auctioneer, before Mr St. John's death. Some of these papers Betsy, much outraged by the sight of them, had furtively rubbed off with her duster, but some remained. Mr Mildmay had something of Betsy's feeling. He, too, when Mr Ascott was not looking, tore off the label from the big old chiffonnier which Mab had called a tomb, and threw it behind the ornaments in the grate – a foolish sort of demonstration, no doubt, of being on the side of the forlorn family against fate, but yet comprehensible. He did not venture upon any such freaks when Cicely came in, in the extreme blackness of her mourning. She was very pale, keeping the tears out of her eyes with a great effort, and strung to the highest tension of self-control. She met Mr Ascott with composure; but when she turned to Mildmay, broke down for the moment. 'Thanks!' she said, with a momentary pressure of his hand, and an attempt at a smile in the eyes which filled at sight of him, and it took her a moment to recover herself before she could say any more.

'Mrs Ascott charged me with a great many messages,' said that lady's husband. 'I am sure you know, Cicely, nobody has felt for you more; but she is very sensitive – that you know too – and I am obliged to interpose my authority to keep her from agitating herself. She talks of coming to-morrow. When do you go?'

'On Saturday,' said Cicely, having just recovered the power of speech, which, to tell the truth, Mildmay did not quite feel himself to have done.

'On Saturday – so soon! and you are going — '

'With my aunt, Miss Maydew,' said Cicely, 'to London for a time – as short a time as possible – till I get something to do.'

'Ah – h!' said Mr Ascott, shaking his head' 'You know how sincerely sorry we all are; and, my dear Cicely, you will excuse an old friend asking, is there no little provision – nothing to fall back upon – for the poor little children, at least?'

'Mr Ascott,' said Cicely, turning full towards him, her eyes very clear, her nostrils dilating a little – for emotion can dry the eyes as well as dim them, even of a girl – 'you know what papa had almost as well as he did himself. He could not coin money; and how do you think he could have saved it off what he had? There is enough to pay every penny he ever owed, which is all I care for.'

'And you have nothing – absolutely nothing?'

'We have our heads and our hands,' said Cicely; the emergency even gave her strength to smile. She faced the two prosperous men before her, neither of whom had ever known what it was to want anything or everything that money could buy, her small head erect, her eyes shining, a smile upon her lip – not for worlds would she have permitted them to see that her heart failed her at sight of the struggle upon which she was about to enter; – 'and fortunately we have the use of them,' she said, involuntarily raising the two small hands, looking all the smaller and whiter, for the blackness that surrounded them, which lay on her lap.

'Miss St. John,' said Mildmay, starting up, 'I dare not call myself an old friend. I have no right to be present when you have to answer such questions. If I may come another time— '

To look at his sympathetic face took away Cicely's courage. 'Don't make me cry, please; don't be sorry for me!' she cried, under her breath, holding out her hands to him in kind of mute appeal. Then recovering herself, 'I would rather you stayed, Mr Mildmay. I am not ashamed of it, and I want to ask something from you, now that you are both here. I do not know who has the appointment; but you must be powerful. Mr Ascott, I hear that Mrs Jones, the schoolmistress, is dead – too.'

'Yes, poor thing! very suddenly – even more suddenly than your poor father. And so much younger, and an excellent creature. It has been a sad week for Brentburn. She was buried yesterday,' said Mr Ascott, shaking his head.

'And there must be some one to replace her directly, for the holidays are over. I am not very accomplished,' said Cicely, a flush coming over her face; 'but for the rudiments and the solid part, which is all that is wanted in a parish school, I am good enough. It is difficult asking for one's self, or talking of one's self, but if I could get the place — '

'Cicely St. John!' cried Mr Ascott, almost roughly in his amazement; 'you are going out of your senses – the appointment to the parish school?'

'I know what you think,' said Cicely, looking up with a smile; but she was nervous with anxiety, and clasped and unclasped her hands, feeling that her fate hung upon what they might decide. 'You think, like Aunt Jane, that it is coming down in the world, that it is not a place for a lady. Very well, I don't mind; don't call me a lady, call me a young woman – a person even, if you like. What does it matter and what difference does it make after all?' she cried. 'No girl who works for her living is anything but looked down upon. I should be free of all that, for the poor people know me, and they would be kind to me, and the rich people would take no notice. And I should have a place of my own, a home to put the children in. The Miss Blandys, I am sure, would recommend me, Mr Mildmay, and they know what I can do.'

'This is mere madness!' cried Mr Ascott, paling a little in his ruddy complexion. Mildmay made a rush at the window as she spoke, feeling the situation intolerable. When she appealed to him thus by name, he turned round suddenly, his heart so swelling within him that he scarcely knew what he was doing. It was not for him to object or remonstrate as the other could do. He went up to her, scarcely seeing her, and grasped for a moment her nervous interlaced hands. 'Miss St. John,' he cried, in a broken voice, 'whatever you want that I can get you, you shall have – that, if it must be so, or anything else,' and so rushed out of the room and out of the house, passing Mab in the hall without seeing her. His excitement was so great that he rushed straight on, into the heart of the pine-woods a mile off, before he came to himself. Well! this, then, was the life he had been wondering over from his safe retirement. He found it not in anything great or visible to the eye of the world, not in anything he could put himself into, or share the advantages of. He, well off, rich indeed, strong, with a man's power of work, and so many kinds of highly-paid, highly-esteemed work open to him, must stand aside and look on, and see this slight girl, nineteen years old, with not a tittle of his education or his strength, and not two-thirds of his years, put herself into harness, and take up the lowly work which would sink her in social estimation, and, with all superficial persons, take away from her her rank as gentlewoman. The situation, so far as Cicely St. John was concerned, was not remarkable one way or another, except in so much as she had chosen to be village schoolmistress instead of governess in a private family. But to Mildmay it was as a revelation. He could do nothing except get her the place, as he had promised to do. He could not say, Take part of my income; I have more than I know what to do with, though that was true enough. He could do nothing for her, absolutely nothing. She must bear her burden as she could upon her young shrinking shoulders; nay, not shrinking – when he remembered Cicely's look, he felt something come into his throat. People had stood at the stake so, he supposed, head erect, eyes smiling, a beautiful disdain of the world they thus defied and confronted in their shining countenances. But again he stopped himself; Cicely was not defiant, not contemptuous, took upon her no *rôle* of martyr. If she smiled, it was at the folly of those who supposed she would break down, or give in, or fail of courage for her work; but nothing more. She was, on the contrary, nervous about his consent and Ascott's to give her the work she wanted, and hesitated about her own powers and the recommendation of the Miss Blandys; and no one – not he, at least, though he had more than he wanted – could do anything! If Cicely had been a lad of nineteen instead of a girl, something might have been possible, but nothing was possible now.

The reader will perceive that the arbitrary and fictitious way of cutting this knot, that *tour de force* which is always to be thought of in every young woman's story, the very melodramatic begging of the question, still, and perennially possible, nay probable, in human affairs, had not occurred to Mildmay. He had felt furious indeed at the discussion of Cicely's chances or non-chances of marriage between the Ascotts; but, so far as he was himself concerned, he had not thought of this easy way. For why? he was not in love with Cicely. His sympathy was with her in every possible way, he entered into her grief with an almost tenderness of pity, and her courage stirred him with that thrill of fellow-feeling which those have who could do the same; though he felt that nothing he could do could ever be the same as what she, at her age, so boldly undertook. Mildmay felt that she could, if she pleased, command him to anything, that, out of mere admiration for her bravery, her strength, her weakness, and youngness and dauntless spirit, he could have refused her nothing, could have dared even the impossible to help her in any of her schemes. But he was not in love with Cicely; or, at least, he had no notion of anything of the kind.

It was well, however, that he did not think of it; the sudden 'good marriage,' which is the one remaining way in which a god out of the machinery can change wrong into right at any moment in the modern world, and make all sunshine that was darkness, comes dreadfully in the way of heroic story; and how such a possibility, not pushed back into obscure regions of hazard, but visibly happening before their eyes every day, should not demoralize young women altogether, it is difficult to say. That Cicely's brave undertaking ought to come to some great result in itself, that she ought to be able to make her way nobly, as her purpose was, working with her hands for the children that were not hers, bringing them up to be men, having that success in her work which is the most pleasant of all recompenses, and vindicating her sacrifice and self-devotion in the sight of all who scoffed and doubted – this, no doubt, would be the highest and best, the most heroical and epical development of story. To change all her circumstances at a stroke, making her noble intention unnecessary, and resolving this tremendous work of hers into a gentle domestic necessity, with the 'hey presto!' of the commonplace magician, by means of a marriage, is simply a contemptible expedient. But, alas! it is one which there can be no doubt is much preferred by most people to the more legitimate conclusion; and, what is more, he would be justified by knowing the accidental way is perhaps, on the whole, the most likely one, since marriages occur every day which are perfectly improbable and out of character, mere *tours de force,* despicable as expedients, showing the poorest invention, a disgrace to any romancist or dramatist, if they were not absolute matters of fact and true. Pardon the parenthesis, gentle reader.

But Mr Mildmay was not in love with Cicely, and it never occurred to him that it might be possible to settle matters in this ordinary and expeditious way.

Mr Ascott remained behind when MIldmay went away, and with the complacence of a dull man apologised for his young friend's abrupt departure. 'He is so shocked about all this, you must excuse his abruptness. It is not that he is without feeling – quite the reverse, I assure you, Cicely. He has felt it all – your poor father's death, and all that has happened. You should have heard him in church on Sunday. He feels for you all very much.'

Cicely, still trembling from the sudden touch on her hands, the agitated sound of Mildmay's voice, the sense of sympathy and comprehension which his looks conveyed, took this apology very quietly. She was even conscious of the humour in it. And this digression being over, 'her old friend' returned seriously to the question. He repeated, but with much less force, all that Miss Maydew had said. He warned her that she would lose 'caste,' that, however much her friends might wish to be kind to her, and to treat her exactly as her father's daughter ought to be treated, that she would find all that sort of thing very difficult. 'As a governess, of course you would always be known as a lady, and when you met with old friends it would be a mutual pleasure; but the village schoolmistress!' said Mr Ascott; 'I really don't like to mention it to Adelaide, I don't know what she would say.'

'She would understand me when she took all into consideration,' said Cicely. 'I could be then at home, independent, with the little boys.'

'Ah, independent, Cicely!' he cried; 'now you show the cloven hoof – that is the charm. Independent! What woman can ever be independent? That is your pride; it is just what I expected. An independent woman, Cicely, is an anomaly; men detest the very name of it; and you, who are young, and on your promotion — '

'I must be content with women then,' said Cicely, colouring high with something of her old impetuosity; 'they will understand me. But, Mr Ascott, at least, even if you disapprove of me, don't go against me, for I cannot bring up the children in any other way.'

'You could put them out to nurse.'

'Where?' cried Cicely; 'and who would take care of them for the money I could give? They are too young for school; and I have no money for that either. If there is any other way, I cannot see it; do not go against me at least.'

This he promised after a while, very doubtfully, and by and by went home, to talk it over with his wife, who was as indignant as he could have wished. 'What an embarrassment it will be!' she cried. 'Henry, I tell you beforehand, I will not ask her here. I cannot in justice to ourselves ask her here if she is the schoolmistress. She thinks, of course, we will make no difference, but treat her always like Mr St. John's daughter. It is quite out of the question. I must let her know at once that Cicely St. John is one thing and the parish schoolmistress another. Think of the troubles that might rise out of it. A pretty thing it would be if some young man in our house was to form an attachment to the schoolmistress! Fancy! She can do it if she likes; but, Henry, I warn you, I shall not ask her here.'

'That's exactly what I say,' said Mr Ascott. 'I can't think even how she could like to stay on here among people who have known her in a different position; unless — ' he concluded with a low whistle of derision and surprise.

'Please, don't be vulgar, Henry – unless what?'

'Unless – she's after Mildmay; and I should not wonder – he's as soft as wax and as yielding. If a girl like Cicely chooses to tell him to marry her, he'd do it. That's what's she's after, as sure as fate.'

CHAPTER TWENTY

THE PARISH SCHOOLMISTRESS

I will not follow all the intermediate steps, and tell how the curate's family left their home, and went to London; or how Miss Maydew made the most conscientious effort to accustom herself to the little boys, and to contemplate the possibility of taking the oversight of them. They were not noisy, it is true; but that very fact alarmed Aunt Jane, who declared that, had they been 'natural children,' always tumbling about, and making the walls ring, she could have understood them. Perhaps, had they been noisy, she would have felt at once the superiority of 'quiet children.' As it was, the two little tiny, puny old men appalled the old lady, who watched them with fascinated eyes, and a visionary terror, which grew stronger every day. Sometimes she would jump up in a passion and flee to her own room to take breath, when the thought of having them to take care of came suddenly upon her. And thus it came about that her opposition to Cicely's scheme gradually softened. It was a bitter pill to her. To think of a Miss St. John, Hester's child, dropping into the low degree of a parish schoolmistress, went to her very heart; but what was to be done? How could she oppose a thing Cicely had set her heart upon? Cicely was not one to make up a scheme without some reason in it; and you might as well (Miss Maydew said to herself) try to move St. Paul's, when the girl had once made up her mind. I do not think Cicely was so obstinate as this, but it was a comfort to Miss Maydew to think so. And after everybody had got over their surprise at the idea, Miss St. John was duly installed as the schoolmistress at Brentburn. The few little bits of furniture which had belonged to them in the rectory – the children's little beds, the old faded carpets, etc. – helped to furnish the schoolmistress's little house. Cicely took back the little Annie she had sent away from the rectory for interfering with her own authority, but whose devotion to the children was invaluable now, and no later than October settled down to this curious new life. It was a very strange life. The schoolmistress's house was a new little square house of four rooms, with no beauty to recommend it, but with little garden plots in front of it, and a large space behind where the children could play. The little kitchen, the little parlour, the two little bedrooms were all as homely as could be. Cicely had the old school-room piano, upon which her mother had taught her the notes, and which Miss Brown had shed tears over on that unfortunate day when Mr St. John proposed to marry her rather than let her go back to the Governesses' Institute – and she had a few books. These were all that represented to her the more beautiful side of life: but, at nineteen, fortunately life itself is still beautiful enough to make up for many deprivations, and she had a great deal to do. As for her work, she said, it was quite as pleasant to teach the parish children as to teach the little ladies at Miss Blandy's; and the 'parents' did not look down upon her, which was something gained.

And it was some time before Cicely awoke to the evident fact that, if the parents did not look down upon her, her old acquaintances were much embarrassed to know how to behave to her. Mrs Ascott had gone to see her at once on her arrival, and had been very kind, and had hoped they would see a great deal of her. On two or three occasions after she sent an invitation to tea in the evening, adding always, 'We shall be quite alone.' 'Why should they be always quite alone?' the girl said to herself; and then she tried to think it was out of consideration for her mourning. But it soon became visible enough what Mrs Ascott meant, and what all the other people meant. Even as the curate's daughter Cicely had but been a girl whom they were kind to; now she was the parish schoolmistress – 'a very superior young person, quite above her position,' but belonging even by courtesy to the higher side no more. She was not made to feel this brutally. It was all quite gently, quite prettily done; but by the time spring came, brightening the face of the country, Cicely was fully aware of the change in her position, and had accepted it as best she could. She was still, eight months after her father's death – so faithful is friendship in some cases – asked to tea, when they were quite alone at the Heath; but otherwise, by that time, most people had ceased to take any notice of her. She dropped out of sight except at church, where she was only to be seen in her plain black dress in her corner among the children; and though the ladies and gentlemen shook hands with her still, when she came in their way, no one went out of his or her way to speak to the schoolmistress. It would be vain to say that there was no mortification involved in this change. Cicely felt it in every fibre of her sensitive frame, by moments; but fortunately her temperament was elastic, and she possessed all the delicate strength, which is supposed to distinguish 'blood.' She was strong, and light as a daisy, jumping up under the very foot that crushed her. This kind of nature makes its possessor survive and surmount many things that are death to the less elastic; it saves from destruction, but it does not save from pain.

As for Mr Mildmay, it was soon made very apparent to him that, for him at his age to show much favour or friendship to the schoolmistress at hers, was entirely out of the question. He had to visit the school, of course, in the way of his duty, but to visit Cicely was impossible. People even remarked upon the curious frequency with which he passed the school. Wherever he was going in the parish (they said), his road seemed to turn that way, which, of course, was highly absurd, as every reasonable person must see. There was a side window by which the curious passer-by could see the interior of the school as he passed, and it was true that the new rector was interested in that peep. There were the homely children in their forms, at their desks, or working in the afternoon at their homely needlework: among them, somewhere, sometimes conning little lessons with portentous gravity, the two little boys in their black frocks, and the young schoolmistress seated at her table; sometimes (the spy thought) with a flush of weariness upon her face. The little house was quite empty during the school-hours; for Annie was a scholar too, and aspiring to be pupil-teacher some day, and now as reverent of Miss St. John as she had once been critical. Mildmay went on his way after that peep with a great many thoughts in his heart. It became a kind of necessity to him to pass that way, to

see her at her work. Did she like it, he wondered? How
different it was from his own! how different the position – the
estimation of the two in the world's eye! He who could go and
come as he liked, who honoured the parish by condescending
to become its clergyman, and to whom a great many little
negligences would have been forgiven, had he liked, in
consequence of his scholarship, and his reputation, and his
connections. 'We can't expect a man like Mildmay, fresh from
a University life , to go pottering about among the sick like
poor old St. John,' Mr Ascott would say. 'That is all very
well, but a clergyman here and there who takes a high position
for the Church in society is more important still.' And most
people agreed with him; and Roger Mildmay went about his
parish with his head in the clouds, still wondering where life
was – that life which would string the nerves and swell the
veins, and put into man the soul of a hero. He passed the
school-room window as often as he could, in order to see it
afar off – that life which seemed to him the greatest of all
things; but he had not yet found it himself. He did all he could
as well as he knew how, to be a worthy parish priest. He was
very kind to everybody; he went to see the sick, and tried to
say what he could to them to soothe and console them. What
could he say? When he saw a man of his own age growing into
a gaunt great skeleton with consumption, with a wistful wife
looking on, and poor little helpless children, what could the
young rector say? His heart would swell with a great pang of
pity, and he would read the prayers with a faltering voice,
and, going away wretched, would lavish wine and soup, and
everything he could think of, upon the invalid; but what could
he *say* to him, he whose very health and wealth and strength
and well-being seemed an insult to the dying? The dying did
not think so, but Mildmay did, whose very soul was wrung
by such sights. Then, for lighter matters, the churchwardens
and the parish business sickened him with their fussy foolishness about trifles; and the careful doling out of shillings from
the church charities would have made him furious, had he not
known his anger was more foolish still. For his own part, he
lavished his money about, giving it to everybody who told
him a pitiful story, in a reckless way, which, if persevered in,
would ruin the parish. And when any one went to him for

advice, he had to bite his lip in order not to say the words which were on the very tip of his tongue longing to be said, and which were, 'Go to Cicely St. John at the school and ask. It is she who is living, not me. I am a ghost like all the rest of you.' This was the leading sentiment in the young man's mind.

As for Cicely, she had not the slightest notion that any one thought of her so, or thought of her at all, and sometimes as the excitement of the beginning died away she felt her life a weary business enough. No society but little Harry, who always wanted his tea, and Charley, with his thumb in his mouth; and those long hours with the crowd of little girls around her, who were not amusing to have all day long as they used to be for an hour now and then, when the clergyman's daughter went in among them, received by the schoolmistress curtsying, and with smiles and bobs by the children, and carrying a pleasant excitement with her. How Mab and she had laughed many a day over the funny answers and funnier questions; but they were not funny now. When Mab came down, now and then, from Saturday to Monday, with all her eager communications about her work, Cicely remembered that she too was a girl, and they were happy enough; but in the long dull level of the days after Mab had gone she used to think to herself that she must be a widow without knowing it, left after all the bloom of life was over with her children to work for. 'But even that would be better,' Cicely said to herself; 'for then, at least, I should be silly about the children, and think them angels, and adore them.' Even that consolation did not exist for her. Mab was working very hard, and there had dawned upon her a glorious prospect, not yet come to anything, but which might mean the height of good fortune. Do not let the reader think less well of Mab because this was not the highest branch of art which she was contemplating. It was not that she hoped at eighteen and a half to send some great picture to the Academy, which should be hung on the line, and at once take the world by storm. What she thought of was the homelier path of illustrations. 'If, perhaps, one was to take a little trouble, and try to find out what the book means, and how the author saw a scene,' Mab said; 'they don't do that in the illustrations one sees; the author says one thing, the artist quite another – that, I suppose, is because the artist is a great person and does not mind. But I am nobody. I should try to make out what the reading meant, and follow that.' This was her hope, and whether she succeeds or not, and though she called a book 'the reading,' those who write will be grateful to the young artist for this thought. 'Remember I am the brother and you are the sister,' cried Mab. It was on the way to the station on a Sunday evening – for both of the girls had to begin work early next morning – that this was said. 'And as soon as I make money enough you are to come and keep my house.' Cicely kissed her, and went through the usual process of looking for a woman who was going all the way to London in one of the carriages. This was not very like the brother theory, but Mab was docile as a child. And then the elder sister walked home through the spring darkness with her heart full, wondering if that re-union would ever be.

Mr Mildmay had been out that evening at dinner at the Ascotts, where he very often went on Sunday. The school was not at all in the way between the Heath and the rectory, yet Cicely met him on her way back. It was a May evening, soft and sweet, with the bloom of the hawthorn on all the hedges, and Cicely was walking along slowly, glad to prolong as much as possible that little oasis in her existence which Mab's visit made. She was surprised to hear the rector's voice so close to her. They walked on together for a few steps without finding anything very particular to say. Then each forestalled the other in a question.

'I hope you are liking Brentburn?' said Cicely.

And Mr Mildmay, in the same breath, said: 'Miss St. John, I hope you do not regret coming to the school?'

Cicely, who had the most composure, was the first to reply. She laughed softly at the double question.

'It suits me better than anything else would,' she said. I did not pretend to take it as a matter of choice. It does best in my circumstances; but you, Mr Mildmay?'

'I want so much to know about you,' he said, hurriedly. 'I have not made so much progress myself as I hoped I should; but you? I keep thinking of you all the time. Don't think me impertinent. Are you happy in it? Do you feel the satisfaction of living, as it seems to me you must?'

'Happy?' said Cicely, with a low faint laugh. Then tears came into her eyes. She looked at him wistfully, wondering. He so well off, she so poor and restricted. By what strange wonder was it that he put such a question to her? 'Do you think I have much cause to be happy?' she said; then added hastily, 'I don't complain, I am not *un*happy – we get on very well.'

'Miss St. John,' he said, 'I have spoken to you about myself before now. I came here out of a sort of artificial vegetation, or at least, so I felt it, with the idea of getting some hold upon life – true life. I don't speak of the misery that attended my coming here, for that, I suppose, was nobody's fault, as people say; and now I have settled down again. I have furnished my house, made what is called a home for myself, though an empty one; and lo, once more I find myself as I was at Oxford, looking at life from outside, spying upon other people's lives, going to gaze at it enviously as, I do at you through the end window — '

'Mr Mildmay!' Cicely felt her cheeks grow hot, and was glad it was dark so that no one could see. 'I am a poor example,' she said, with a smile. 'I think, if you called it vegetation with me, you would be much more nearly right than when you used that word about your life at Oxford, which must have been full of everything impossible to me. Mine is vegetation; the same things to be done at the same hours every day; the poor little round of spelling and counting, never getting beyond the rudiments. Nobody above the age of twelve, or I might say of four, so much as to talk to. I feel I am living to-night,' she added, in a more lively tone, 'because Mab has been with me since yesterday. But otherwise – indeed you have made a very strange mistake.'

'It is you who are mistaken,' said the young rector. warmly. 'The rest of us are ghosts; what are we all doing? The good people up there,' and he pointed towards the Heath, 'myself, almost everybody I know? living for ourselves – living to get what we like for ourselves, to make ourselves comfortable – to improve ourselves, let us say, which is the best perhaps, yet despicable like all the rest. Self-love, self-comfort, self-importance, self-culture, all of them one more miserable, more petty than the other – even self-culture, which in my time I have considered divine.'

'And it is, I suppose, isn't it?' said Cicely. 'It is what in our humble feminine way is called improving the mind. I have always heard that was one of the best things in existence.'

'Do you practise it?' he asked, almost sharply.

'Mr Mildmay, you must not be hard upon me – how can I? Yes, I should like to be able to pass an examination and get a – what is it called? – *diplôme,* the French say. With that one's chances are so much better,' said Cicely, with a sigh, 'but I have so little time.'

How the young man's heart swelled in the darkness!

'Self-culture,' he said, with a half laugh, 'must be disinterested, I fear, to be worthy of the name. It must have no motive but the advancement of your mind for your own sake. It is the culture of you for you, not for what you may do with it. It is a state, not a profession.'

'That is harder upon us still,' said Cicely. 'Alas! I shall never be rich enough nor have time enough to be disinterested. Good-night, Mr Mildmay; that is the way to the rectory.'

'Are you tired of me so soon?'

'Tired of you?' said Cicely, startled; 'oh no! It is very pleasant to talk a little; but that is your way.'

'I should like to go with you to your door, please,' he said; 'this is such an unusual chance. Miss St. John, poor John Wyborn is dying; he has four children and a poor little wife, and he is just my age.'

There was a break in the rector's voice that made Cicely turn her face towards him and silently hold out her hand.

'What am I to say to them?' he cried; 'preach patience to them? tell them it is for the best? I who am not worthy the poor bread I eat, who live for myself, in luxury, while he – ay, and you — '

'Tell them,' said Cicely, the tears dropping from her eyes, 'that God sees all – that comforts them the most; that He will take care of the little ones somehow and bring them friends. Oh, Mr Mildmay, it is not for me to preach to you; I know what you mean; but they, poor souls, don't go thinking and questioning as we do – and that comforts them the most. Besides,' said Cicely, simply, 'it is true; look at me – you

spoke of me. See how my way has been made plain for me! I
did not know what I should do; and now I can manage very
well, live, and bring up the children; and after all these are the
great things, and not pleasure,' she added, with a soft little
sigh.

'The children!' he said. 'There is something terrible at your
age to hear you speak so. Why should you be thus burdened –
why?'

'Mr Mildmay,' said Cicely, proudly, 'one does not choose
one's own burdens. But now that I have got mine I mean to
bear it, and I do not wish to be pitied. I am able for all I have to
do.'

'Cicely!' he cried out, suddenly interrupting her, bending
low, so that for the moment she thought he was on his knees,
'put it on my shoulders! See, they are ready; make me
somebody in life, not a mere spectator. What! are you not
impatient to see me standing by looking on while you are
working? I am impatient, and wretched, and solitary, and
contemptible. Put your burden on me, and see if I will not
bear it! Don't leave me a ghost any more!'

'Mr Mildmay!' cried Cicely, in dismay. She did not even
understand what he meant in the confusion of the moment.
She gave him no answer, standing at her own door, alarmed
and bewildered; but only entreated him to leave her, not
knowing what to think. 'Please go, please go; I must not ask
you to come in,' said Cicely. 'Oh, I know what you mean is
kind, whatever it is; but please, Mr Mildmay, go! Good-
night!'

'Good-night!' he said. 'I will go since you bid me; but I will
come back to-morrow for my answer. Give me a chance for
life.'

'What does he mean by life?', Cicely said to herself, as,
trembling and amazed, she went back into her bare little
parlour, which always looked doubly bare after Mab had
gone. Annie had heard her coming, and had lighted the two
candles on the table; but though it was still cold, there was no
fire in the cheerless little fireplace. The dark walls, which a
large cheerful lamp could scarcely have lit, small as the room
was, stood like night round her little table, with those two
small sparks of light. A glass of milk and a piece of bread stood

ready on a little tray, and Annie had been waiting with some impatience her young mistress's return in order to get to bed. The little boys were asleep long ago, and there was not a sound in the tiny house as Cicely sat down to think, except the sound of Annie overhead, which did not last long. Life! Was this life, or was he making a bad joke at her expense? What did he mean? It would be impossible to deny that Cicely's heart beat faster and faster as it became clearer and clearer to her what he did mean; but to talk of life! Was this life – this mean, still, solitary place, which nobody shared, which neither love nor fellowship brightened? for even the children, though she devoted her life to them, made no warm response to Cicely's devotion. She sat till far into the night thinking, wondering, musing, dreaming, her heart beating, her head buzzing with the multitude of questions that crowded upon her. Life! It was he who was holding open to her the gates of life; the only life she knew, but more attractive than she had ever known it. Cicely was as much bewildered by the manner of his appeal as by its object. Could he – love her? Was that the plain English of it? Or was there any other motive that could make him desirous of taking her burden upon his shoulders? Could she, if a man did love her, suffer him to take such a weight on his shoulders. And then – she did not love him. Cicely said this to herself faltering. 'No, she had never thought of loving him. She had felt that he understood her. She had felt that he was kind when many had not been kind. There had been between them rapid communications of sentiment, impulses flashing from heart to heart, which so often accompany very close relations. But all that is not being in love,' Cicely said to herself. Nothing could have taken her more utterly by surprise; but the surprise had been given, the shock received. Its first overpowering sensation was over, and now she had to look forward to the serious moment when this most serious thing must be settled, and her reply given.

Cicely did not sleep much that night. She did not know very well what she was doing next morning, but went through her work in a dazed condition, fortunately knowing it well enough to go on mechanically, and preserving her composure more because she was partially stupified than for any other reason. Mr Mildmay was seen on the road by the last of the little scholars going away, who made him little bobs of curtsies, and of whom he asked where Miss St. John was?

'Teacher's in the school-room,' said one unpleasant little girl.

'Please, sir,' said another, with more grace or genius, 'Miss Cicely's ain't come out yet. She's a-settling of the things for to-morrow.'

Upon this young woman the rector bestowed a sixpence and a smile. And then he went into the school-room, the place she had decided to receive him in. The windows were all open, the desks and forms in disorder, the place as mean and bare as could be, with the maps and bright-coloured pictures of animal history on the unplastered walls. Cicely stood by her own table, which was covered with little piles of plain needle-work, her hand resting upon the table, her heart beating loud. What was she to say to him? The truth, somehow, such as it really was; but how?

But Mr Mildmay had first a great deal to say. He gave her the history of his life since August, and the share she had in it. He thought now, and said, that from the very first day of his arrival in Brentburn, when she looked at him like an enemy, what he was doing now had come into his mind; and on this subject he was eloquent, as a man has a right to be once in his life, if no more. He had so much to say, that he forgot the open public place in which he was telling his love-tale, and scarcely remarked the little response she made. But when it came to her turn to reply, Cicely found herself no less impassioned, though in a different way.

'Mr Mildmay,' she said, 'there is no equality between us. How can you, such a man as you, speak like this to a girl such as I am? Don't you see what you are doing – holding open to me the gates of Paradise; offering me back all I have lost; inviting me to peace out of trouble, to rest out of toil, to ease and comfort, and the respect of the world.'

'Cicely!' he said; he was discouraged by her tone. He saw in it his own fancy thrown back to him, and for the first time perceived how fantastic that was. 'You do not mean,' he said, faltering, 'that to work hard as you are doing, and give up all the pleasure of existence, is necessary to your – your – satisfaction in your life?'

'I don't mean that,' she said simply; 'but when you offer to take up my burden, and to give me all your comforts, don't you see that one thing – one great thing – is implied to make it possible? Mr Mildmay, I am not – in love with you,' she added, in a low tone, looking up at him, the colour flaming over her face.

He winced, as if he had received a blow; then recovering himself, smiled. 'I think I have enough for two,' he said, gazing at her, as pale as she was red.

'But don't you see, don't you see,' cried Cicely passionately, 'if it was you, who are giving everything, that was not in love, it would be simple; but I who am to accept everything, who am to put burdens on you, weigh you down with others beside myself, how can I take it all without loving you? You see – you see it is impossible!'

'Do you love any one else?' he asked, too much moved for grace of speech, taking the hand she held up to demonstrate this impossibility. She looked at him again, her colour wavering, her eyes filling, her lips quivering.

'Unless it is you – nobody!' she said.